It's 1977. The safety
The swastika some

ENGLAND
BELONGS TO ME

By Steve Goodman

England belongs to me,
A nation's pride
The dirty water of the river!
No one can take away her memory
Oh-oh, England belongs to me!
COCK SPARRER

LOW LIFE

Dedicated to the spirit of the skinhead cult and especially gangs gone past including New Milton Punks, Skins and Bootboys (1972-77), Stonebridge Park Skins, Punks and Clash City Rudies (1977-79), Borough Of Christchurch Skins, Guildford, Aldershot and Camberley Skins, Borough Of Bournemouth Skins and Punks, Poole and Camford Heath Skins (all 1979-81), Gillingham and Sheppey Skins (1981), Orpington and Bexley Skins and Punks, the Last Resort crew and the Kidbrooke Skins and South East London firms (1981-84). Life was never dull for a moment!

England Belongs To Me (pbk)

© Steve Goodman

ISBN 1 898928 00 2

Published by Low Life, Scotland.
Printed by Loader Jackson, England.

This book is a work of fiction. The characters and events are purely imaginary. There is no such place as London.

Low Life is an imprint of
S.T. Publishing, P.O. Box 12, Dunoon, Argyll. PA23 7BQ. Scotland.

It's 1977. The safety pin is a fashion accessory.
The swastika something far more dangerous.

ENGLAND
BELONGS TO ME

By Steve Goodman

We're just bored teenagers
Seeing ourselves as total strangers
Bored teenagers - bored out of our skulls, bored out of our minds!
BORED TEENAGERS - THE ADVERTS (1977)

CHAPTER ONE

DEREK Peterson stood there with Wardour Street stretched out before him. Barely twelve o'clock, and already he was bored shitless. Apathetic to the point where not even Soho's enchanted seduction could entice any enthusiasm. The seventeen year old youth looked on unaffected as the world carried on around him, its people flowing chaotically like driftwood on the Thames.

The blare of a taxi horn grabbed at his attention. The hooker, who had blundered out in front of it, ignored the need for apologies by giving a two fingered salute and telling the hapless driver where he could stick his cab.

A middle-aged woman stopped in front of Derek, her shopping trolley in tow. Derek just looked at her with the same disinterest, thinking to himself, *I ain't fucking moving.*

For a few seconds the lady stood there expectantly. Then, realising the youth wasn't going to extend the courtesy she required, she wheeled the trolley around him and shambled off muttering to herself. Stupid cow! Not that Derek was always disrespectful to the elderly, but the woman must have seen him from some way off, so why didn't she aim to go around him in the first place? After all, he wasn't moving so it wasn't a hard thing to do!

"That's right, honey. Be sure to get the Queen in the picture . . . "

The American drawl was strong enough to cut through the rest of the hustle and bustle to reach Derek's ears. Turning his attention to the speaker, his eyes were greeted by a family group posing, while the mother stooped, camera in hand.

"Isn't this great?" asked the father, oblivious to the grimaces of his daughter and son as he gathered them close to him, like some giant psychedelic cuddling teddy bear. *Jesus, Hawaiian shirt and khaki safari shorts!* You don't get any more clichéd than that. Derek wouldn't have believed that Hollywood stuff if he wasn't seeing it with his own eyes.

Following the camera angle, his eyes shielded from the sunlight with a hand, the reference to the Queen became more apparent. Overhead and centre stage to row upon row of Union Jack bunting, was a large banner featuring the head and shoulders of Queen Elizabeth and Prince Philip in tasteful cameo frames. Golden scrolls, proudly proclaimed The Silver Jubilee. *Whoopie!* The sarcasm sounded in his thoughts. It wasn't as if the Queen was ever going to be popping down to Soho for a vibrator or anything else that would enable her to witness this loyal display. Yet there was always the walking yen or dollar that would!

As the camera snapped, a pigeon seated above the banner deposited a Trafalgar Square Special on the Queen's face. A thick white streak ran down and marred the solemn regality of the pageantry. *Probably heard about the GLC plans to cull them before the Jubilee parade,* Derek mused to himself.

"Hey Pops, is that one of them punk rockers?"

The girl's words, drew Derek's attention back to the family, just in time to see that the girl was pointing at him and the mother lightly slapping her hand down with the words, "You know it's rude to point."

Punk rocker! Me?!

The basic niceties of pointing or not went right over Derek's head, but the girl couldn't have insulted him more if she'd asked her old man if that was a wanker over there. Turning to glance in the nearby shop window, he tried to understand the basis of her mistaken identity. Any thought of her nubile charms had gone west - *No chance darling, you've blown it!*

He was relieved to see the same reflection looking back as he had seen in the hall mirror on his way out this morning. *How could she confuse me with a punk?*

It was beyond his understanding. Staring out from dark blue eyes, he could see the black hair, cropped tight in a number three, crowning a face that, though young and fair of skin, was ruggedly handsome thanks to a strong bone structure. Any danger of it making him look gaunt, was belied by the roundishness of youth. At 5' 9", he had an average sort of frame that leant towards a muscular build, largely thanks to his job on the market selling fruit and veg. Setting up the stall, breaking down cases and the like, all day long, had its fringe benefits in the fitness stakes.

As far as he could tell, his clobber was totally different from that of the punks. Black and yellow striped Fred Perry, scarlet braces holding up a pair of British Army lightweight fatigues, and all capped off by shiny oxblood Airwair Doctor Martens.

Punk? Don't be such a stupid bitch!

Any chance of Soho providing the answer to his boredom had been destroyed by that uneducated comment. Still, it had hinted inadvertently at another possibility. According to the national dailies, the Kings Road was almost as action-packed as Brixton's Railton Road - The Frontline as it was known to locals.

Anywhere there was a possibility of confrontation was good news for a bored social mercenary. Turning on his heels, he headed back through Leicester Square, aiming for the tube stations on the Charing Cross Road.

Emerging from the bowels of Sloane Square, Derek silently promised a smack in the mouth to the next person to shove him. Brixton, like the East End, had a strong sense of bonhomie with an undercurrent of casual violence. It was there in the way you grew up, the schoolyard, street corner and local clubs. You learned young to push back harder when pushed. Anything less and you were condemning yourself to spending your life as a perpetual victim.

In this, Derek was the South London equivalent of a fighting Cockney Sparrer. He could take it and dish it out. Which was partly the reason he took to the skinhead culture. It provided an outlet, like the throwing down of a gauntlet. His choice of fashion was a beacon to other hooligans who needed little excuse to provoke a fight.

Thankfully, the ticket examiner at the gate was lax and not really paying attention to the offered tickets. At least this way, the station could speedily vomit forth the struggling mass of humanity where they could carefully regain the pretension of civilised behaviour that was strangely removed by travelling or driving through the capital.

Back in the open, Derek felt at liberty to relax again. The sun was shining and people were everywhere. All different classes and backgrounds. Curiosity prompted him to join a crowd in the pedestrian square. Pushing to the front, Derek discovered that it was a troupe of Majorettes that were attracting so much attention. They were going through a baton twirling number accompanied by a small drum and trumpet corp, probably as part of the Jubilee festivities.

Unlike the assorted tourists, he wasn't interested in how quaint it all was. He wouldn't have been interested at all if it wasn't for the fact

7

that some of the Majorettes were more his own age. Sixteen, perhaps seventeen year olds, proudly thrusting their breasts forward, while flashing their satins as they marched on the spot. Even fingering the baton took on a whole new meaning when they were that age.

The sly glances and flashed smiles, exposing pure pearly whites, at whatever young guy took their fancy, showed they knew all too well the effect they were causing. *Jesus, she's horny*, thought Derek at the sight of the teenage Sergeant Major marking the head of the column. Long silky blonde hair, lily-white thighs, and an aloofness that confirmed rather than denied the girl's awareness of her sexuality and its influence.

Derek would have fallen head over heels in love if he had stayed any longer, but a couple of police officers scrutinising him from across the parade ground began to make him feel uncomfortable. Not because of any guilt complex - innocent or otherwise never figured in the indignation of a SUS law shakedown. He just wasn't in the mood to play the smart-mouthed kid and risk being arrested. For that reason, he reluctantly turned and wormed away from the front of the crowd, out towards the Kings Road proper.

* * *

"Think the old skinheads are coming back?" PC Winstead asked his beat companion.

"Maybe . . . "

* * *

Away from the glaring eyes of big brother, the young skinhead felt more at liberty to enjoy himself. The Kings Road buzzed with a vibrancy quite different from that of Wardour Street. It was alive and exciting, rather than the simulated sordidness of Soho. The latter was the preserve of gangsters and clippers - female grifters posing as prostitutes and taking the punter's money without fulfilling the promise. Here the pretension was less about abusive manipulations and more on being self-expressive. The girls glowed bright and bubbly with a naive sparkle in their eyes - refreshing when compared to the hardened and haggard street wisdom of those who frequented the likes of Rupert Street, Dean Street and its surrounding area.

Christ, there's a lot of people here, Derek complained to himself, as he was forced to weave his way along the crowded pavement. Across

8

the road, between two number nineteen buses, he saw a gang of bootboys he recognised from Chelsea's Shed end. Holding up a hand in a loose wave, he mouthed "Alright son!", knowing that calling it across the traffic snarl would be a wasted effort. In response, the returning wave was accompanied by rhythmic clapping and a group chant of "The Chelsea! The Chelsea! . . . "

Derek smiled. It was heart-warming to feel like you belonged to a top dog outfit. There was no one who could challenge Chelsea's supremacy. Not after the off they had had with Manchester United's mob in the backstreets around Manchester's Piccadilly Station. That had been one hell of a fight, but it had sorted out the bullshit the tabloids were pushing that the Red Devils were contenders for the title of top yobs.

Having their source ridiculed, the 'papers were quickly pushing Harry the Dog and The Millwall Treatment as Chelsea's latest number one enemy. Based on one undecided off outside the away end at Stamford Bridge, Derek was sure one-armed Babs and his gang would have tamed the Lions when he broke through the police wall of link-armed officers by sinking his teeth into the nearest policeman's bicep. Yet the temporary breach had been a minor one, and only about twenty Chelsea boys had got through before the police re-established their barrier. It was a confrontation that would have to wait until next season to be settled.

Next season? Pearson and Greenoff's goals in Man United's F.A. Cup win over Liverpool were still fresh memories. Next season might just as well be a million light years away for all the difference it made to a Saturday afternoon in May.

Thoughts of what delights August would bring faded to the back of his mind as he passed through a tight knot of indecisive shoppers, and found himself in an open section of pavement where a group of punks were having fun with a brace of Japanese tourists. The punks, four guys and two girls were lounging around a 1959 Thunderbird parked tight against the pavement.

"Photograph this, man . . . " called a punk holding his hands out as he stooped on the car's bonnet. He was dressed in a greatcoat, of the type worn by frontier men in Sam Peckinpah Westerns, set off by zip-covered trousers and a World War Two leather flying helmet complete with goggles.

The orientals just looked on bemused as another punk, seated on the pavement with his back against the car, looked at his companion

9

through a set of opera glasses he had stolen on a college trip to the Albert Hall. "What you s`posed to be?" he asked, as a cider bottle dropped out of the bottom of the fly-boy's coat. Bouncing off the bonnet, it shattered on the pavement, with a crash that attracted all nearby attention.

"The Enola Gay, what else?" his now drinkless friend replied before asking the Japanese, "Did you get that man, eh?"

Taking their silent bewilderment as being a negative response, he turned to his companions again. "Consistent ain't they? Never saw it the first time. Never saw it this time . . . "

"Who's gay?" asked a punk girl, turning just enough so that Derek could get a clear look at her. Her lightly hued skin spoke of mixed parentage, while her face was a mixture of Anglo-Eastern, possibly Phillipino. Her hair mimicked a crop for length, but was coloured peroxide blonde with black irregular shaped spots worked in to give a leopard skin pattern. Large false eyelashes and mascara, worked delicately into the shape of cat's eyes, finished the feline effect.

From the ground upwards, a pair of red plastic sandals, the kind worn by kids at the beach, led into holed stockings. An outsized shirt was worn as a dress and given shape by a kid's plastic belt with red hearts and the words I LOVE YOU looping around. The shirt itself sported the typical slogans of punks. BOOMTOWN RATS . . . SEX PISTOLS . . . ANARCHY NOT APATHY . . . although these played minor league to the larger declaration of PRICK TEASE sloping from the right shoulder in two lines of carefully worked text.

"Whatcha looking at?" sneered the girl, snapping Derek out of his intense staring.

Caught off guard, his mouth worked off its vocation. "Hey girl . . . If you don't know, what you asking me for?"

"Nice one mate!" chipped in the guy with the opera glasses, as he giggled at the glowering punkette.

Tasty chick, thought Derek as he continued on his course to the Chelsea Potter.

Fucking arsehole, thought Suzi as she watched the skinhead leaving.

The public bar seemed more subdued than usual. Not that there was a negative atmosphere. Everything was very much alive, but there was something different about the place. Holding a five pound note up to

10

attract the barman's attention, Derek looked around. There was a large group of punks sitting and standing around the two oak tables in front of the bay window. Glasses and half-filled ashtrays crowded the table tops.

What they were talking about was largely lost to the general hub, bar the input of one rather loud bird who, though not a punk herself, seemed very settled in the company of the others. There was something said about a guy called George and what a jerk he was.

Further along, there was a group of football lads standing in front of a table used by a couple of tourists who seemed to be wondering what planet they'd been beamed down to. Behind them was a display case with a couple of vases, the landlord's idea of maintaining the pottery theme.

Through the lads, Derek was afforded a temporary glimpse of a guy chatting up a bird who he had accosted on her way out of the toilets. Someone was playing the fruit machine and the tables by the jukebox were also occupied.

That's it! Derek thought. The jukebox was silent. Worse than that, the glass cover had been smashed and covered temporarily with cardboard. Glancing first at the barman, who was bending down to examine the row of bottles in the cold drinks cabinet, then to the people who propped up the bar with him, Derek tapped the punk next to him on the shoulder. The guy turned around with an inquisitive expression on his face. He was about nineteen, with satin black spikey hair that hinted quite strongly at being dyed.

"Has there been a fight in here recently?" Derek asked.

"Strange question pal, why do you ask?"

Derek grinned. "Yeah, thinking about it, it was a pretty bizarre thing to ask someone you don't know. It's just the jukebox was working last time I was here!"

"Oh, that," said the punk looking over at the wrecked machine, then back to the skinhead. "Sid did it last night. Went rabid on some acid and stuck a stool through it."

"Why'd he do that?"

"Oh, he just thought someone was trying to wind him up by putting on *Lucy In The Sky With Diamonds*."

"Were they?"

"Nah. Some stiff in the other bar had put it on . . . "

11

"So what happened to Sid?" asked Derek, for no other reason than to keep the conversation flowing. It was a good tactic for making friends and chatting up girls.

"He was pulled by the Old Bill before he could get down the tube!"

Derek shrugged in a gesture of "well that's life ain't it". Luckily the barman had by now spotted his five pound flag and gave him the opportunity to change the course of the conversation. There was a limit to the amount of things you could say about a Sid you didn't know.

"Yes?" enquired the barman.

"Light and lager for me!" Turning to his newly acquired friend, Derek then asked, "You want a refill?"

"Yeah, sure", enthused the punk, draining the remains of his drink in a series of rapid gulps. "Usual, George", he said holding the empty glass up as if for inspection before banging it down with a dull thud on the bar top.

"Bitter, isn't it?" George asked as he scooped the glass up. Derek placed the fiver on the scratched veneer as the punk nodded and sent the barman about his business.

"By the way, me name's Derek, Del to me friend's!"

"Alright Del. I'm known as Snake-Eyes by most people . . . "

"Yeah, why's that then?" Derek asked, accepting the offered handshake.

"Ahh!" said Snake-Eyes in a knowing fashion. "When I'm pissed, me eyes go as dead as those of a snake. Someone mentioned it once and it kind of stuck! So, how come you ain't got into the punk thing?" Snake-Eyes asked, warming to Derek's company.

"I'm happy with being a skinhead, I guess", Derek responded as George returned with their drinks. Del accepted the light and lager and drained the first mouthful. He had been looking forward to sinking a beer, and that first draft was like nectar to the gods.

"That's one pound sixty-four please!"

The skinhead nodded at the five pound note. While George took the banknote to the till to process the change, Snake-Eyes held the glass up in a typical drinker's salute, to which Derek raised his eyebrows in lax acknowledgement.

"Skinheads and all that are a bit old hat, don't you think?" asked Snake-Eyes. "After all this is Nineteen Seventy-Seven!'

"Maybe", Derek agreed, not taking any offence at the punk's words. After all, the guy wasn't saying anything he hadn't heard from other quarters many times before. "But there's more skinheads about now than there has been for quite a while. Anyway, there's an old saying about what goes around, comes around!"

"Old sayings are for old folks though!" Snake-Eyes pointed out with a level of personal conviction.

Derek was aware of the anarchic sentiments of punk and what it translated into at street-level. The December confrontation between Bill Grundy and The Sex Pistols had proved the inevitable when two worlds collide. Though in this case, he disagreed with the concept. Skinheads now were football geezers - bootboys who realised that at grassroots level, both cults were one and the same yet didn't feel comfortable with the diversity evolving within the bootboy movement. From the jean-jacketed teenies to the iridescent crushed-velvet jackets of the Townies to Pringle boys with their high-waister trousers.

For those who returned to the skinhead look, it appeared that bootboys were not so much evolving as devolving. Although Derek had an insight into why things were, he didn't say anything to Snake-Eyes. Mainly because he didn't completely understand it himself. If asked why he was a skinhead, he'd respond, "I wanna be different!" or something like that.

Yet the return of skinheads was for the same reason as the cult's instigation back in Sixty-Eight and Nine. It was a return to purity - began originally by those mods who resented the intrusion of psychedelia into modernism and its dilution of the cult's principles. They had evolved the skinhead look from an enforced introversion, a necessity to return to basics to preserve ideals. If Derek had been aware of this, he might have seen the similarities between those mods who became skinheads then, and the bootboys who were becoming skinheads now.

The arrival of George with the change proved enough of a distraction to prevent any further thought on the matter. Three pound notes and a small selection of coins were jammed, uncounted, into Derek's jean's pocket. Snake-Eyes had sparked the desire for open conversation in him, so he was more intent on what the next topic was to be than checking the change for inconsistencies.

In the course of an hour and a half, and with the aid of a couple of additional beers, Derek and his newly acquired drinking companion, brushed over many subjects including life in their home area. Snake-Eyes came from the Broadwater Farm Estate in Tottenham and from what Del could gather, it was much the same as his own Brixton

13

manor. It too had a large coloured population, was easy going in the main, but with the odd mob or two that were best avoided.

When Derek indicated his preference for reggae music, old time and the current vogue of Rockers and Dub, Snake-Eyes was quick to point out there was a Rasta DJ who worked at the Roxy Club in Covent Garden. Spinning reggae as a contrast to the energy burst of live punk bands.

"Yeah?" Derek said, genuinely taken aback. There had been no indication of such in the press coverage of punk - not that he was surprised by that. Judging by the press hounds who had sniffed around the Chelsea crew at the Kings Arms on the Fulham Broadway, hacks were never much the wiser on leaving than they were on arrival. It seemed that one or two tales and a few names were all they needed to fuck up their "in-depth" feature.

Snake-Eyes had been able to name the DJ when asked, but Don Letts wasn't anyone Derek was familiar with from the Sound System clique. Although not an expert on the subject, he was quite knowledgeable about who was who within that scene.

"Yeah, the stuff that guy plays is good. Dub, roots and oldies. You should give it a go, Del!"

Derek was already one jump ahead of the offer. The possibility of a night out at a club where the only concession to reggae wasn't just Bob Marley and the charted material of the last two years, would make one helluva change. Disco music wasn't really his cup of tea, yet that's where the women were at. So unless a life of celibacy appealed, there was usually little choice.

"Yeah. Who's on there tonight?" Del asked in a non-committing way.

"Umm . . ." Snake-Eyes murmured as he placed his glass down while he scratched his head and tried to remember. "Dunno . . . Oh wait, tell a lie. It's X-Ray Spex, Wire and The Xtraverts." Nodding, he picked up his drink again.

"Good bands?" The names meant nothing to Derek.

"Oh yeah. X-Ray Spex have this brilliant girl vocalist called Poly Styrene . . . "

A name like that was too much for Del. It hit him square on the funny bone and he was chuckling before he had time to check himself. "You pulling my leg?"

"Nah, straight up!" Snake-Eyes answered with a grin. "She's known as Poly Styrene. You'll find a lot of punks operate under nicknames!"

"Like what?"

"Well, for instance - Johnny Rotten, Sid Vicious, Captain Sensible, Rat Scabies, Tory Crimes, you know."

"Sounds like something out of a Superman comic!"

"You're probably right about that. Anyway, X-ray Spex are good, Wire have a real bass heavy sound - if you like dub you should like that, man. Though their lyrics tend to be vague and not really there at all."

Derek raised an eyebrow, noting the confused interpretation. "In what way?"

"Dunno really. Kind of abstract lyrics. One liners that don't really mean anything on their own. I've got a tape of one of their gigs and it's the kind of stuff that you can listen to on your own and it makes you think of different things at different times. Know what I mean?"

"No!" came Derek's reply.

Snake-Eyes realised that Derek was taking the piss out of the depth of his explanation. Maybe it had sounded a bit involved. "Well, fuck you then!" he said, dismissing any further explanation at the same time as Derek's attitude.

"What about the last mob?" Derek asked. It was his way of letting Snake-Eyes know that he was being light-hearted rather than offensive.

"You'd like 'em I guess. Very similar to a terrace chant style!"

"How's that?"

"You taking the piss again?" asked Snake-Eyes suspiciously. He only continued when Derek assured him he was not. "Basically punk music with terrace lyrics, similar to glam. You know, Gary Glitter, The Sweet and all that. Bit more aggressive though!"

"Sounds good!" Derek commented, not really sure what a more aggressive version of the Glitter sound would be like. Still, he was intrigued nonetheless. After all, Gal had been a hero of aspiring jack the lads everywhere, really.

"Gonna give the Roxy a go then?" asked the punk.

"Why not?" mused Derek, hiding just how deeply the idea appealed to him.

Snake-Eyes was more openly enthusiastic. "That's it mate. We'll change you into a punk in no time!"

"No fucking way! I'm too dedicated to what I am. No offence, but I've found my thing, if you know what I mean?"

"Yeah, each to his own I guess!" agreed Snake-Eyes.

I'm tired of being told what to think
I'm tired of being told what to do
I'm tired of fucking phonies
That's right - Im tired of you!
MR. SUIT - WIRE (1977)

CHAPTER TWO

THERE was barely half an hour to afternoon closing time when a commotion at the doorway announced the arrival of a gang of skinheads from East and South London.

"Friends of yours?" asked Snake-Eyes, trying to sound nonchalant in spite of his unease. He never trusted skinheads in groups of more than two or three. When there were more than that, experience had taught him, though thankfully not personally, that the shorn-headed bootboys were unpredictable and schizophrenic by nature. One minute they were your best mate, the next they were kicking your brains out for the slightest thing, whether imaginary or real.

"Hey, don't get nervous mate," Derek said with a conviction that his words would stay gospel. "They ain't gonna touch ya!"

Snakes-Eyes nodded, but said nothing. He looked over at the skinheads with cold eyes. A technique he had learned from being a punk and living on the edge. The difference between not looking and appearing weak, and looking too intensely and provoking a confrontation, was a fine line to walk.

"Oi! Del! Del!"

Snake-Eyes looked at the skinhead guy calling out as he came towards them from the middle of the gang. He was stocky in build, but chubbyish as the form was derived from bulk rather than tight muscle. Derek moved to greet him and Snake-Eyes astutely assessed them to be firm friends. The warmth of greeting was unmistakable even when masked by the macho strong handshaking, the shoulder slapping, and excitable exchanges with their tinge of sarcasm.

"How are you, you old tart?" The other greeted Del with boisterous profanity.

"Not so bad, Jay. What you been up to? I ain't seen ya since the off with Southampton?"

"Not surprising mate, I got three months for that one!"

"No shit?"

16

"Straight up! I was cornered by the Saints mob, on the station. You know, where the footbridge is."

"Southampton Station?"

"Yeah!"

Derek nodded as a hazy picture of the platform layout formed in his mind. Memories of a train disgorging a thousand plus Chelsea fans, police lining the way out of the station where there was a horse and police car escort from there to the Dell, Southampton's football ground.

"Well, I got separated during the attack on their end. Then I found myself mixed in with their boys so I stashed me scarf quickly and pretended to be one of theirs. I'd have got away with it too if the guy I spanked in the battle hadn't turned up at the station. All of a sudden there's a hundred or more lads, suddenly sussed on the fact I was the enemy . . . "

"Fuck . . . " said Snake-Eyes, falling silent when Jay looked at him suspiciously, wondering whether the punk was being a nosy eavesdropper.

"Jay . . . This is Snake-Eyes. Snake-Eyes, Jay!"

Jay nodded in response to Snake-Eyes' raised brow greeting.

"So what happened?" Del wanted to finish the story of Jay's arrest.

"Well, there I was, they had just sussed me out. I thought, fuck I'm dead. They weren't in a hurry to pile in as they knew they had me stone-cold. Then there was this one ugly cunt. Stocky, with a face like a bulldog's. Christ, he was an animal. Anyway, he started towards me. I don't know what came over me, but I grabbed this parcel off this trolley next to me and started laying into him. Apparently the parcel contained the joining bar of a factory cart, and the guy ended up in hospital with a fractured skull! I was nicked because the police appeared behind me at the same time I whacked the geezer. Open and shut case. Must have been the easiest bust they had ever made."

"Fucking unlucky pal . . . " Derek was amused since it was the sort of stunt he had come to expect from Jay.

"Not really. The police did me a favour by supporting my version of the circumstances that I was in the middle of a big mob who wanted to kill me. I guess they felt obliged to give me a term, but it could have easily been two or three years. I mean malicious wounding isn't small potatoes . . . "

"You're right there!" said Derek, tapping him on the cheek with a playful punch. "Good to see you back out. This your getting out do is it?" Del asked with a sweeping arm indicating the other skinheads.

17

"Oh it's a getting out party all right. Not for me though," explained Jay, taking time to point out one of the larger skins. "Him!"

"Don't know him . . . " Del admitted after a cursory look. The guy was a new face to him.

"Not surprising mate. He was banged up in Angola . . . "

"Angola . . . That's Africa ain't it?"

"Well it ain't fucking Margate is it?"

"I ain't stupid mate - bit surprised, that's all! What the fuck did he do to get bird there?"

"He was involved in that mercenary expedition back in Seventy-Five. When everything turned to shit. He found himself in front of a people's tribunal. Got ten years for his involvement."

"Christ!"

"Well, he was luckier than most. A lot of them were executed!"

Derek was only half listening to Jay's words, his attention being diverted to the object of the conversation. The guy was around twenty five, making him instantly one of the top three for age. There was a strength of mannerism about the bloke, aided by his muscular build and massive arms. Just by the way the guy held sway over his court of immediate skinheads, Del could see that the guy had a particular self-styling that exuded the confidence of a leader.

"What's his name then?" Derek had already made his mind up to introduce himself into the group.

"Simon Ward. You wanna come over and check him out. He's got some great stories about his time in the mercs and the Angolan jail!"

"Yeah! Snake-Eyes?" He glanced at his punk friend.

"Nah, I'm off in a minute. I'll see you down the Roxy tonight if you get there!"

Del had the feeling that the guy was covering up a sense of unease. Yet there was no point in pushing the issue. What was there to gain? "Okay mate - catch ya there!"

Jay led while Derek followed on behind. As they arrived at the spot commandeered by the skinhead mob, Del could hear Simon talking about a jailbreak in a place called Luanda. He could only hazard a guess that he was referring to his manner of repatriation. He didn't want to disturb the recantation - it seemed prudent to leave introductions till later. For the moment, it was a matter of joining the listeners as Simon did the talking.

" . . . Anyway, they came to us and said we were being transferred to a military compound. I didn't like the sound of that. Seemed to me there was a big chance of getting one in the neck as soon as we were in the bush. So I made me mind up to make a break for it if I saw an opportunity.

"Sure enough, as we were touching the outskirts we got held up by this bus. I guess it had broken down or something as there was a lot of shouting and cursing going on. Anyway, I knew it was a now or never kind of thing. The guard was talking to some bitch who was giving him the come on. As he leant out to feel her up, I kicked him in the back."

Pausing, Simon gathered his thoughts before continuing.

"I don't know if you're familiar with the army three tonner, but it's a fair drop from the tailboard to the ground. He ended up dropping on his face, kind of wallowing around stunned, you know?"

A round of nodding assured him they did.

"Before he could get it together, I jumped down on his arm and booted him in the face. Then, snatching up his rifle, I legged it. I reckon the tart was a bit shocked by it all as she only started screaming after I had got a couple of hundred yards. By the time the remainder of the escort had broken off the argument with the bus driver, I was pretty well out of it. They only managed a few shots and I was around the corner and gone. It was easy getting away, but staying out of their hands, now that was another game entirely. They had the area tightened up within thirty minutes and it looked like the entire conscription was out looking for me . . . "

"Whatcha do then?" piped up a young skinhead whose front teeth protruded slightly - just enough to lend a rodent-like appearance to his thin face.

"I hijacked a cart carrying fertiliser to hide in - nearly suffocated on the smell, but it was the only one that wasn't gonna be searched too readily . . . "

"Did you kill the driver afterwards?"" asked rat face.

Simon looked the kid over and decided that perhaps he wasn't taking the piss, and was as naive as he sounded.

"Nah, what was the point? I pointed out that should he think of running to the authorities, he'd likely be arrested for not giving me away at the roadblock. It was enough to convince him that pretending he hadn't seen me was the best solution to his predicament."

"What did you do after that?" asked Derek, wanting to hear more on his escape.

19

"Went to the Dutch Mission. They allowed me to clean up and supplied some fresh clothes and the first real food I'd seen in years. You might think prison food here is terrible, but it ain't anywhere near as bad as the shit they were dishing up in that jail. Every day was the same. A boiled corn mash . . . "

Simon shuddered at the memory of the tasteless grey mess, still convinced that it was swill the pigs had rejected.

"Their houseboy was lent to me as a guide as he knew the border areas. Four days later, we wandered into Matadi. He went back across the border and I cadged a lift in an army truck to Kinshasa. Found the British Embassy and the Consulate General, a guy called Reid, and arranged to get on a U.K. bound flight. I got the impression that he didn't like me. For being a merc, that is. Yet there was no way he was going to throw me back to the Marxist rulers in Angola."

"First day back then?" Del asked, marking what Jay had said about the pub crawl being a getting out party.

"First day out. I spent about three days in the company of Home Office officials and members of MI5 . . . "

"What was that in aid of?" It hadn't occurred to Del that there might be repercussions back home.

"We had some trouble in the bush the authorities wanted to know about and whether I was involved or not. Then MI5 were interested in the political stability of Angola and Zaire . . . "

"What was the trouble in the bush?" the rodent asked, butting in without due consideration.

"None of your business, you nosy little shit!" Simon's voice came on aggressive all of a sudden, with a warning tone that stated flatly he wasn't going to discuss it.

The young skinhead glowered bright red and muttered something. Simon's arm shot out and his hand snatched the guy's collar up in the closing of his fist which he pressed hard against the kid's cheek.

"Always talk clearly if you're gonna say something - otherwise I might think you called me a cunt. You wouldn't want me to think that would you?"

Whatever anyone's feelings about size differences, they didn't matter in this situation. Simon appeared to be ice cold when menacing, and there was something about him that made the hardest feel uncomfortably inadequate in comparison. The kid was shaking his head, eyes wide in fright.

"Got anything else to say?" he asked.

Again the kid's head shook.

"Good!"

A little force was put into the fist to warn as well as to push the young skinhead away. Glancing around at the faces surrounding him, Simon took each one in turn, slowly. Studying the features of each individual skinhead. For the others, it seemed he was searching for some sign of resentment. If they had been privy to Simon's thoughts they'd have found the assumption to be correct.

All morning, he had been gauging the mob, noting who stood prominent and who the followers were. Then, when he decided it was time to make a play, as long as they accepted his authority, the leadership of the gang was his. The current figurehead - Mad Dave Shepperton - was a close friend by virtue of schooling together. Knowing he always had the edge on him meant a power-sharing partnership would be readily accepted by Dave.

As he scanned each face, the owner did his best not to feel self-conscious whilst portraying a laid-back and unchallenging persona. Finally satisfied, he drained his glass before he had even considered buying a refill.

The rodent saw a chance for some redemption. Reaching over, he asked Simon what he was drinking.

Simon knew he had made his impression stick on the young guy, so it didn't hurt to give a bit. "Pint of Carlsberg - cheers, mate!"

The youngster smiled in response. The "mate" spoke volumes merely from the highlighting tone. It said okay, you've learned your place so I'll forget you were winding me up. That was sufficient enough to swing the rat's mood from miserable to elated relief. It felt great to know he hadn't made the long-term enemy he thought he had.

As he left the circle to get the lager, Del followed his progress and became aware of the fact that the incident had attracted the attention of the rest of the pub's clientele. Undaunted, Del stared on, till they became aware of his staring back.

Fuck 'em!

Right at this moment it felt good to be a skinhead. His day had come to live the part he had looked up to as a kid. All the skinheads back then had treated him like a gang mascot. It was natural that the ways of the cropped haired ones had made such a big impression on him. He loved the cult with a dedication that bordered on religious mania.

21

The remainder of the session passed in a more relaxed fashion, with everyone managing at least another one if not two pints. A couple of skinheads were already blotted, having hijacked a bottle of Jim Beam from one of their parents' drinks cabinet. Staggering about, the crazy pavement of blood-shot eyes spoke volumes, as did the inability to focus properly.

The gap between last orders and chucking out time hardly seemed like the requisite ten minutes, but whether right or not, the landlord and his male bar staff were not going to take too much shit.

Early on in his tenancy, the governor had learned that pretty barmaids were meant for the lounge and part-time barmen-come-bodybuilders were what the public bar needed. It had been an expensive lesson to the tune of seven hundred pounds in fixture repairs. The first time he had experienced the after match Chelsea clientele when the team had lost. He might have got away with it, but for the arrival of a group of Sunderland supporters. The glasses that before had been used to drown sorrows were now broken with malice into some teenage northerner's face.

Straight after that, he had started employing bar staff recruited from the local gym. He paid over the odds, but the additional insurance premium paid off in peace of mind. There hadn't been much in the way of mob action in The Potter for months. Things were quiet, just the way he liked them to be. Also, clearing the bar was no longer the long-winded task it had once been. Now there were parallels for astute observers to compare the tactics to that of a beating party on a grouse shoot. Except in this case the push was towards the door, rather than on to the guns of the hunters.

Outside, the more timid members of the general public stepped up their pace, as the unruly crowd of mixed street cults spilled forth from the twin doors. Simon was back in the company of Dave towards the head of the skinhead contingent, while Del followed on further back.

Going through the doors, his attention had been drawn by the shape of the arse of the punk bird in front. She was a large but well shaped girl, wearing a satin waist coat and a dog collar, with a pink bow-tie fixed on the front by virtue of the clip-on clasp. She looked okay facially when Del had noticed her in the bar, and from the back her wet-look mini-skirt was enticingly provocative. Squeezing on the firm flesh like a second skin, it highlighted the sheerness of her panties by the visibility of the elastic lines. She wasn't aware of Derek's interest, but it wasn't something the girl would object to. Being noticed was her intention and anything to that end was a desirable course.

"So what do ya think?" asked Jay as they slipped past the governor and head barman and out on to the street.

"Think of what?" asked Del, not too sure if he was referring to the chick in front of them.

"Simon!" answered Jay, wondering where Del had gone astray. Not having the same enthusiasm for casual appreciation of the female form, the enticing carrot dangled in front of Del had gone unnoticed by Jay.

"He's something else altogether, mate. I got the feeling things will start hotting up with him on the scene . . . " Having adjusted to the difference in lighting, he regarded Jay for a moment and knew that he was going to ask him to clarify his perception.

"Don't you like the idea then?"

"Didn't say that did I?" replied Del. "We didn't become skinheads to avoid trouble did we? Part and parcel of what we are ain't it?"

"Sorry mate, thought you were turning soft for a minute . . . "

"Fuck you!" joked Del, pushing Jay in a rough-handed but playful fashion.

* * *

Up ahead, Dave and Simon were discussing employment opportunities. Dave mentioned that he knew some people who'd hire for muscle, if he was up for it. Simon made it clear that he didn't want to get lumbered with a shit security guard number, prompting Dave to outline that the jobs were more in the line of bouncing and personal bodyguards. "The fact you've had active service will put you in the top grade. Experience with and in face of firearms is a desirable commodity you know."

"Yeah, as long as it ain't bent. After the hassle I've had with the Home Office, they're liable to call for full term if I'm brought up on something heavy!"

Looking around, Simon noticed that several of the younger skinheads were hanging on his every word even though they weren't being addressed personally. It was an incredible buzz to be back and to walk straight into a prominent position. Life, after the mundaneness of the Luanda jail, was looking incredibly good.

Just in front of him, the leading group of punk girls stopped on the corner. The slight exchange of words and manner of uncertainty told Simon something was wrong.

"Teds!" yelled the girl with satin black hair.

"Let's go!" Simon said, breaking into a run and pulling Dave along by the shoulder until he matched him for pace. The rest of the mob fell in behind as they scrambled for the corner.

The scene soon opened up before them, with a fight already in progress. An outnumbered group of punks were taking a hiding from the rock and rollers. The main action was going off on the left hand side of the street, on the pavement outside a small row of shops and between the cars parked against the immediate curb. A quick head count showed a force of about 25 teddy boys, most in their late teens and early twenties. With a four to one advantage, the fight was more like a massacre.

Only one punk seemed to be giving a good account of himself. Caught on the opposite side of the street in the delivery yard of a department store, he was keeping six teds at bay by whirling a bullet belt above his head and lashing out at anyone who got too close.

The dash had dropped down to a deliberate forward march, with fists at the ready and jaws set in grim determination. Del pushed his way to the front, while Jay spread out about fifteen feet towards his left. Only a few of the teddy boys were aware of the tables having been turned.

The skinhead and punk army moved with silent resolve up until Jay decided he was close enough to strike. He had already decided his target was the nearest group of teds holding a punk over a car bonnet by both arms, while the others were punching him and hitting him with heavy belt buckles.

"HAVE 'EM!"

It was Jay's favourite one-liner for kicking off any aggro. Like a war cry of some ancient tribal group, it had the desired effect of triggering off the coiled anticipation. Dashing forward, the group was quickly narrowed to a specific target. The teddy boys were now all aware of the other mob's presence, but it was too late to affect a retreat.

Del moved off the pavement and rounded the cars, intent on having a go at the few individuals who were scrapping between the motors. A large chunk of the relief force broke after the six teds who were attacking the belt-swinging punk. One startled ted made an ill-fated dash for the High Street, only to be drop-kicked through the department

24

store's big display window. The whole pane smashed with an unbelievably loud crash. The ted lay still, sprawled in the middle of a cosy living-room setting, blood pouring from his lacerated face.

"Strike one!" cried the American punk with glee, unbothered by the condition of his victim, or the fact that the security alarms were now clanging away like some demented banshee.

The punk who had earlier been keeping the rock and rollers at bay, now felt confident enough to take the initiative and go on the attack. Ducking forward in a low bob and weave, his belt coiled upwards like a striking snake, fetching one of the distracted teds a telling blow to the side of head. "Fuck!" was all the ted managed, as he folded with his hand covering the battered temple.

"Fuck you son!" snarled the punk, angered that a few seconds ago he himself would have copped it. After whipping his victim across the back of the head, he added a Doc Marten to the face for good measure.

The other four teds were indecisive. Any chance of getting back out of the delivery yard's gates was totally gone, as the thirty or so punks spread across its mouth meant they were trapped. Two of them seemed resigned to their fate. One even managed to put a brave face on it by beckoning the enemy with his hands and calling out, "Come on you fucking garbage!"

The other two broke for the far end of the yard, in a hope that there was some way out over there. As soon as the teds' resolve broke, the attacking group of punks tore for them. The first two disappeared under the weight of the assault, with the noise of it all causing increasing panic amongst the other escaping teds.

* * *

Dave and Simon ripped through the middle of a dozen strong group of teds. With other skinheads following through, the scene quickly dissolved into a multitude of individual actions.

Derek, having rounded the cars from the road side, recognised that one of the punks the teds were trying to give a kicking to was the girl with the leopard spotted crop from earlier on. Any indecision over where to strike was quickly resolved. Their brief encounter was enough to generate a loose sense of kinship within Derek - and besides, he never liked seeing a girl take a beating from a guy.

The girl was trapped between parked cars, doubled over and trying to protect her face from the fists that sought to cause damage. Moving fast, Del ducked between the cars and grabbed at the head of the nearest teddy boy. The element of surprise was complete. The ted wasn't really aware of the fact that he had been grabbed until his face was slammed hard into the boot of a Capri.

It gave Del a sense of satisfaction to both hear and feel the impact that turned the guy into a limp sack of shit that slid to the floor. The grin that crossed his face was short lived though, when his head was jarred back by a well placed fist.

Fuck, that smarts, thought Derek, as he grabbed at the car's rear wing, hoping to be able to steady his buckling legs. Feeling exposed, it was lucky for him that the punkette had gained enough respite to come alive like a wild cat. Fists flailing, scratching and kicking, the girl's uncompromising attack denied the ted the chance to administer the coupe de grace that Del was open to.

Suzi lacked the physical stature to produce anything decisive, and with her energetic burst on the wane, there was the uncomfortable sensation that she had bitten off more than she could chew. Thankfully, rescue from the old adage came in the shape of Dave Shepperton who hauled the ted off his feet with a growling, "Come here!"

Dave threw his victim to the pavement and jumped on top to sit astride him, delivering a punishing volley of blows as he did so. It gave Del the chance to recover, just as the sound of a distant police siren reached his ears, and was joined a few seconds later by one a lot closer, somewhere out on the Kings Road.

"PIGS!" yelled Del as a warning. Grabbing the girl by the wrist, he said to her, "Come on, let's go!"

It had just dawned on her who the guy was. That bloody skinhead with all the lip. "Get off me!" she replied indignantly, trying to break his hold.

"You wanna get nicked do ya?" asked Del, tightening his hold and hauling her out from between the cars. For twenty yards or so he had to forcibly drag her. Right up until the screech of rubber announced the arrival of a police transit at the mouth of the side street. Even before the vehicle had stopped, the rear doors were thrown wide open and the first officers were out and running into the affray. Not daring to look back, the girl now matched Del's pace evenly.

The police managed to catch some of the combatants who were just too caught up in their own situations to realise that the game was up. One punk tried to break through the forming line and get clear on to

26

the Kings Road, but his luck ran out when he was brought down and struck with a truncheon. Handcuffed and still stunned, he was thrown bodily on to the floor of the Transit.

With others overtaking him along the only open avenue of escape, Del momentarily considered dumping the girl. She was hampering his chance of avoiding capture, but it wasn't in his nature to be that self-centred. Rounding the corner and finding themselves momentarily out of sight of the police, Del noticed the way the parked cars thinned for a rubbish skip which was sitting on the kerb in front of an old shop unit undergoing repair and refurbishment.

The whitewashed windows gave no indication of the nature of the interior, but on getting closer he quickly confirmed what he had suspected. The door wasn't quite flush with the frame. So, in spite of appearances, it wasn't locked.

"This way girl!", he called, ducking between two parked motors, where he halted and let a bunch of punks and skins pass in front of them. Once clear, he dashed for the shop front and booted the frame. It jarred under the force of the blow and shuddered as it swung open, exposing floor boards covered in a mixture of cement and plaster dust.

Not waiting to look more, Derek and the girl hurried in. Del dived after the small wooden prop the builders were using to create the illusion that the place was secure. This time he jammed it against the door hard and tight., ensuring that it wouldn't give as easy a second time.

From the sounds outside, Derek got the impression that the police had arrived in the area., He felt a nervous buzz rising like an old friend. A playful grin flitted across his face. It was something that the people who played the game straight could never understand. That rush of adrenaline from being on the wrong side of the fence.

In spite of popular press perceptions, there was nothing moronic about Del. Nor was he particularly malicious. It turned his stomach as much as Joe Publics to read about gangs attacking kids and old folks at football grounds, burglars beating and raping elderly victims. Mostly, Derek fought against those who wanted to fight against him.

Unlike politicians and generals, status in this arena was won by personal abilities and not off the backs of those who ended up being represented by field after field of poppy flowers. It might not be right, but it was certainly more honest than those who etched their names in the history books in the blood of others. Still, it's always been the prerogative of politicians to approve violence performed on their behalf while condemning that which is detrimental to their shepherding of the masses.

Only just got away with that one! Derek told himself.

The punk girl was looking at him as if she didn't know what to do next. She opened her mouth, but before she could speak, he quickly raised a warning finger to his lips. Then, using the same digit to motion towards the rear storeroom, he made it clear that it was the best place to get out of the way of anyone who might look too closely through one of the thinner whitewash smears.

Nodding in comprehension, the girl gingerly picked her way through the dust, her wrinkled nose underlining her displeasure of their new surroundings. If Del had been in a position to see her face, then he may have thought she was being snobbish, but he would have been well off the mark.

The musty smell of dampness and fungus triggered a half forgotten memory from her childhood. While playing with some friends in a block of domestic garages, she had found a dead tramp, lying as if asleep on a decaying sofa. As a seven year old, the discovery had deeply affected her and it had taken two years for the nightmares to subside.

Being older and more capable didn't do anything for her irrational sense of unease. The same smell was as inherent here as it had been at the time of her trauma. The fact that she hadn't been sent screaming from the place defined the only difference that being older made. Once in the back, she was thankful that the smell subsided to little more than a faint trace.

Sunlight came into the room from a small window above a sink full of building debris and covered in dust. In the corner of the room another heap of rubble, belonging to a partially demolished wall, spoke of the intent to remove the dividing barrier and open up the floor space. As Suzi looked at the debris, Derek pushed passed her and began rummaging around.

"Excuse me!" she said, trying to work out what he was about. When he opened the cupboard unit under the sink, she thought it best to ask rather than second guess. "Whatcha doing?"

Derek looked back over his shoulder, maintaining his semi-crouch. "Sometimes they leave the power tools on site."

"So you thought you'd help yourself?"

"Something like that!" Derek agreed as he turned his attention back to the cupboard's recesses.

Thirty quid or so for a ripped off drill wasn't to be sneezed at, but the temptation to question her attitude was set aside when all he could find was a rock solid packet of floor cleaner and a yellowed newspaper. Out in the light, he looked to see what had made front page news four years ago.

"How long we gotta be here?" Suzi demanded as she folded her arms around her chest to ward off the sensation of being cold. The goose pimples had formed within seconds of coming into the shop and out of the sun.

"What don't you like in here?" Derek asked flippantly.

"What do you think?" She was getting annoyed with the skinhead's attitude.

"It's better than a cell ain't it?" Derek pointed out as he tossed the 'paper aside. Moving towards her, he could see she was shivering. "Cold?" he asked.

She reacted by moving back a step. "Yeah, but that ain't an invitation to try and warm me up . . . " Her eyes showed a measure of determination, coming from a mix of discomfort and aggression.

Derek checked himself. She obviously wasn't in the best of moods, but rather than fight back against the girl's temper, he just smiled disarmingly. "Hey, I was only gonna give you this!" he said, peeling off his Harrington and holding it out to her. "It's a bit thin, but better than nothing!"

She looked at the jacket and then the skinhead's smile, and felt a bit bad for having prejudged him. If the prospect of an extra layer hadn't been so attractive, she'd have refused out of embarrassment. But taking it, she sheepishly thanked him and added, "Sorry, I guess I'm still a bit wound up from those fucking teddy boys!"

"Hey, no problem," answered Derek, feeling a measure of relief that he had covered up his original intention so convincingly.

"So what's your name, girl?" Del had decided to adapt his approach to one a bit more laid back.

"Suzi . . . And you?"

"Derek, but Del's what I get called more times than not . . . "

He offered her his hand and she accepted it with a grin. The formality of a handshake between street kids was strange enough, but the setting and circumstances took it out of all sense of normality.

Nodding towards the way they had come, Derek told her, "Best we give them time to calm down. Then we can slip away without too much trouble."

"So what we gonna do till then?" Suzi asked.

Del wondered if that was an invitation, but didn't dare risk the peace. "Let's take a look around the place. I'd lay odds we'll turn something up that's worthwhile."

Having no luck downstairs, they went up the stairs to the flat overhead. Del found a tin of royal blue paint and amused himself by painting BRIXTON SKINS on the stairwell wall. Suzi wandered off on her own, but soon called out to him. Wondering what she wanted, he placed the can and brush down and followed the sound of her voice. He found her in the bathroom holding a drill and an angle grinder in her hands.

"These what you were looking for?" she asked, delighted with being the one to find them first.

"Yeah, that's 'em!" His eyes fell on the panel she'd removed from the bath's cladding. "Any more in there?"

"Yeah, something like this one!" Suzi replied, indicating to the angle grinder by holding it up. As Derek moved in to check out the little hidey-hole, Suzi added, "You gonna cut me in on the action?"

"You're sharp, ain't ya?" Del said with an appraising look.

"Well, I did find 'em!"

"Okay, I'll cut you in - no worries!" He could have argued the toss, but what the hell. The actual split hadn't been mentioned and he still had more than just a business partnership in mind.

A canvas plumber's bag provided them with a means to carry the tools away from the Kings Road. Despite making sure the street was clear of police, Del wasn't a hundred percent relaxed until he was safely on the tube.

Meanwhile, Suzi had been talking about how she had lived in Oxford and had moved to London a year ago. Now she was sharing a squat with some other punks, just around the back of Camden Parkway.

Suzi was warming to the skinhead's company and he to hers. Derek thought there was a chance they could unload the tools in a second-hand shop on the other side of the Camden canal and then perhaps they could go back to her place. After all, he was going to the Roxy that night so they might as well go together.

30

Career opportunities are the ones that never knock,
Every job they ever offer you is to keep you out the dock
CAREER OPPORTUNITIES - THE CLASH (1977)

CHAPTER THREE

THE second-hand shop was owned by an old whizzen man with a chubby face and snow white bushy eyebrows.

"Thirty-three pounds the lot!"

Del looked at Suzi, but she just looked back. It was obvious to Del that with him and her together, the old guy had to know the goods were nicked, so there was hardly likely to be any mileage in haggling. Del nodded his agreement and the old guy snatched the bag from the counter top. Then, turning his attention to the till, he fished out the agreed amount and handed it to the young skinhead.

Derek took the money and nodded by way of a begrudged thanks. He didn't like the idea of being ripped off, but it was getting late and they weren't going to find a better offer with all the shops closing for the day.

"Tight-fisted bastard!", grumbled Derek, holding thirteen pounds out to Suzi.

She laughed. "Bloody criminal if you ask me!"

Derek knew she was poking fun at the fact the tools had been stolen in the first place and he gave her a playful push as she was jamming the money into her pocket. "Shut the fuck up!"

She put on a macho voice and danced around like Sugar Ray Leonard, her fists clenched and circling. "Gonna make me, son!"

Derek caught the sense of fun and joined in with some bobbing and weaving of his own. While he worked soft and slow jabs to her abdomen, she tapped him repeatedly on the jaw, supplying her own sound effects as she did so. "Bop, bop, bop!"

Trying to be clever, Derek dropped back, only to slip on a discarded half-eaten mango.

"The winner!" Suzi declared, arms held high in victory.

Derek had lost his sense of fun thanks to a dull aching throb in the knee that had taken the force of his fall. He gingerly testing it for weight-bearing, but ended up hobbling helplessly since it refused to co-operate.

"Hey, you all right?" Suzi asked as she grabbed him around the waist and held him up.

"Thanks," he grinned weakly, trying to pretend it didn't hurt as much as it did. "Me knee's given up on me."

"Aaah!" Suzi cooed.

Derek looked into her face, looking for any sign that she was taking the Michael, but as their eyes met, there was a strange and mutual sensation. As if they were seeing beyond the surface, perhaps into the very soul itself. Not only that, but it was drawing them together with an irresistible pull.

For Derek, Suzi's hand on his waist seemed to generate an electrical buzz of its own that flowed through him like a trembling power surge. His free hand settled above her hip and sparked the finality of their union. Romantics would refer to it as falling in love. A little presumptuous maybe, but falling certainly captured something of what was happening between them. The sensation of being drawn together was as strong as any pull gravity had on the proverbial apple.

Their lips met and defined the limit of their physical draw, yet their emotions flowed far beyond, like a spiritual union of kinetic energies. They held each other tighter, abandoning themselves to the sensations that had come alive within them. When they broke, both trembled slightly from the buzz of emotions let loose.

Suzi smiled and murmured, "You're a smooth operator!"

"Well, you didn't object!" Derek pointed out, looking into her eyes to make sure he wasn't being held solely responsible for what had happened.

Suzi shook her head lightly in agreement. Holding the smile, she kissed him again. "Shall we get a bus back to my place?" she asked.

"Sure!" The way Derek felt, anything at all was okay.

They stayed in Suzi's room at the squat until seven-thirty, listening to her collection of demo tapes of American and English new wave bands. Now Del could understand the connection that Snake-Eyes had made about new wave being a more vibrant version of glam rock.

He could appreciate the sounds of the American outfit, The Ramones, but the rehearsal tapes of The Clash and The Sex Pistols left a little to be desired. Still, Suzi had explained that they had been recorded on her portable deck and it wasn't really up to the job. She

32

was trying to get copies of the demos made for the record companies, but it was proving hard to get around the groups' managers.

Derek could only nod in agreement. The ways of the music business were alien to him. Apart from the recent spate of reggae concerts by Toots And The Maytals, Misty In Roots and artists of that stature, Derek hadn't been interested in even going to gigs. He enjoyed bands like The Sweet and Slade, but their shows were now few and far between and usually sold out well in advance. Discos and sound systems were the staple diet of his socialite aspirations.

"I've gotta get something to eat!" Derek said, feeling a knot gnawing at his stomach, reminding him that he hadn't eaten since breakfast. If you can call a cup of coffee and a slice of toast breakfast.

"Yeah, sure. Just gotta call round on a friend. Then we'll go to the Wimpy!"

"Where's that?" asked Derek as he got up off the mattress on the floor which served as a bed. What little furniture there was in the room looked like it had been salvaged from the bin men, but Suzi had still managed to create a homely aura.

"Out on the High Street, going up towards the Music Machine," she replied before heading for the door. Once in the hallway, Suzi snapped a heavy padlock into place and they were on their way.

Just outside the squat, they met some of the other residents coming in.

"Who's he?" demanded one of them.

Del looked around the faces. Black spikey hair adorned each of them and the speaker was suffering from a severe crop of acne.

"He's with me," snapped Suzi. "You got a problem with that?"

It was obvious to Del that Suzi and the guy didn't like each other.

"Should've checked it out with us first. We've got stuff in there!"

Suzi went to speak, but Derek placed a hand on her breast bone, moving between her and the guy.

"You saying I'd nick something of yours?" Del asked evenly, a sense of cold determination hanging over every word.

It was obvious that the guy hadn't expected Del to take a part in the situation with the odds stacked against him four to one. Caught on the hop, the punk could only compromise. "It's not an accusation. Just I don't know you from Adam!"

"My name's Del, not Adam!" he replied in grim sarcasm.

"Since when have you ever checked anything out with me before you do it?" Suzi then demanded of the guy.

"Okay, forget I said anything!" said the punk rocker, a bit put out that the other three were remaining silent. He would have something to say to them later on the matter.

"Yeah, don't make it sound like a favour, Greg. You know I'm right!" Suzi pointed out.

That for her closed the matter, and she left by the garden gate. Derek held Greg's gaze for a second or two then followed Suzi. Out on the pavement, he relaxed the readiness of his muscles.

"Fucking wanker!" Suzi muttered.

"Tell me about it!" Derek used the Jamaican-English phrase for understanding, but Suzi took it as an invitation to unload the aggression caused by the confrontation.

"He's always giving me grief. The other three ain't so bad, it's just they follow his lead. If it weren't for him, things wouldn't be bad at all."

"Why don't he like ya, then?" asked Derek, comprehending their was something more to the story than just a personality clash.

"He thought he could fuck me, cos I weren't with anyone . . . "

"So he got the hump when you told him to piss off?" Del continued , taking a stab at the remainder.

"Nah, he ignored it. He only got the hump after I'd kicked him in the bollocks."

Though Suzi had said it in all seriousness, Del couldn't help laughing at the way it had been delivered.

Derek wondered where she was taking him as they twisted and turned down several streets, moving away from the main drag, rather than towards it. When they finally arrived at the friend's house, it turned out to be a little more classy than the rest of the neighbourhood. The most obvious sign of alteration from the original design was the inclusion of double glazing, with its sleek modern lines lending a pronounced sense of contrast to its surroundings. Although suffering from the same ageing, the door wasn't standard council stock either. It was far more flashier, made as it was in mahogany, and decorated by panels and a large brass griffin-shaped door knocker.

As they stood on the step, Suzi used the griffin with zest to bang on the door, alerting not only the occupants, but probably half the neighbourhood as well. Moments later, the sound of the lock being drawn was followed by the door swinging open.

"Suzi!"

Derek hadn't been sure who would open the door, but the house's appearance had killed off the possibility of Suzi visiting another punk or anyone else of a street oriented nature. Nothing though could have prepared him for the gorgeous blonde bombshell now standing in front of him. Casually dressed she would have caught his attention, but in the leather mini-skirt and lacy V-necked t-shirt showing just the right amount of cleavage, it was almost too much for him.

She looked him in the eye and purred to Suzi, "Where did you find this hunk?"

Derek felt as if she had taken his breath away.

"Cut it out, Gill. You're embarrassing him!" Suzi didn't seem too bothered by the woman's come on looks. Derek took that to mean it was par for the course and therefore probably didn't mean anything.

Gillian stepped back and ushered them into the hall. "Go through to the kitchen," she said as she closed the door. Not that Suzi needed the instruction. She had been there enough times to know the procedure. Derek just adopted a relaxed attitude. It seemed best considering he didn't really know what was going on.

In the kitchen, Gillian began filling up the electric kettle. "Coffee?"

"Yeah . . . Del?" Suzi pulled his head round to face hers, noticing that he had been looking at Gillian's arse.

"Sorry?" He condemned himself with his lack of attention to what was being said.

"Coffee?" Amusement registered as a wry smile.

"Oh yeah, yeah . . . Sure, why not?"

Gillian knew she was the cause of Derek's caught in the act behaviour. Her mannerism and mode of dressing were deliberate ploys to gain a measure of control. It was strange how so many men turned to putty at the flash of a bit of thigh and an encouraging word. It had taken her all of three days to alienate herself from the rest of the women in the neighbourhood. Their husbands had been falling over themselves to do her a favour.

What did she care if the bitches were just too lame to understand that she wasn't the enemy. They were just too stupid to see that it was their own slide into insipidness that was at the heart of the wandering lust. Calling her a slut behind her back didn't change that fact. Both her and Suzi had a sense of kinship because they shared similar attitudes. One by nature, the other by desire, but sisters under the skin nevertheless.

Once the coffee had been placed in front of them and Derek had taken a healthy draft from it, Suzi got down to the business at hand. "Is Clive about?"

Gillian looked up and shook her head. "Don't matter though. Usual arrangement?"

Suzi nodded, while Derek gave up trying to comprehend the ins and outs of what was going on. Things soon became clearer when Gillian returned to her seat with a plastic container from the cupboard above the breakfast bar. Removing the airtight lid, she tipped some of its contents on to the laminated surface of the kitchen table. Little blue pills, about the size of cheap aspirins.

"Blues?" asked Derek, receiving an affirmative nod from both the girls.

"So how many you after?" Gillian asked Suzi, extracting a roll of plastic change bags.

"Give us sixty. I'll come back for more tomorrow if I need them!"

Without ceremony, Gillian bagged up the required sixty tablets. Scribbling Suzi's name on a scrap of paper that came from the container, she said, "Four a quid, that's fifteen quid tomorrow night, okay?"

"I know!" Suzi could afford a certain air of flippancy. She knew she was one of the few who were extended credit. For as long as the coffee lasted, they talked about minor things. Like the fact that Gillian hadn't seen her husband for the past two days. Not that she seemed bothered. As she explained to Derek when he asked, "He spends a lot of time away from home, when he's not in jail!"

Complaining about it didn't seem to cross her mind and she wasn't disconcerted by the part-time nature of her relationship. "It'd be stifling to try and be anything more than we are!" she pointed out, with a profound sense of wisdom that Del considered to be in advance of her twenty-six years.

Later, as he and Suzi headed for the Wimpy bar, he asked her if she thought Gillian was really happy with her lot.

"As happy as she's going to be!" Suzi replied.

Derek nodded. The response had made as much sense as the situation. Perhaps she was happy, but it was still a strange set-up.

In the Wimpy, and after mixed grill and chips paid for out of their booty, Suzi dipped into the bag supplied by Gillian. With one eye on the Asian waiter, she separated three of the blues. "Hold out your hand!" she said to Derek, dropping them into his palm as he did so.

36

"Take 'em," she said softly, dropping some into her own mouth with the mannerism of a peanut eater.

Derek looked at them momentarily. He'd never done anything but smoke a bit of hash before, but to ask questions might seem a bit wimpish.

Sod it!

He swallowed them with a mouthful of the bitter coffee that the fast food joint seemed to excel in. He shuddered involuntarily, as he always did with any form of tablet.

"A spoonful of sugar . . . " said Suzi, turning the container up and allowing another measure to fall into his cup.

"Helps the medicine go down!" added Del, remembering the old Hammerstein flick.

Suzi pointed her finger with an agreeing smile. "Exactly!"

From behind the counter, the waiter viewed them suspiciously. He had seen Suzi's playful action and feared that it would prelude something a bit more exuberant. Suzi had seen him watching, but thought nothing of it. The bloke was an insignificant closet case.

"Let's go, huh?" she said, getting up and stamping her feet to get rid of the pins and needles that were threatening.

Del slid out after rejecting the compulsion to finish the coffee, and brushed the creases out of his jeans. As they headed for the door, Suzi poked her tongue out at a gaggle of pre-teen girls watching a little too intently from a window table.

After several drinks in the Duke of Wellington on the north side of Wardour Street, Suzi and Derek headed off towards Covent Garden and the Roxy. The streets were as full of life in the evening as they had been that morning when Derek was on the other side of Shaftesbury Avenue wondering what to do.

The street that housed the Roxy was also home to a row of warehouses, lock-ups and nondescript doors that held a sense of intrigue for many a passer-by. The cobblestones gave it a forgotten world atmosphere and only the march of time prevented it being a living museum. Del knew the street well from the early morning pick-ups of produce for the stall he worked on.

Down towards the bottom end, one of the doors led into the collection of knocked together cellars that formed the basis of the Roxy club. Even before they reached the door, Derek knew where it was by the small group of punks outside, trying to get a friend up off the floor.

"Problems?" asked Suzi as they drew closer.

A large punkette looked up from her efforts of tugging on the guy's leather jacket. "Yeah. The stupid jerk's been hitting his old man's morphine!"

"Over done it a bit?" Derek noted, as the guy's spikey head lolled around like a puppet with its strings cut.

"He's always over doing it - fucking junkie!" She grabbed his lapels and violently shook the limp punk. "You hear me - you fucking junkie!"

Derek could see the grey skin and glazed eyes of someone caught in a compulsive decline. It didn't take much to work out the guy wasn't going to straighten out. He was just someone marking time until the end.

Suzi side-stepped the scene with a parting shot of "See ya in there!"

As they entered the club, Derek's interest was taken up by the welt of graffiti that adorned the walls of the descending staircase. He'd been to a few discos and clubs, but nothing of this nature. There was an air of unconventionality to the place, as if the DIY nature of the punk movement was present in every aspect, like a living spore. Never more so, than in the fashion perceptions.

The sheer variety impressed Derek. Imaginations had been fired up and cut loose. Old men's jackets adorned with safety pins and chains, fetish wear, old school clothes, plastic bin liners. Anything and everything was brought into play and used to extend and intensify their self-portrayal.

In all, Derek reckoned on about a hundred and seventy punters in the club. It was throbbing, but not jammed out as yet. Suzi began her sales pitch straight away and it was soon obvious to Derek that there were many regulars for her wares.

Over by the stage, Snake-Eyes promise was being fulfilled by a Rastafarian DJ who announced himself periodically as Don Letts, while fusing old time commercial reggae with deep roots and steppers. Derek was enjoying the scene, and the exhilaration of the amphetamine was just beginning to grip him when Suzi returned with three cans of lager on their plastic binder.

"Enjoying it?" Suzi asked.

Derek nodded.

"Good!" She was pleased they had common ground. Taking one can for herself, she handed the others to Derek. "Take them, you'll be feeling thirsty soon!"

"Thanks!" he said, aware of the thirst beginning.

"I'm gonna have to float around for a while . . . try and sell this gear. You wanna come or you gonna be all right here?"

Derek held up the cans of lager as an indication that he was okay now. Suzi responded with a knowing wink and went about her business, leaving Derek to crack open one of the cans and take a good swig. The beat of a Joe Gibbs dub tune, *No Bones For The Dogs*, appealed to his sense of rhythm and drew him into a lazy skank. There was something about the tune that held the essence of early reggae while trading on a par with the established hit style of the Town & Country label as represented by *Up Town Top Ranking* and *Money In My Pocket*.

Having finished her initial sweep of the joint and having off-loaded two-thirds of her supply, Suzi was now more at liberty to relax and let the remaining trade come to her. From what she could make out, not a moment too soon either. She'd spotted two punk girls getting in close to Del while over the other side of the club - not that Del had noticed the interest he was being paid. Still, it wouldn't hurt to let them know that he was taken before they got any ideas of cutting in ahead of her.

Del smiled at her as she approached. Her hands touched his face and they kissed. Even as they embraced, Suzi's eyes were on the two girls. The one with the inverted swastika drawn on her left cheek smiled briefly - as much as the safety pin through her other cheek would allow anyway. Suzi winked, then allowed her eyes to close and enjoy the embrace for its own sake.

The DJ clicked out and the main PA came on with a whistle that hummed out as a crackle. The opening band were on the stage, the bass player spilling slops from his glass as he staggered about. Much to Derek's amusement, the guy looked ready to be thrown out by the bouncers rather than getting set to perform.

As Derek watched, the lead singer swayed on the microphone stand like an idle chimpanzee. "Okay, closets. They say we're morons. Clueless klutzes without an original idea between us. Not surprising really . . . We're the Xtraverts and this is *Blank Generation*!"

Derek, not knowing what to expect from these punk bands, jumped involuntarily as the first guitar stabs burst out and the drum roll struggled to gain altitude in the audio fog. Suzi giggled and Derek could only smile weakly.

The roll emerged into a heavy beat, not so far from that of terrace chants, something that struck Del straight away. Suzi, knowing the words, sang along.

"Blank-blank-blank-blank-blank Gen-ner-ration!
What-what-what-what you gonna do?
No-no-no-no-no sophistication
They - all - laugh at you!"

A crowd had emerged from nowhere to fill the vacant space in front of the stage, all dancing in a wild and ecstatic manner. The pogo saw many varieties. The Hanged Man, referring to the angle of the head as it rested, crooked against the shoulder, to The Epileptic, with arms and legs jerking in spasms. One guy even had his girl on the floor and was throttling her in time to the music - something they had picked up from watching *The Rocky Horror Show*.

Derek was feeling great, speed aside, and the place suddenly had the same electricity as Stamford Bridge on a Saturday afternoon. A pyrotechnical display of emotion that created illusions of individual invincibility, while bonding those present into a coherent group.

"Do you like it?" Suzi asked, noticing his teeth were grinding, but not sure if it was the speed or the music.

"Like it? I love it!" Derek declared.

"That one's trouble . . . " Bobby the head bouncer mentioned as he leaned against the bar rail, popping peanuts into his mouth from the complimentary bowl provided.

Nicky Dawson looked at him quizzically. "Which one?"

Bobby regarded the young charge he had personally taken under his wing. "That skinhead over there! "His index finger gave the briefest of indications.

Nicky followed the direction shown, and through the dancers he saw Simon stagger on the three steps that separated the booths and tables from the trendy nightclub's dance floor. "Wanna throw him out?" he asked, keen to show the right attitude to the new job.

"No . . . slow down," said Bobby laying a restraining arm on Nicky's shoulder. "Take a look to the left of the jockey's platform."

Doing as he was told, Nicky saw a group of half a dozen skinheads and a few other likely lads. "Mob handed, eh?"

"Got it in one, Nicky my boy!" Bobby was being sarcastic in a warm sense. "Always look before you leap!"

"Even so, I reckon we can take 'em," said Nicky weighing the group up for physical build.

"You could be right, but here begins the first lesson. Not only do we have to sort trouble out, but we have to do it discreetly. That's the difference between our company and a run of the mill minder."

Bobby regarded the young body builder with the paternal sense of a father teaching his son the family business. Which had an essence of truth because Nicky was Bobby's twenty year old nephew and more the kind of son he had hoped his own boy would have been. Thanks to Maria, Ian was never going to be a typical East End guttersnipe what with her private schools and university plans for him. Not that Bobby minded the cost. His security business provided the kind of money usually associated with a South Kensington address.

* * *

Simon regained control of his feet, and continued towards the booth of girls he had seen across the dance floor. Paula saw him lurch past the disc jockey and she silently prayed to the gods that he wasn't headed for her.

She had been aware of his stares for the last 20 minutes. Her best friend Sarah had correctly supposed that the guy had his eye on Paula. *Shit, why me?* she thought as Simon steadied himself with both hands on the edge of the table.

"Hello darling - what you drinking?"

Sarah couldn't help burst out laughing. Even when the skinhead glared at her, she wasn't going to be pushed into an introvert retreat.

"What's so funny?" Simon asked, holding her eye contact.

"Corn on the cob - that's what!"

"Do what?" asked Simon. The subtle nature of the blonde girl's tongue went straight over his head in his present condition.

"'Ello darling!" Sarah responded with the corn she was referring to.

"All right, so originality went out the window a few pints ago - so what?" Even seven parts cut, Simon managed to formulate what he considered a reasonable response. "Who am I to knock tradition?"

"Hey, don't give the guy a hard time, he's just trying to be friendly!" said Paula.

Sarah regarded her suspiciously, thinking she must have lost her mind.

"Yeah, that's right. Give me a break will ya?" complained Simon, sensing her objections didn't hold true for everyone. But he missed the sly wink that Paula passed Sarah as he sat down at their table.

"Gin and tonic."

Simon looked at the girl quizzically.

"You asked me what I was drinking!" reminded Paula.

"So I did. You want another?" he asked, looking at her face, but not quite getting her eyes into focus. *Were they green or grey?*

"That's nice of you to ask!" Paula said as if the offer had only just been made.

"My pleasure sweetheart, believe me!" With that, Simon left for the bar.

"You fucking crazy?" Sarah asked, after she made sure the skinhead was out of earshot.

"No, I'm just out to have a laugh!" replied Paula.

"With a drunken slob like that?"

"There's more to having a laugh than dropping your knickers!"

Sarah didn't like the way Paula had said that. Was her remark supposed to carry a personal meaning? Sometimes she wondered if they really were best friends. It was as if she was only there to be a fall guy. Still, there was no point pulling her up about it now. Past experience had taught Sarah that Paula would never retract in front of others. It was best to hold off till the following day and ask what she meant then.

As Simon took his turn at the bar under the watchful eye of the Dawson clan, Paula took her tweezers and compact from the make-up case in her handbag. From behind the compact's mirror, she took one of half a dozen Red Star blotters and, using her tweezers, sloshed the acid tab around in Simon's half finished lager.

"You're a bitch!" Sarah said, her eyes sparkling with a sense of shared mischief.

Simon found them to be totally different on his return. More talkative and hanging on his every word. Paula was enjoying building the guy up for his trip by making great play on her preference for horror movies. As they talked, the DJ carried on spinning the latest disco imports from the U.S. interspersed with European acts like Baccara.

"Okay! Let's turn to the Caribbean where the music is as hot as the sun! This is Bob Marley & The Wailers and *Could You Be Loved*."

The other lads who had turned up with Simon decided it was right to leave him the space to go solo, and saw the reggae track as their cue to occupy the dance floor. Simon was too engrossed to care about the music. A slight sobering effect was occurring as the speed buzz prior to the full hallucinogenic stage began to bite. "Excuse me girls - gotta shake hands with the vicar."

As he moved towards the toilet, Bobby tapped Nicky on the shoulder. "Action stations, kid!"

Following Simon, Bobby let him go into the toilet. "We'll get him on the way out!" he said to Nicky as he moved to lean against the mirror wall.

Inside the toilet, Simon was feeling a bit strange, something he put down to the fact he'd been drinking all day. The neon lighting seemed intense and caused a certain amount of spots and blotches, as if it had a fault that caused it to flicker. The textured artex on the wall around the urinals seemed to flow around as if liquid rather than solid.

"Shit . . . time to stop drinking!"

Nicky had been waiting to the left of the toilet door, and as Simon came through, he grabbed him with a headlock. Surprised and shocked, Simon grappled the arm that was tight against his windpipe. Even with his vision fogged by the pressure of the hold, he could see Bobby moving in from the left. Still struggling, he gauged the bouncer's approach and at the right time, his foot flashed up and found the soft part of the guy's groin.

Pain flashed through the big man's frame at the speed of light, and a silent scream exploding in his mind as his hands went to the source of the pain. Simon grinned as the bouncer staggered in search of support.

Nicky threw Simon from him, sending the skinhead crashing and bouncing into the wall. Even before he had fallen, Nicky had driven him to the floor and was punching him with a fury. His first blow had been a good one and Simon was too stunned to offer any affective resistance. Nicky would have happily shredded the skinhead, but another doorman restrained him. "Don't play with him! Sling the bastard out!"

Grabbing him together, they hauled the skinhead's semi-conscious form to the entrance door where they launched him like a rag doll down the stairs and on to the street.

"Go and sort Bobby out," the doorman said. "I'll make sure this one doesn't get back in!"

Nicky nodded and returned to the foyer.

On the pavement, Simon thrashed about until he found out where his feet were. Coming up on awkwardly splayed legs, he shook his head in an effort to clear the fog. Then he dabbed his face with the back of his hand, looking at the blood that came from his split lip. "Fucking cunts!"

"You'll get more if you try and come back here!" called the doorman who had been watching him flounder around like a fish out of water.

Simon turned and glared manically, but the bouncer remained aloft and unimpressed.

Spitting out what blood there was in his mouth, the skinhead moved away down the main street, muttering to himself. "Fucking do 'em next time!" he promised.

In spite of the pain, he was feeling quite elated. There was something warm and radiant about the throbbing from his lip and bruises. The street seemed enormous and expansive, yet intriguing rather than threatening. The lit shop windows up ahead sparkled like beacons.

There's something weird going on here!

A tantalising tingle ran through him like an ebbing wave, drawing up and pushing outwards.

"Jesus!"

Simon was a bit shocked by the sudden rush, but it was a pleasant sensation. So good that he laughed involuntarily. One of the tunes the DJ had been playing looped through his mind, its rhythm so compelling that he felt unable to resist the beat. His walking took on a bopping kind of step and, noticing the cracks in the pavement, it became his task to avoid them. Hard work considering their disrepair.

As he reached the traffic lights, a patrol car pulled over. The two police officers had been watching his antics as they came up behind him. The cop in the passenger seat wound down his window and called over to Simon, "Oi, son - a word!"

Looking up from the interesting pavement, Simon saw the white car with the wicked glowing red band along its length. *It's the pigs,* thought Simon. The connection between pigs and the police gave a certain logic to Simon's dismissive reply of, "Not by the hair of my chinny-chin-chin!"

"What the fuck . . . ?" the driver of the panda car said to his buddy.

44

"He's on something - look at his eyes!" the other answered.

"Are you the piggy that went to market or the one that stayed at home?" Simon asked in an earnest sort of way.

"No, I'm the little pig that arrested the young arsehole!" the cop replied as he and the driver opened their doors and stepped out on to the street.

"Oh oh, heavy shit!" mused Simon. He knew he should be worried, but frankly he couldn't give a damn. It was merely film life, celluloid clichés in the flesh.

"You been out tonight, son?" asked the officer standing in front of Simon, while the driver rounded the car with one hand on his truncheon. This fact didn't escape Simon's attention and a semblance of sobriety returned. He looked at the cop, then the pavement and back to the cop. "Well I didn't stay in did I?"

"Don't smart mouth me!" the cop angrily spat out, making a grab for the skinhead.

Simon stepped back out of range, his hands up in an attempt to pacify the policeman. "Hey you asked a question. I gave you a straight answer!"

"Okay, you're coming with us!" snapped the driver.

"I wouldn't do that if I were you, Constable!"

All heads turned to the intruder. Simon recognised the voice as belonging to an American, but had no idea who the man was.

"I'd suggest you leave, sir. This is no business of yours!" said the driver as he faced the guy who was in his mid-forties and wearing a pair of blue slacks, a cream coloured sports shirt and an expensive pair of Italian shoes. A white jacket was slung across his shoulder. His hair was greying and a bit thin on top, but his face was hard set and lean, like his physique.

"I think I'll stay and see that justice is served, if you don't mind!"

Simon liked the guy's style. Much to the irritation of the patrolmen, he had the same uncaring frame of mind that Simon himself felt.

"I do mind, sir. Either you leave or we'll arrest you as well!"

"On what charge, may I ask?" he asked, peering at the cop through gold rimmed spectacles. The threat was water off a duck's back for all it appeared to mean to him.

"We'll think of something!" promised the second officer.

The American peered thoughtfully at the policeman for a second then spoke. "Perhaps I can save you some embarrassment by telling you that any charge you care to make up will be set aside via diplomatic immunity. Then your ass will be grass once I start hollering about your dubious techniques!"

To assure the pair that he was in a position to carry out his threat, he opened his wallet and held it under the noses of the two officers. Simon enjoyed the look of dismay that crossed their faces. The American had the same sense of satisfaction, knowing that he had deliberately played them into a corner of their own making.

"Ah . . . shit!" the cop said, looking at the I.D. card then comparing its photograph to the person in front of him. There was no mistaking the guy was who he said he was - a trade attaché to the American Embassy.

Silently the driver cursed, knowing it was going to take some backtracking and sweet talk to get them out of the situation. "Sorry about that Mister Ritter. My partner does tend to get a little excited. In view of your status there is little point pursuing a charge of obstruction. So if you'll excuse us, sir, we'll just take this yobbo with us . . . "

The cop reached to grab Simon's collar, but the skinhead reacted by ducking slightly, and moving away. The intense look on his face spelled entertainment as far as the two bored patrolmen were concerned.

"Come on, son . . . " the second cop said, not really wanting the youth to comply. He moved forward, his hand already resting on the handle of his truncheon.

The American had other ideas, and stepping in between the officers and the skinhead, he held up his hands. "Hold your horses. I don't think you quite appreciate the situation here. If you arrest this man, I'll have to come down to the station as a witness . . . " He looked at the cops and saw that the older one understood straight away. For the benefit of the younger and more naive policeman, he continued to spell it out in full. "If that happens, I'll have to tell - now how does it go? Ah, yes! The truth, the whole truth and nothing but the truth! How do you think we can overlook the threat of false arrest if we've got to do that?"

He smiled in a benevolent manner. It was enough to convince the Sergeant that there were better things to do. His partner wasn't so ready to walk away. Craning his neck, he called after the driver. "Sarge! Ted?! We can't let them do this?"

"Don't you understand?" the Sergeant replied as he opened the car door. "He's the one that got away!"

Angrily, he slammed the door and started up the motor. The young cop looked at Simon, then back to the car when his mentor called out, "Come on Robby, we've wasted enough time here!"

Not to be outdone, the young cop glared past the American at Simon, who was looking back with mild amusement "I'm gonna have you, son!" he warned.

"Not until we've been going steady!" Simon smirked back.

Anger boiled within the cop, but his Sergeant's impatience was more pressing. "Robby! Get your arse in the car!"

"Goodnight, SIR!" he snapped at the American as a final gesture.

"And to you cunt-stable!" retorted Simon, happy to take advantage of the situation.

With a malicious glare, the cop returned to the patrol car and an angry exchange with his partner. Simon and the American watched as the police car pulled away and cut up a Volvo estate as it sped through the lights.

"It's not clever to mouth the law!" the American said, pushing the glasses back up the bridge of his nose. It was an irritation that they kept slipping, but as his optician had explained, that was one of the drawbacks of having what was called a Roman nose.

"They asked for it!" Simon said, not really giving a damn about the advice offered. Now that the tension was draining from him, the fractured light show was returning and his eyes winced as they tried to focus.

"You should leave the acid out as well, son. It'll fuck your brain up!"

"I ain't taken any!" Simon answered back. He knew that much was true, but he was still at a loss to explain the sensations he was feeling. Then it dawned on him. "The fucking bitch!"

The American laughed. "Slipped you a mickey huh?"

"I'll kill her!" Simon went to return to the club, but the American laid a restraining hand on his shoulder.

"What and get into another fight with the security?"

Looking at the American, he found the man's face suddenly brighter and enlarged, like the centre of the universe. Strangely, this visual phenomena didn't interfere with his reasoning. "You saw that, huh?"

"Yeah, I followed you out! Good job I did really!" responded the American.

"Can't argue with that . . . " agreed Simon as he shrugged the guy's hand off. "But why did you follow me? What was you doing in the

47

club for that matter?" Apart from the Yank's age, an East End dive wasn't exactly high on a socialite's calendar.

"Questions, questions . . . " the American said, weighing up Simon.

"Cut the shit and get to the point!" Simon had several ideas running around his mind, and he didn't like the prospect of any of them, especially if the guy was a nonce.

"Okay, I'll be straight with you. I've been asked to find someone for a job that some friends of mine have in mind. Kind of out of the ordinary. So I came out east to find someone to fit the bill!"

"Muscle?" Simon asked, pointing to himself.

"Uh-huh."

"What sort of job?"

The American looked at him and decided that perhaps right now wasn't the best time for a detailed explanation. Reaching into his pocket for his wallet, the American took out a business card and handed it to Simon. "Give me a call in the morning . . . I'll explain it then!"

"What does it pay?" Simon asked.

"It pays well!" responded the American as he folded his wallet, replaced it and walked away.

* * *

Snake-Eyes had arrived by the time Wire were on the stage. He came over and greeted Derek, who by now was speeding like a jet. "You made it then?"

"Yeah!" nodded Derek like one of those toy dogs that occupy the rear window of many a tasteless driver's car.

Snake-Eyes nodded to Suzi. "You two together?"

"Uh huh!" she responded, her eyes darting wildly between the two guys.

"When did this happen?"

"This afternoon," Del said, "When we was dodging the law!"

"Oh yeah?"

"Yeah!" Suzi added, hugging Del's waist.

"Guess you could call it love at first fight!" Del said with a light-hearted smile.

"Daft sod!" laughed Suzi.

Turning his attention to the band, Derek began to appreciate the immense power of the band, egged on by a droning bass sound fuzzed beyond recognition. His head moved in time to the rhythm dirge.

"Hey I'll catch you two later," Snake-Eyes shouted in his ear. "Gotta see if I can pull something!"

"Yeah, sure man. Check ya later!" Del said, holding a thumb up.

Suzi looked around and saw an assembly forming around a group who had just arrived. "Del, come here. I want you to meet some people!"

Pulling him by the hand, he followed her into the midst of the clique. "Joe . . . Meet me boyfriend!" she called as the guy held up a hand in recognition.

"Alright mate?"

"Joe, this is Del. He got me out of a bit of aggro this afternoon with the teds". Then to Del she said, "You remember that tape I played you this afternoon?"

"Which one?" asked Del as he shook Joe's offered hand.

"The Clash at Sheffield!"

"Oh, yeah."

"Yeah, well this is the singer - Joe Strummer!"

"Nice one mate!" Derek told him.

"We're better than that tape makes out - it's a fucking awful recording!"

"Yeah, where's me copy of the demo then?" Suzi asked. "You keep saying you'll sort one out for me!"

Joe looked at her in an apologetic way. "You know what Bernie's like . . . He won't let no one have a copy in case it gets bootlegged!"

"Are these others members of the band?" Derek wanted to know.

"Yeah. The guy over there with the greasy hair's Mick Jones. Next to him's Paul Simonon. Terry's not here!"

"Never is, is he?" Suzi said, knowing all about the drummer's aloft edge.

"Well, it's his way. He's just like that you know! We're rehearsing tomorrow . . . You coming?" Joe asked, as Paul butted into the conversation and said, "Hey Joe, there's a guy over here who wants to do a piece on us . . . "

"Okay, I'll be there in a minute . . . Well?"

"Since when have I ever needed an invitation?" said Suzi.

"Okay - see ya tomorrow!" With that Joe turned and joined Paul and a chubby looking guy over by the bar.

"Okay this is our last one and it's called *1- 2 XU*!" the singer informed the crowd as he wiped the sweat dripping from his brow.

A joker in the audience jeered, "About fucking time!", as the squalling wall of noise flooded from the PA.

"Come on, I'll teach you how to pogo!" Suzi declared.

"Nah!" Del was feeling a bit conspicuous still, yet his smile said he really didn't mean the objection he was making.

That was the way Suzi took it anyway. "Come on . . . don't be a closet case! Enjoy yourself!" she bemoaned, grabbing his arm and pulling him along.

"You talked me into it!" Although self-conscious to begin with, Del slid into the activity quite well. He was grateful for the fact that he had something to apply the charge running through him to. Unlike the precision of the disco delights, it didn't seem to matter how you behaved to the energy. Like swimming, you just dived in and let yourself go.

Before the next band came on, Suzi disappeared and returned with another batch of lager. It seemed to Derek that the idea was to bring your own - a good thing to remember for next time.

X-Ray Spex were good in Derek's opinion. The inclusion of a saxophone player set them apart from the other two bands, as did the singer who was a chubby half-caste with a mouthful of metal courtesy of a National Health brace. Her hair was wild, like a destroyed and close cut affro, and she was decked out in a bin-liner dress and torn t-shirt minus its sleeves. She grappled with the microphone like she wanted to throttle it, climb along its chrome length and reach out into the audience.

"I like this outfit!" Del called into Suzi's ear, as the band tore into a rendition of *Identity*. The reference to skinheadism had caught his attention straight away, not that the lip service was solely responsible for him liking them. Their sound was a very vibrant form of pop rock and the sax added a transitional line of melody that could accentuate or bind the output into a glossed delivery.

Suzi took several sideways glances at Del as the concert progressed. It was obvious that he was enjoying the experience and that meant a lot to her. It also tickled her sense of irony that they had come together by chance. She probably wouldn't have looked twice if it had been any other way.

* * *

50

Simon forced the key into the lock after wavering around it for a few seconds. It had been a bit of a job to get back to the bed and breakfast he had been booked into earlier that day, mainly because of the drug's continued effect.

The B&B accommodation had been arranged courtesy of the Home Office rehabilitation services and was little more than a glorified bedsit, a prize shit-hole of the first order. At least the grumpy old bastard of a landlord did him the favour of staying away in his ground floor room.

Climbing the stairs with great difficulty, he turned the second lock and nearly fell over groping for the light switch. The flood of light made him wince as it shone off the white walls, giving the room an even colder sensation. Tonight it was something Simon was grateful for as it produced its own semi-sobering effect.

He sat down on the bed in the sparsely furnished room and undid the laces of his boots. The business card given to him by the American was placed on the bedside cabinet. Others might have questioned such a twist of fate, but not Simon. Active service had taught him nothing was strange and things that seemed crazy usually had their own sense of logic anyway.

Callen, his Commander In Chief, had been an out and out psychopath who was given the chance to indulge his megalomaniac tendencies. As the laces slipped snake like through the eyelets, his mind drifted to the time when Callen got hold of the Dutch Sergeant's pump-action shotgun.

Simon had been watching from the shade of a Wills Jeep, his back against the tyre and a can of light-ale in his hand. While he supped the tepid liquid, Callen discussed the gun's capabilities with the Sergeant and called one of the native regulars over to prove his point. Ordering him to open his mouth, the barrel of the gun was placed inside. Like the Sergeant, Simon thought Callen was just going to test the soldier's loyalty . . . right up until the back of the man's head exploded, and blood, brain and shredded bone splattered over them like a violent cloudburst.

"Fucking bollocks!" Simon had screamed as he jumped up and sent his can of ale flying.

Colonel Callen didn't even bat an eyelid when he responded coldly, "I think you'll find that was the man's brains. His bollocks are a lot lower!"

The Dutch Sergeant had laughed, while Simon scowled at him. Other potential witnesses had scurried away rather than get caught up in a confrontation. He'd heard that the Colonel had strange tendencies, but it was the first time he had experienced them in the flesh.

"Go and get a bath, soldier!" Callen had ordered. Simon wouldn't usually let someone take him for a fool, yet a voice in the back of his head told him that Callen wasn't someone to be messed with. The order provided a measure of vindication for a retreat in the face of an impending catch 22 situation.

"Crazy fucker!" his voice echoed around his head as he finished easing the boots off. Swinging his feet up on the bed, he began to explore the past three years as disjointed images popped into his head. The approach by Banks, the final luxury of the air flight, the awful truth of the "modern arsenal" they had been promised. Little more than decommissioned Lee Enfields donated by the British government, bren guns and grenade launch cups - laughable if it hadn't been his arse on the line.

His first action upwind had been to relieve a dead MPLA fighter of his Kalashnikov rifle. A supply of ammunition wasn't hard to secure either. The rebel forces were poorly trained and lacking in the principle team work of a true fighting unit. Any action, no matter how minor, would yield an extra four or five clips at least. Besides which, the Russian semi-automatic was quite adapt at taking mismatches in munition sizes without jamming or destroying the breech mechanism.

Simon found that the acid trip really kicked hard when the light was switched off. Robbed of outside sensations, the mind was at liberty to wander through reality and fantasy at will. Like a freeform artist, the lack of discipline blurred everything together. Not that Simon cared. Now that he understood the nature of the ailment, he was happy enough to let it runs its course. At least it wasn't fatal like the bout of malaria that had taken Pete Hounslow to the end of the road. A youngster like Simon, Pete had joined the expedition out of necessity. The military and civilian police were after him for desertion and armed robbery.

Sleep was a long time in coming. Though aware of a physical need, the mind refused to succumb . . .

* * *

Suzi and Derek joined the flow of people out of The Roxy. The market was still deserted bar a watchful patrol car which monitored the club-goers from a distance. Still speeding, sleep seemed like a nonentity, so they joined a group of Sidcup punks in a jaunt to the coffee bar under the arches.

For the next couple of hours, they chatted freely with Derek thirstily buying milk by the gallon. He idly stroked Suzi's thigh under the table, but the amphetamine quashed the essence of passion into some distant unattainable thing.

At around three in the morning, and on Suzi's insistence, they got a cab back to the squat. The driver had insisted on the three pounds fifty upfront before he'd even select first gear, thinking they looked likely candidates to do a runner.

Back in Camden Town, Suzi was thankful that the others weren't up. It saved having another argument with them. "Home sweet home," she said to Del, switching on the stolen street hazard light that served in the absence of electricity.

Derek watched her in the yellow strobe as he lay on the mattress. He found her sexy in a veiled kind of way. Perhaps it was the differences in the way she made herself appear compared to the majority of girls. There was something alive and alluring, an air of independence rather than submission.

Not that Suzi was out and out defiant. She still responded to her emotions in the same way as anyone did. Yet neither of them could muster much interest in sex. Exploring hands didn't stimulate the strength of response they should have. Like a simmering pot, boiling point wasn't quite reached. Sleep induced a break as dawn's light painted a glowing square on the wall over the mattress.

Shit! was the last thing Derek could remember thinking.

I don't wanna holiday in the sun
I wanna go to the new Belsen
I want a piece of the history
Now I've got a reasonable economy!
HOLIDAYS IN THE SUN - SEX PISTOLS (1977)

CHAPTER FOUR

SIMON woke feeling like shit.   The strange room set him immediately on edge, making him wonder where the hell he was. A cold perspiration covered his brow as he stared wildly around, but from the recesses of his mind, a recollection of all that had taken place began to form.

Angola was far behind him and instant relief allowed the mental replay to begin from the time spent in the Home Office's debriefing centre and the return to London with the travel warrant and cash provided. Meagre though it was, it would see him through.

Then he'd looked up his old mate Dave Shepperton and found him to be a skinhead. They had joked that Simon already had the hair for it thanks to the Angolans following Russia's lead in shaving the heads of all prisoners. Dave had even sorted him out with a spare of jeans, a t-shirt and a pair of braces. Further on there was the piss up, several fights, the American . . . and something about a job

Looking over at the cabinet, there was the card Simon was hoping to see. Howard Ritter, underscored by a Queensway address and a telephone number. Not knowing what time it was, he didn't really care about waiting. Ringing the guy would provide him with a distraction if nothing else.   Dressing as quickly as the after effects would allow, he went out in search of a telephone box.

Howard was woken by the trill of the phone in the living room. Getting up, he grabbed the dressing gown from the back of the door and headed for the phone. Picking the receive from its cradle, he stifled a yawn. "Hello?"

"Is that Howard Ritter?"

It was obvious the enquiry was being read off a card from the slow pronunciation of his name. He needed no second guess to realise that it was the skinhead from the night before. "Yes, it is!"

"We met last night. I'm . . . "

"Yeah, I know who you are!" Howard replied.

"Great, you mentioned something about a job?" Simon said testingly. He knew it might still be early, but if the guy really wanted him for the job - what ever it was - then there was room for a little push on his behalf.

"I don't want to discuss it over the phone. Look, um . . . "

"Simon!" the skinhead supplied as he watched a guy pass the telephone box and headed towards the corner shop.

"Okay, Simon. You have my address on my card so maybe we can discuss it over breakfast. How long will it take you to get to Queensway?"

"I dunno? About an hour, I guess!"

Howard gave him directions from the tube station and added, "I'll see you in an hour then!"

Howard was in the middle of cooking when his doorbell rang. Putting the frying pan on the back ring, he rubbed his hands on the tea towel and went to answer the door. Opening it, he looked at Simon and then stepped back. "Come in!"

Simon could smell the odours of food cooking and it reminded him that he hadn't eaten since leaving the government centre two night's before. Following the American into the kitchen, he sat down at the table as indicated, while Howard returned the frying pan to the heat.

"Feeling better?" Howard asked as he turned the rashers.

Simon looked at the guy hovering over the stove. "Drained like shit, you know?" Simon responded, his eye falling on the set table before him and the glasses of orange juice.

Howard had seen the eye movement. "Help yourself to the juice. It's the best thing after a tab!"

That was the invitation Simon had needed to feel relaxed. He swallowed half the tumbler's contents in a series of gulps before he felt satisfied enough to take his time. "You mentioned something about a job?" Simon came right out with it as he peered into the glass at the creamy liquid.

"Yes I did, and you wanna know what it involves?"

Looking up at Howard, Simon nodded. "Yeah, something like that!"

"Okay, point one. I know you're a merc fresh out of Angola."

"How?"

"I've got a contact in the Home Office and did some checking, but that isn't important. I don't know how aware you are of the political situation here in England, but it's fair to say I have some friends here who think it's not good."

Simon had the feeling that the point was a long way off, but what the hell. This was his place, his job offer - his dime!

"Now, they want to do something about it, but cannot be seen to be doing something about it because their public acceptance is still a fragile entity . . . "

"What are we talking here? National Front?" Simon was aware of their presence. There had been several members on the books in Angola.

"Yes, I suppose that is a valid supposition. Well, anyway . . . excuse me a minute while I plate this up will you?"

Moments later, Simon was tucking into a steaming hot plate of bacon, eggs, hash browns and beans. A cup of filtered coffee was also lined up in formation with the juice.

Seated opposite Simon, Howard returned to the point of the conversation. "It was decided that action could only be taken in the third party which is where you come in. We need your talents on the street working for us!"

"I ain't a hitman!" Simon said, jumping to the conclusion that the American was talking in terms of Mafia type contracts.

"Oh, nothing like that is called for. Not that it'd be a bad thing mind you. No, what is on the table is limited to acceptable harassment - roughing up certain individuals, breaking up meetings and putting certain operations out of action. Things of that nature!"

"So where do you fit into this?" Simon asked, sawing at the bacon with his table knife.

"Well not meaning to boast, but I created this little plan. It occurred to me that whilst their hands were tied to a need for public acceptance, there was no way they could be seen to be actively involved.

"I don't know if you've seen the way they organise their marches? At no point can a riot be blamed upon their members' behaviour because they restrain themselves until the left-wing factions have attacked and been seen to attack. In this way, they absolve themselves of responsibility for what takes place.

"Several members though have been expelled for overstepping the bounds of acceptable behaviour. My idea was to use this expelled element to create the appearance of a breakaway faction with its own identity, a more extreme version of the NF. Not only will it divorce the party from any political attacks we have ordered, but it will also have an additional benefit of making the National Front appear all the more middle of the road in comparison."

"It won't work - the press are going to suspect a connection," Simon pointed out.

Howard nodded, smug in the fact that it had already been taken into account. With his hands held together like an evangelist, he smiled triumphantly and said, "We've already considered that possibility. The Executive Council is drawing up an additional list of selected members who will act as unwitting sacrifices, thereby creating the impression that they are also targets of this splinter group."

"Devious!" Simon allowed. He could see that Howard wasn't one to be taken for granted.

"Now you're probably wondering where you fit into this. Well, for all good feints to work, it's necessary to have some fall guys. In this case it's going to be the leaders and members of this new group. You will be our plant if you like, within that organisation. You'll be the only one aware of the true nature of its existence!"

"So, why me, eh? Surely one of the ex-members would be happy enough to carry out the facade?"

"Yes, sure, but they can't be trusted. They're too . . . how shall I put it . . . full of themselves. Too loud with their mouths and loose with their talk. No, we need someone we can trust implicitly. Does this sound like you?"

"What you mean is someone who'll stay silent if caught. Name, rank and serial number, yeah?" Simon said, pushing the finished plate away and sliding the coffee into its place.

"Got it in one!" Howard declared.

"Where do you fit into this then?" asked the ex-mercenary.

"I've several roles. Financial courier for the new movement. I've managed to persuade the American Aryan Fellowship to finance the operation. It wasn't hard . . . they feel a certain affinity with hardcore extremists. Then I'll also be your contact and paymaster, acting as go between for the real intent. I'll relay instructions on targets as and when necessary!"

"Okay, how do I get into this group? Don't they resent an outsider being brought in?"

"You're already in. I suggested that they should have a membership modelled on Braun's S.A. - the brownshirts of Hitler's Germany. It was a simple suggestion to make with regards to the romantic notions they have for the Third Reich, and they jumped at the idea of a Sergeant At Arms and Recruitment Officer who has seen active service against the Marxist forces in Africa!"

"Okay, now about pay?" Simon asked, looking Howard square in the face. It was a negotiation tactic he'd learnt sometime ago. To look away was an indication of weakened resolve. 'Never sell yourself short' was his watchword.

"The party will pay you fifty pounds a week, for as long as they require your services . . . "

"It would seem that you need me to carry this thing off, so I'm not going to sell myself short. Seventy pounds a week is the price I'm going to ask."

Howard smiled with vague amusement. "I'm not sure they'll go for that!"

"Well best of luck in finding someone else then!" Simon was magnanimous.

Howard wasn't too put out by the skinhead's attitude. He hadn't expected anything else following the character assessment he had made. Persuading the Executive to up the ante might prove difficult. Yet failing that, he could always juggle the financing of the group to accommodate the extra eighty a month. Nodding, Howard held out a hand to shake on the deal. "Agreed!"

With business out of the way, Howard felt at liberty to continue with his breakfast. "I'll be going to meet with the Executive later. You're at liberty to stay here, or there's a public house down the road. I'll be back at around two p.m. to pick you up and introduce you to your leader.

"Oh yeah, who's that?"

"A guy by the name of Ralph McLare!"

"What's he like?"

"What can I say? Um, a bit chubby . . . Something of a dreamer. He'd be real harmless if it wasn't for a slight pathological penchant for a dictatorial order . . . "

"A nutter then?" Simon asked. He wasn't sure if he liked the idea of working with a screw loose. Not after the escapade in Angola.

Howard read the veiled concern correctly. "Hey, no worries on this guy. His nature is reserved for outsiders. Once you've demonstrated a willingness to support his dream, you'll find him gullible beyond belief!"

"We'll see," Simon responded, indicating that he was going to hold certain reservations in check.

* * *

Derek woke rapidly. The speed in his system hadn't yet dissipated. A glance at his watch told him it was half-past eleven. Suzi was still asleep, but a series of muffled sounds from downstairs told him that the rest of the squat was up and about. Using his fingers to pinch across the bridge of his nose, he rubbed the sleep glue from the corners of his eyes.

Quite what there was to do now, he didn't know. Later there was the lunchtime session at The King George on the Portobello Road, a pub favoured for the landlord's acceptance of raucous behaviour as normal. For now though, he would have to look closer to home for entertainment.

Looking around the room, his eyes fell upon the cassette recorder. A touch of music wouldn't hurt. Ensuring the volume was on the number two setting before pressing the play button, Derek waited to hear the rest of the Ramones tape. Distant chords burst forth as he set the machine down on the floor next to the bed.

Surrounding the mattress was a number of press clippings and magazine articles on the punk rock scene. After flicking through a few, his eyes wandered to Suzi's semi-clad form. Her t-shirt had ridden up during the night, exposing her flat midriff.

Idly, he traced a fingertip around her navel. Goose pimples were forming, but whether because of the cold air or the sensation of touch Del wasn't in a position to know. From the natural indentation, he slowly drew a line to the hip bone with his finger, exploring the curve that it apexed. His breathing began to match the rising excitement as the compulsive attraction took hold.

Even in her state of slumber, Suzi was beginning to adopt a responsive posture, turning into the touch as if to receive a more intimate contact. Del smiled, allowing his hand to rest on her side and slide slowly down to cup and tickle her buttocks. A slight flicker of her eyelids coincided with a tensing of the muscles that lay under his touch.

"Umm . . . that's nice!" she said in a sleepy tone. Moving to hold him, the feeling of his rising erection against her bone caused her to gasp. A tingling feeling travelled through her, bringing with it a flash flood of emotions. "God!" she moaned.

Her grip on his neck increased and he responded by moving his mouth to hers. His tongue pushed past her lips. Suzi teased him by sucking on it lightly for a second or two and the increase in pressure told her she had struck the right chord. Her free hand pushed into the back of his boxer shorts and trembled as she felt him in the flesh rather than her imagination. Then, moving her hand round to the front, it was Del's turn to let a heavy breath escape from his lungs.

Her cool hand coiled around his penis, causing him to think he was going to explode there and then. Even more so as she squeezed him gently. Hooking the top of her underwear with his thumb, he gently eased them down.

"Make love to me you bastard!" she hissed into his ear, probing the opening with her tongue.

Del nearly tore her knickers in his eagerness to comply. Her legs wrapped themselves around his hips as he sank into her, leaving passion to weave its compulsive magic . . .

Derek lay back, trying to catch his breath as he listened to the blood beating against his temple in perfect time with his pounding heart. Suzi kissed him lightly, then getting up, she asked him to excuse her for a minute while she got cleaned up.

Derek nodded. All in all, he was feeling quite pleased with himself. It had taken a while to get it together, but it had been well worth it. Suzi was as good as she was sexy.

Flushing the used tissues down the toilet, she gazed at her own naked form in the mirror which leant against the wall. It did her ego good to think she had what it took to turn a guy on. *Don't get carried away,* she told herself as she slipped into her knickers.

"What are we doing today?" she asked on returning to the room.

Del shrugged, as if to say he didn't mind. "Gotta go to Portobello Road first to meet the rest of the lads. Then we could go to this band practice if you want?"

"Yeah. Later I need to go to the launderette."

"What for?" asked Derek.

Suzi looked at him with mild amusement as she started to dress. "What d'you think? I've got no clean clobber!"

"I like you better without clothes!" Derek answered.

"Yeah, well I wanna go out without getting arrested!"

The King George played host to the usual hotch potch of Irish, blacks and college kids, spread out in the booths and around the tables that dotted the circumference of the horse shoe-shaped bar. It was a smallish affair as London pubs go. Not a priority for refurbishment by the brewery, it had seen better days, but the clientele lifted the spirit of what would otherwise be a gloomy place.

As Del expected, the Trojan Crew was in residence around the pool tables. Alan Chambers, a skinhead from Harlesden, was applying chalk to the cue he held, while the others were engrossed in conversation and passing jibes.

"Del!" he shouted as he saw Derek round the bar. "Who's the chick?"

"Suzi." The girl beat Del to the answer.

Alan liked her forward nature. "I'm Alan. If you get tired of this sad sack, you can find me here any Sunday!"

"Yeah, fuck you too!" Del said light-heartedly. Alan was predictable if nothing else.

"Del mate, where were you?" The voice was Robert's who was sitting in the booth between two girls. One of them was Jan, the only true skinhead girl this side of the Sixties, and the other was Rebel, after the track by David Bowie.

"When?" Del called back.

"Yesterday period, son."

"Kings Road mate!"

"Yeah, any good?" Robert asked, tipping Suzi a salute with his glass.

Rebel pulled his arm around her shoulder, as if to make her claim clear to the newcomer.

"Yeah, I guess. It went off again!"

"What with the teds?" Alan asked as he eyed the cue ball, gauging a side-slice for a double.

"No, the fucking girl guides, who'd you think?"

"Them teds are getting too leery!" said a skinhead sitting on a bar stool by the dartboard.

"Hey, I don't notice you going down Bobby Sox's to put them in their place!" The ridicule came from Stanley, one of the gang's black skinheads. It was a well known fact that you'd need a tooled up gang of top notch boys before you'd even contemplate an attack on the Willesden rock & roll club. Besides being packed to the hilt, it was a haunt for all ages, with some right mean dudes from the past still totting cut-throats. The story of the local Chelsea bootboys who had to scatter from a rumble because two teds in their late thirties pulled shotguns from the boot of a car, had become legend in street cult lore.

"After you Stanley!" called the young skin.

"They don't call him Manly Stanley for nothing, geezer!" retorted the Hounslow skinhead who was playing Alan at pool.

There were half a dozen members of the T.C. present, but fully crewed it could boast numbers of twenty or so. Despite being scattered throughout the north, west and south of London, they had became a gang through repetitive association rather than an outward declaration.

"They call me that cos I'm a shit hot lover, not a fighter!" chided Stanley. That wasn't strictly true - Stanley was every bit as vicious as the next bloke when the circumstances called for it.

"You drinking?" Del asked Suzi.

She turned and looked at the bar, trying to decide what she fancied. Her eyes fell on the bottle of Bailey's Irish Cream tucked back between the till and the spirit glasses. "Yeah, get us a Bailey's please, babe."

"And a lager please, darling!" Alan called, adding, "Kissey, kissey," as Del looked back at him. The laughter that rippled around her made Suzi feel a bit embarrassed.

"Leave her alone!" called Rebel. "Just cos you've no feelings Alan, don't mean no one else has!"

Suzi looked over at the bootgirl who held her thumb up, as if to say, "I'll look out for you." After half an hour, the two girls were getting on like a house on fire.

Stanley had a message for Del from Leroy, a rasta DJ who had been a friend of Del's brother when they were counted in the number of the original Brixton and Clapham skins. He was running a reggae blues night in his house and wanted Del to come down tonight.

Del nodded his thanks and sidled up to the booth where Suzi was chatting to Rebel. "Here, girl . . . " he called, breaking into their conversation. Suzi looked up into his face. "What time you thinking of going to the launderette?"

"I dunno . . . 'bout six, why?" she replied.

"Got to go to a reggae do tonight. You fancy it?"

"Oh yeah! Where?" Rebel asked, cutting in.

"Leroy's place, over Brixton!"

Rebel nodded her understanding. Leroy was well known to all of them in one degree or another. He ran one of the few blues nights where there was no bad vibes for white folks. Not only that, but because of his own past, he understood the skinhead adherence to Jamaican music and went out of his way to make them welcome.

"Well, I guess around six o'clock," said Suzi. "We'll be done about eight!"

"Two hours?" Del asked in disbelief.

"Too late?" Suzi asked, thinking that perhaps it was better to make washing night another day later in the week.

"Nah, it's not that . . . It just seems a long time to wash a few things."

"Oh, I see. No, it's not the washing that takes the time, it's the bloody dryers. The old cow down there has them turned down so far they're nearly blowing cold!"

"What a bitch!" declared Del. "Tell you what, I'll hold her down and you can stripe her, okay?"

"Fuck off messing about!" she said laughing.

"Was I messing about?" Del asked Rebel.

"Name one time you've been serious!" Rebel replied.

At around half one, Suzi cornered Del. "I think we should be going now."

Derek was in half a mind to stay, yet the prospect of doing something different was a strong lure. "Alright, girl!"

The tube ride to Camden Town wasn't anything out of the ordinary, and it wasn't long before they were entering the old Camden shunt yard, with its archways under a viaduct which either lay dormant or had been converted for use as lock-ups.

The one used as a rehearsal studio was probably an old shunter's lobby, if the presence of a kitchenette was anything to go by. Even before they had entered the building, the sound of music had greeted them in the yard.

"It's not The Clash," Suzi declared, straining to identify the chords and believing it was probably Matt Dangerfield and his new outfit. For several months after the demise of the London SS he had been talking about bringing another group together and he had even demonstrated some new material to her acoustically.

Inside there were around sixty or so people. Although his arrival came under scrutiny, Derek refused to feel intimidated by the them and us syndrome. At least being with Suzi guaranteed a modicum of acceptance and for half an hour she took great pleasure in introducing him to everyone. The names swam around his head, threatening to blur into one another. Malcolm, Bernie, Johnny Rotten, Matt, Sid, Vivienne, Helen, Steve and so on.

Joe was one of the few who resorted to a hand shake. "See you've made it then?"

"How could I refuse the invite?" Del asked.

"We're going to be doing our set in a minute. Stick around and see what you think!"

Suzi rounded up a couple of cups that had been scattered around the place and made some coffee, while Derek watched Sid and his outfit, minus a lead guitar, jamming on the spotlight section at the far wall that served as a stage. The bass chords were basic and Sid's drumming tended towards power as compensation for a lack of finesse. Yet, as with the night before, Del found a root appeal in the rawness.

When Suzi returned, she found Del talking to Paul Simonon about which ska tunes they knew to be good. Del was enjoying himself because it was a subject he could easily relate to. His brother had been a skinhead during the transitional period of rocksteady to reggae, whilst an uncle of theirs had encouraged an in-depth interest in the ethnic rhythms by virtue of having been a mod era DJ when imports made the sound's identity.

From the two, Del had acquired a knowledge that out-ranked his years, as well as an inheritance of hand-me-down vinyls which formed an extensive collection. The first thing he had done after his uncle had presented him with several thousand singles was to use the woodwork lessons at school to provide a storage unit. Making it hadn't been a problem, but getting it from the school to his home three-quarters of a mile away had been a task that required much bribery and cohersion of friends to achieve.

Paul was laughing when Del explained how half way home, he had fallen out with his friends and the shelf unit had stood in the middle of the pavement while they argued. "I'd have been done up like a kipper if they had left me to it. I mean, there was no way it was going anywhere without help!"

"I've done you a coffee," Suzi butted in, handing the cup over to Del.

"Cheers, girl!" he said, cheerily accepting the hot liquid.

"Where's mine then?" Paul asked tongue in cheek.

"You want one?" asked Suzi in all seriousness.

Paul grinned and shook his head. "Just wanted to see if you'd lose your cool!"

Sid had finished using the equipment and Mick Jones had tapped Paul on the shoulder, indicating it was time to rehearse. A couple of R&B numbers were used as a warm-up device, before Mick piped in, "Do the set now?"

Joe nodded, microphone dangling in a loose grip which soon tightened as he tapped out the tempo of the "One - two - three - four!" chant provided by Mick. A crescendo explosion of guitar and drums burst forth to fill the building.

Suzi smiled. She liked the impact of *White Riot* as well as the revolutionary sentiments it expounded. She didn't pretend to share the political awareness of Mick or Joe, but she knew there was the potential for a wind of change that offered excitement and freedom if nothing else.

The content of the lyrics escaped Del in the blur of the jerry built P.A., but the aggressive power was perceivable not only in the sound, but also in the expressive sneering of Mick, the affected aloofness of Paul, and the muscle tones of Strummer's arms and his facial tension that promoted the distinct display of blood vessels at the temple. It was a rabid attack on apathy, a battering ram in comparison to the soft tones of the syrupy chart music that had come to represent the worthlessness of the times.

"So, what do you think?" Suzi asked, her own enthusiasm showing in the way she was speaking.

"I think they're really good!"

"That's what I like about you," Suzi joked, "You're really expressive!"

Derek grinned with her. "Something tells me you're taking the piss!"

"Hey, would I do that?" she asked in false earnest.

Derek was enjoying himself at the epicentre of the punk culture, the heart of the beast so to speak. There was a profound sense of honesty, a lack of the pretension that had come to typify the conceited nature of music's elected demi-gods.

Once the set had been completed, the band dispersed around the hall to unwind. A few girls jammed together while Suzi and Del went over to talk to Joe. In the course of the conversation, he mentioned a gig in Manchester which seemed to appeal to Del.

"You wanna go?" Suzi asked. She had known about the gig for a few weeks, but hadn't thought about going until now.

"Maybe . . . How we gonna get there?" Del responded.

"Dunno, train I suppose!"

"Hey, if you can get to it, I'll make sure you're on the guest list!" Joe offered. "Sort it out with Matt. I think him and Keith are coming so maybe you can go with them."

"That's your job," Del told Suzi.

"Okay I'll sort it out next week," said Suzi looking at her watch. "Anyway, I guess we'd better get back and sort out the laundry if we're gonna go out tonight."

"Why, what's the time?" Del asked, wondering just how long he had been there. It didn't seem long at all, but then again a voice at the back of his head provided a whisper of doubt.

"Half six . . . If we go now, we'll get out of the laundrette about half eight. Drop the stuff back . . . I guess about nine o'clock we'll be ready to go."

Del guessed it would take an hour, an hour and a half, to get over to Leroy's place, depending on how long they had to wait for tubes. So they would be in Brixton around ten or half past - not too bad because the house would just be starting to get the clients in as Leroy called the party-goers.

"Where you going tonight?" Joe asked out of curiosity.

"Popping over to a mate's blues party. He runs the Ethiopian Express Sound System . . . "

"Is it an open affair, or invite only?"

"Nah, open. He charges a pound on the door, but I'll warn you, they're popular . . . gets packed by eleven o'clock!"

"Tell you what," Joe said, "Give me the address and if we can come, I'll see if the others are up for it."

"You got a pen?" Del asked.

Joe shook his head, but turned to Bernie who had just come up to the group. "Lend us your pen, Bernie."

With the pen and an old tube ticket, Del scrawled the address as best he could. "If you get any problems, just say you know me - Del, alright!"

"Yeah sure. I can't say for certain if we'll be there, but it's handy to know!"

Del nodded, while Suzi's light tug reminded him that time was getting on. "Look I've gotta go, but if you get over Brixton tonight I'll see you there, alright?"

"Yeah sure. Hey listen, feel free to come over here any time you want!"

"Thanks!" Del appreciated the offer and he left with Suzi feeling the afternoon had been worthwhile. As he told her, this punk lark seemed all right.

The laundrette had seen better days and it was both grubby and dingy. The woman who ran it was a real mutt in Del's opinion. Suzi had chuckled at the description, but agreed that it was highly suited to the overweight woman with the dress sense of *Coronation Street's* Hilda Ogden.

The off-licence next door provided a means by which to soften the boredom, but the old bag didn't allow drinking on the premises so they had to sit on the low wall by the end of the shop parade with their bottle of cider. During their liberation, a carload of normals had mouthed it off as they sped past, giving Del the needle. He hated that. Being challenged in a way that couldn't be responded to, bar calling "Wankers!" after them.

Suzi had thought it of little consequence, but she could see how much it aggravated her boyfriend. So she took it upon herself to take his mind off it. "Forget them . . . come and kiss me instead!"

Del looked at her and smiled. Her intent was obvious, but welcome nonetheless.

* * *

Howard had returned from a profitable meeting with the Executive Council and was feeling in high spirits. Everything was coming together without a hitch and they had readily agreed that the scheme was worth the extra expenditure required by their man on the inside.

Simon had seen him pull up and was at Howard's door waiting for him. "Well?" Simon enquired.

"The game's on my impatient friend!" Howard told him as he shuffled past into the hall. "If you'll pour us a couple of glasses of bourbon, I'll arrange an immediate meeting with your glorious leader. Then I'll explain the arrangements for passing you instructions. Oh, take this!" Howard said, fishing a brown envelope from the waist pocket of his sports tweed.

"What's this?" Simon asked as he examined the small packet.

"Your first week's pay . . . I convinced them it would be a good show of faith to pay you up front."

"Cheers!" Simon was happy with the surprise. Stuffing the envelope into his pocket, he went to the drink's cabinet and fixed two measures of Jack Daniels, while Howard talked to Ralph McLare on the phone. Simon felt like there was someone up there looking out for him. No matter how bad things got, something occurred that always turned things around.

It had been the same up the jungle, during a fire-fight. A rebel trooper had skirted the fire-zone and come up behind them. From a range of sixty feet, the semi-automatic would have turned his position into a buzzing swarm of death. Yet an incoming mortar round had landed in the intermittent distance, showering Simon with a hail of soft earth and blinding the silent assassin with shrapnel.

As the rebel rolled around screaming in pain, Simon realised just how close he had come to signing off. It had unnerved him enough to dispatch three shots into the enemy soldier. Watson had remarked that the same god that looked out for Callan was looking out for him too.

Leroy's house was eight houses along from the corner, but before they had even turned into his street, Del and Suzi could hear reggae music with absolute clarity. Suzi was amazed at how loud it was being pumped out. She had never been to a real sound party before and as they walked up to path to Leroy's door, her eyes drank in the sights like a child let loose in Santa's grotto.

For what was just a standard terrace house party, it was amazing how many people had turned up. Even the front garden was full of faces, both black and white, and inside the house it was difficult to move thanks to the sheer weight of bodies. Suzi was also surprised by how many people acknowledged Del as he made his way through to where he had been told Leroy was.

They found him holding court in the only room that was off-limits to party-goers in general. Leroy called it "my yard", while others called it the smoking room because of Leroy's habit of making the biggest reefers you were ever likely to see.

"See you got my message, man?" Leroy said, as Del led Suzi through the rastas and young girls who populated what was, in estate agent terms, the master bedroom.

Leroy was a biggish sort of guy with a muscle tone that was beginning to slacken. A thick bush of dreadlocks covered his head and he also had a small black beard. He had been one of Del's brother's closest friends and was with him the night he was stabbed to death in a Soho pinball hall. Del hero-worshipped his big brother, and Leroy was one of the few people who fully understood the young skinhead's sense of loss.

"Yeah, Stan told me you wanted a word," Del replied as he accepted the mouth-piece Leroy offered him and took a long drag from the bong.

"I was wondering if you would like to do a few dates with my sound?" Leroy knew he didn't really need to ask because Del had long shown an interest in DJing.

"Yeah, course I would! But why do you need me though?"

"The reggae scene, it build up a need for revival sounds, sounds which I no longer possess. Therefore, I tink to myself, that guy Del have the sounds the people wanna hear and together we can make the people come alive and jive!"

"What sort of old stuff?" asked Del, showing his enthusiasm for the idea.

"Sweet rocksteady and killer tunes from the decade we call Seventy. Pick and mix from the best, and Jah and I will do the rest."

"Brilliant! Thanks a lot, Leroy!"

"Hey, I thank you. You'll be paid the going rate for number three DJ - be here about six on Friday okay."

"Yeah , I'll be here for sure." Del was well pleased.

Sometimes I feel like I don't fit in this world
Sometimes high, sometimes low,
That's my life . . . I just don't know!
MY LIFE - THE DOGS (1978)

CHAPTER FIVE

"SHIT!" Despite the hangover, Del was in a panic, thinking he was late.

Suzi woke up wondering what the rush was about. "What's the problem?" she asked.

"I'm late for work!" Del said, hoping around, trying to squeeze his foot into a resistant Dr. Marten boot.

"Didn't even know you worked!" Suzi answered with a yawn. Around her she could see other sleeping bodies in the half-light of the early morning sun that offered a narrow beam of illumination from the chink in the curtain.

"Didn't I tell ya?" he asked, looking down on her, trying to recall if it had been mentioned over the weekend.

"No, you didn't say anything."

"Oh, well I do. Selling veg over at Islington Market, you know? And I'm late!" he added, stealing a look at his wristwatch before strapping it on.

"This early?" Suzi cried. Her own watch told her it was four- thirty. "Jesus, it's more like bedtime for nightclubbers! Who the hell is there to sell to at this time of the morning?"

"Monday morning ain't it?" Del asked, more as a statement that an actual question.

"Yeah, so?" She failed to see the point.

"Buying day . . . Gotta go down Covent Garden and help the governor sort out this week's stock!"

"Do I see you today?" Suzi asked, while Del carried on getting dressed.

He thought about it for a second. "You got the money to get up town?"

"Yeah, after I've paid for the pills!" she considered aloud.

"Okay then . . . " he said, pulling on his jacket. "Meet me at Leicester Square, by the statue in the gardens about five o'clock. I wanna get a tattoo done if there's time."

He paused long enough to give her a kiss and then left Leroy's house at a brisk march, heading for the High Street and the number 11 bus.

Covent Garden was its usual throbbing hub and bustle. Getting the best on offer was an art in itself, but Derek and his boss moved around like professionals at an auction. If Del spotted a supply that was good, he'd find the Irishman and tell him what it was, who the supplier was and how much they were asking. The boss trusted Del's judgement, not least because he had spent some time teaching him the ropes and how to spot the little tricks like sorting out if the displayed stuff was a hook for a dodgy consignment.

After the Irishman was satisfied with the week's stock and it was safely in the back of the van, they took off for the arches and a spot of breakfast.

"Morning Tom, morning Del," called the proprietor as they entered. "The usual is it?"

"The full works, Bob!" Del replied in confirmation.

A couple of lorry drivers known to Tom called him over. They were a couple of West Country men who were contract drivers for the operators at the fruit and veg market. Del was pleased to see them there as it meant his boss would get involved in a couple of hands of poker, and he could take it easy until half seven or so.

Del liked Bob's cooking and, digging in, he soon realised just how hungry he was. The full works for him meant a plate of liver, bacon, sausage, fried egg, bubble, mushroom and beans, while Tom on the other hand, would manage on a bacon sandwich - which soon had the lorry drivers complaining that his fingers were making the cards greasy.

"Stop complaining boys . . . Just cos your luck is bad!"

"If I didn't know better Tom, I'd say you was marking the cards with that grease on purpose," said one of the drivers.

"Get tae fuck!"

Del watched Tom's cards, between taking mouthfuls of food. A pair of threes, a couple of faces and an unconnected ten didn't seem much to be playing on. Tom though was a wily old sort with a streak of leprechaun luck about him. If there was anyone who could fall in shit and come up smelling of roses, it was him.

71

Bob dropped a copy of *The Sun* in front of Del as he passed by from cleaning one of the window tables. "The last punter left it behind . . . Thought you could use it!"

"Cheers Bob!" Del was grateful for the distraction. Watching cards was only interesting for a limited amount of time, and he was soon engrossed in a story about public school pupils being expelled for using cannabis.

As time whiled on, and the empty plate had vanished and the empty mug had been replaced by a refill, Tom decided that perhaps it was time to think about getting over to Islington and setting up the stall. "Feeling fit Del?" he asked as he got to his feet.

"You off Tom?" one of the driver's asked.

"Time waits for no man and I've got a business to run," Tom answered.

"See you next week!"

"Fancy winning some of your money back do you? Don't fool yourself, man. I've been blessed with the luck of the Irish!"

"We'll see, we'll see!" the other driver said in response.

With a stretch and a satisfied belch, Tom unlocked the van door and leant over to let Derek in. The skinhead youth lay back in the passenger seat and closed his eyes. He felt sluggish from all the food and all he wanted to do was go back to kip.

Tom was soon nosing the van into the little cul de sac, formed by three blocks of garages, with a forecourt. Parking the van in the corner near the exit, he told Del to get the stall set up, while he stowed the fresh produce.

Del knew that it meant he had the shit job later of sorting out the usable waste from last week's remaining stock. Anything that looked like it could be sold was mixed in with the poorer grade stuff. It was a standard market trick to have the real choice produce on display whilst serving customers from a box of inferior goods under the back of the stall. Unless the customer objected, he or she had to put up with the slight of hand switching that went on.

Pulling the stall out of the lock-up was no mean feat, but it rolled well and steered easily when on the move. Until one of its iron wheels got caught in a pot-hole. Tom watched the skinhead grunt and groan as he tried to rock it free, then with a laugh, he put his shoulder behind it and helped work it free. "Watch where your steering it next time!" he warned.

"Yeah, fuck you too!" Del murmured under his breath as he strained like a cart horse.

Pulling out on to the street, he was all cheery, a typical marketeer. "Alright you old tosser!" he called to the middle-aged guy who ran a utensils stand outside the chip shop.

Reaching their pitch, Del took several attempts to nestle the stall against the kerb. Personally he preferred to get there early and pull straight in.

"Have a good weekend, Del?"

Without looking up, Del knew it was the young girl from the neighbouring pitch. Her father had had a flower stall in the market for fifteen years and now he was teaching the trade to his daughter. He looked up and saw her staring at him with that same wistful expression he'd seen countless times before. She had just left school, hadn't quite learned the refinements of dealing with the opposite sex, and the heart on her sleeve was plain for all to see.

Not that Del objected. She was a pretty looking girl and her attentions were good for his ego, but it wouldn't be proper for him to take advantage of her naivety while they were neighbours in the same market. A subtle hint was called for. "Yeah, not bad. I met a girl Saturday, down Kings Road!"

"A skinhead girl?" Toni asked, brushing the fringe of her auburn hair from her eyes. The look she gave him was unmistakable, but Del ignored it and just shook his head. "Nah, her name's Suzi - she's a punk rocker."

"Pretty?"

"Yeah, I guess so . . . I like her," he said as he continued to set out the display boxes on the ground and the rest of fruit and veg on the stand.

"Maybe I'll get a chance another time!" Toni said.

"Yeah, maybe," Del agreed. He didn't have the heart to tell her that the chance was never likely to come. Still as he'd told Tom when he'd last stuck his nose in, it didn't hurt for the girl to have her fantasies.

With the stall ready, he gave the girl a wink to be going on with and turned to face the thoroughfare.

"OLI-OLI-OLI-COLLIE!"

He had placed both hands to his mouth like a megaphone and was soon calling out the rehearsed street traders' banter that the office workers seemed to like so much.

"LOVELY JOVELY TOMMY TOMATOES!" came the answering cry from Kevin on the stall further up on the other side. That's what Del liked about the market. No matter what mood you started the day in, you always ended up feeling good about things after half an hour of the hue and cry.

* * *

Howard was getting ready for a nine-thirty appointment at the offices of Samuel Jones Esq., a backstreet solicitor who handled business premises sales and leases. He had arranged to look over a small office unit over a new and used tyre salesroom in Bow.

"What shall I do in the meantime?" Simon asked.

"Whatever you like. I'll be back here about two-thirty to pick you up. Then you and Ralph can start moving in and get the party HQ sorted out."

"Why two-thirty? I thought you said the lease was gonna be straight forward?"

"It's not only that," Howard answered as he adjusted his tie to his satisfaction. "There's the print run to sort out and the company name for the mail order side. Gotta keep everything above board. Once the objections to the party start, they'll be looking for any angle to disrupt its activities. So you see, it's necessary to ensure you're beyond reproach in all aspects."

Simon nodded. He remembered the fiasco of the recruitment drive for Angola which had descended into a farcical episode of cloak and dagger ducking and diving.

Checking his watch, Howard saw it was still too early, but a leisurely drive to Ralph's Place in Peckham before heading out east seemed a reasonable prospect. If he was still running early, he could get a coffee there.

Howard had left a key with Simon so he was at liberty to come and go. For his part, Simon was pleased with the way things were working out. Here he was, fresh back to the U.K., and already he had a job, doing the kind of thing he enjoyed. The general consensus might have been that he was a hired thug, but he didn't give a toss. He knew he was addicted to adrenaline and it was something he didn't care to change. He loved the way he felt in the middle of action and to survive was to feel invincible.

74

* * *

Suzi had gone to pay Gillian the money from the weekend's dealing. "What's up?" she asked, seeing that Gillian wasn't her usual bouncy self.

"Nothing much . . . He didn't come home again, that's all."

Suzi stayed silent. She knew how depressing things got when she let them get to her.

"You want some more, do you?" she asked reaching up for the jar that contained the pills.

"Yeah, the usual amount. Hey, don't worry too much about Clive," she said referring to Gillian's husband by name.

"It's not that . . . Just I sometimes wonder if we are together or not. It's like I hardly ever see him these days - bastard!" There was a venomous bite to her final word. "Here you go Suzi, there's another sixty there," said Gillian holding out the package.

Suzi accepted them and after a quick hug, left the house. Half way down the street she glanced back at Gillian watching from the living room window. She didn't like seeing her friend down like this.

"You must be Simon!" the portly man exclaimed. "Howard has told me so much about you!"

"I trust it wasn't all bad!" Simon replied, as he accepted Ralph's outstretched hand.

"No, not at all. I think it's quite exciting to have a real mercenary in our team." Turning to Howard, the would-be führer then started to thank Howard for all he had done for the cause, but Simon was more interested in the young lady standing by Ralph's side. Howard had told him that Ralph had managed to attract a young German girl to his side, but Simon had no idea she was going to be this beautiful.

Howard, having played his active part on behalf of Ralph's dream, decided that it was time to take his leave. "Okay, I'll quietly drop out of it."

"Yes, okay - thanks for everything!" Ralph rose from his seat to give him a comradely hug. Greta smiled and used her fingers to wave goodbye.

"See ya, Howard!" Simon called as the American opened the door and stepped through it.

75

With Howard gone, Simon settled into the position as Sergeant In Arms of the Great Britain Party, discussing recruitment techniques with Ralph and confirming that he should be able to provide a reasonable starting force from his position within the skinhead scene.

"And now we have this new HQ," Ralph enthused, "nothing will stop our rise to glory!"

"Yeah, it's a good place," Simon agreed looking around the office.

Greta was already busy sweeping and tidying the place up while Ralph sat down and started to sort out a list of expelled and disillusioned members of his former party. It was part of his plan to contact them and offer them positions within his new organisation.

"Once we get the flyers and the manifesto books, it'd be an idea to leaflet some public areas," Ralph mused. "Markets, football matches and such like."

"Don't forget you have to book the hall above the library," Greta said to remind Ralph.

"I'll do it as soon as I have sorted out who is on our side . . . Excuse me, Simon. I have to call up a bunch of old friends!"

"Come with me," Greta said to Simon. "I want to find out what the local shops are selling as we need some tea and coffee, things like that!"

Simon looked to Ralph for approval.

"You go ahead Simon," Ralph said. "I've got things to do!" Then into the telephone receiver, "Hello, is Dave Sykes there . . . ?"

Greta was already in the doorway waiting for him.

"Okay, lead on," he said.

She turned and descended the staircase that led to the door on the sidestreet. "Don't be so uncomfortable!" she said. "When things warm up, you'll be my bodyguard. Ralph has already promised me your protection!"

"Nice of him to tell me about that!" Simon said.

"What's up? Don't you want to protect my body?" There was a sly innuendo in her words.

"Maybe!" Simon allowed as they turned into the High Street and walked past the front of the tyre company.

The speed had been safely stashed under the mattress at the squat so Suzi felt comfortable about the two beat bobbies who were looking over at her from beyond the garden railings. An old lady was sitting next to her, feeding the square's pigeons from a plastic bag of carefully prepared breadcrumbs.

She had only been waiting a few minutes when Del came into sight. He was smiling as he walked up to her, causing her to do likewise. Standing up, she received his hug and kissed him.

"Good to see you, girl!" he said looking into her eyes.

"Good to see you too!" she responded.

"Sorry we can't hang about too long. I don't know when the studio closes," Del said referring to the tattoo parlour in Greek Street. "We can get a drink and relax afterwards though."

"Sure," Suzi agreed. Anything was okay by her as long as they were together.

The tattoo parlour turned out to be closed when they got there which angered Derek. He had been keying himself up for it, only to fall at the final fence.

"Bollocks!"

"Can't you get it done another time?" Suzi asked.

"I wanted to do it now!" he said.

His despondent kid routine made Suzi smile. "Aaah . . . Never mind!"

"Fuck off taking the piss!" Derek responded.

"Okay, promise . . . What shall we do now?" she said looking into his eyes.

"Go and get this drink I suppose. There's The Wellington over on Wardour Street . . . should be all right for us."

The Wellington worked well as a West End bar because it provided a cache of cosy snugs that allowed different worlds to come together while remaining secluded from one another. The city's army of office workers were well represented, as were staff from the nearby Shaftesbury Avenue theatres who were on their breaks between the matinee and evening performances. Several clippers and a couple of real working ladies with their pimp added a splash of garish colour to the otherwise sober gathering.

Del pushed past people to claim a portion of the bar in a bid to attract the bar staff's attention. The guy in the suit on the bar stool next to him had looked to see who was pushing and had caught sight of Suzi. Turning to his companions he said, "Look at that will you?"

His friends turn to look at the punk girl. A couple of them laughed and one went as far as saying, "Jesus, is it male or female?"

77

Both Suzi and Del took offence straight away. Del shoved the guy hard square on his chest. "You wanna take the piss out of me, cunt?"

The guy looked shocked and didn't even see Suzi sweep up the nearest glass and throw the contents over him. "Not so clever now, eh?" she sneered as he stood there dripping with beer.

One of the city gent's friends made a move for Suzi, but Del stepped in and lashed out with his fist. "No you don't!" he snapped as the blow bounced off the lax jaw. It gave him a feeling of satisfaction to see his opponent stumble and fall into a group of drinkers gathered around a nearby table.

Not that Del's sense of achievement was to last long. A fist crashed into his face, momentarily blinding him. Still unable to see clearly, his hands grabbed wildly and found a jacket. Pulling the weight towards him, he moved to the left and lashed out with his right foot. The planned move achieved its intended result by dumping the attacker on the floor, where a boot in the solar plexus ensured that he wasn't going to get up in a hurry.

Del's sight had cleared by the time he put the boot in, but before he could do anything else, he was being hauled around by the lapel. Without even thinking about it, Del allowed the momentum to carry him beyond what the handler had intended, and he didn't stop until his forehead had crashed into the guy's face.

The bloke was obviously in a lot of pain, and as his hand went up to ease the suffering, Suzi crashed the empty glass over his head, gashing the scalp and causing a healthy flow of blood that stopped the remaining office bods in their tracks.

"Call the police!" shouted the barmaid.

Del was mindful that Suzi had just opened them up for charges that provocation wouldn't diminish. "'It's all right . . . We're leaving!" His eyes were on everyone in the room. "Don't take the piss unless you can take the consequences!" he warned the rest of the mouth's friends.

Together, Del and Suzi fled the pub and ran. Out on Shaftesbury Avenue they managed to jump on a bus that was pulling slowly through the traffic lights. It was their only chance to get clear of the city before the police were out looking for them. It didn't even matter where the bus was going as long as it was away from the city centre. Once clear of the action, the tube network and its subterranean labyrinth would soon take them to wherever they wanted to go.

Slumping into an upper deck seat with his chest heaving, Del could see the crowd of young office boys arrive on the Avenue. Too late to do anything though since the bus was now accelerating towards Charing Cross Road and had already put a couple of hundred yards between them.

"What'd you glass him for?" Del asked Suzi.

"Thought he had you . . . I didn't realise you was gonna nut him!"

"Trust me, girl . . . They were loud, not fighters!"

"Yes please?" the bus conductor butted in.

"Two tens please," Suzi requested.

Del settled back as his breathing began to even out. The fact that a police car flashed past on the other side of the road meant that they hadn't been sussed getting on to the bus. A couple of days spent low key and they would be in the clear.

I'm waiting on a street called death,
Turn left at Soho Square!
KILLING TIME IN SOHO - THE SOFTIES (1977)

CHAPTER SIX

THE print run arrived at the offices of the Great Britain Party at around eleven o'clock Tuesday morning. While Ralph wrote out the cheque for the delivery man to take back to the printers, Simon took the top leaflet from one of the boxes and gave it the once over.

The party logo designed by Greta occupied the right-hand corner and was printed in red and black. The party's name was boldly printed across the top in large gothic letters. Moving to sit at the spare desk, Simon absorbed himself in the text.

Countrymen! Now is the time to rally to the defence of this nation, for we are under attack like never before.

This time it is pointless to watch the coast for our enemy's approach or the skies for his bombers. Today, the enemy lurks within! From the stock market where patriotism is for the colour of currency and not the national colours, and the proud traditions that they represent, to the industrialists who import cheap labour from the Third World to appease their Zionist bankers and profiteering vultures.

True Britons languish on the dole for the want of a proper wage and acceptable conditions while Parliament and its corrupt politicians are just as responsible for maintaining this criminal abuse of a nation and its people. It shouldn't go on any longer!

We at the Great Britain Party believe the time for radical change has come. Rather than the fatted calf of international finance or the puppet state of any superpower, we wish to see England stand independent and strong. With a strength derived from its people and a unity and loyalty felt at all levels.

By rekindling the spirit of national pride and eradicating those who seek to corrupt and abuse our inherent rights to security and prosperity from belonging to a strong and single-minded nation, we shall put the Great back into Britain!

Further details and the full party manifesto can be acquired by sending an SAE (11" x 8") to The Great Britain Party, P.O. Box 134,

Stratford Post Office, East London.   Full membership details included in manifesto booklet.

STOP PRESS: Public Meeting of the GBP to take place at Stratford Library (upstairs function room) at 7pm, April 4th 1977.

"Stirring stuff!" Simon declared, putting the sheet back in the box.

"The virtues of being a public speaker my boy!"

God, I wish he wouldn't say that - "My boy!" Simon thought to himself. It was as if he was McLare's rent boy, especially when said with the feminine edge that his leader displayed.   Yet there was the girl, Greta. Was she really having a relationship with McLare or was she a smoke-screen without fire? It was hard to tell as they were both a bit strange for Simon's liking.

Ralph took the leaflet Simon had been reading and fixing his reading glasses to his nose, he began to admire it.   The content was deliberately void of excessive right-wing ideology in a bid to attract as wide an audience as possible amongst the discontented working classes. They needed to be coaxed in the right direction before the GBP could adopt a more paramilitary stance. At the back of Ralph's mind, there was a certainty that a Munich Putsch would be required for the final destruction of the old order.

Looking up, Ralph said to Simon, "Okay, now we have these, if you can arrange some people to handle distribution, we can target some of the street markets which I guess will be as good a place to start as any. Greg said he and his boys would be able to help!"

Greg had turned up at the office a few days ago. He had a background of football violence and led a ten strong crew at West Ham. Simon had agreed with Ralph's assessment that he was a handy recruit. He could tell that Greg wasn't a pretender because of an air of suppressed sadism in his manner. Simon hadn't actually said much to him, but didn't feel he was going to be a threat to his position. He got the impression that as long as there was action, Greg would be happy.

Simon nodded.   "Yeah, I'll sort out half a dozen lads tonight to handle it!"

He knew there was a regular source of hands at The Black Horse in Leytonstone which had become something of a haunt for the new wave of skinheads.

"I feel like celebrating!" Ralph declared. "But, I guess we'll have to make do with toasting our success with tea - I really must organise a small bar here at some point!"

81

"Tea will be fine!" Simon said, placing his feet on the corner of the desk and leaning back in the seat. His mind was already going over the skinheads he could entice into the movement. There were several who sprang to mind with the correct attitude already installed. Once he had formed a core, subsequent recruiting would be a doddle.

Suzi wasn't happy about laying low for the whole weekend as Del had suggested. The prospect of spending three days banged up in the squat just didn't appeal to her, especially when Del's appearance on Saturday had intensified the loathing between her and the other residents. Del hadn't been able to guarantee that if she did go up town she wouldn't be arrested, but if she bleached the leopard spots out of her hair and changed her clothing, there was every chance that she wouldn't be lifted. After all, they were looking for a punk girl and a skinhead and London was awash with both.

So, having bleached her hair and opted for ski-pants, a black bra and yellow stringed vest, she caught the tube to Sloane Square. A World War Two gas mask canister served as a handbag and she nervously fumbled for a cigarette in it when she walked past three policemen and a WPC.

Lighting up, she decided that they had had enough time to challenge her if they were going to, and she breathed a sigh of relief as she exhaled the smoke. Putting the cigarette packet back in the canister, she snapped the lid shut and headed for Malcolm McLaren's Sex shop which played a focal role in the punk scene. If her friends were going to be anywhere, they were going to be there!

Outside the shop with its smoke glass windows, a gathering of the clan was perceivable from the near distance. Joey, the punk with the leather flying hat spotted her approaching and called out. "Floozie!"

She smiled as he bounded up to her with arms held out wide. "Alright, Joey!" she said laughing as he swept her up in his arms and spun her around a few times.

"I thought you'd got nicked by the Old Bill!" Joey exclaimed, putting her feet back on the floor.

"Nah, not me mister!" Suzi chirped.

Joey was one of her best friends. They shared a similar sense of humour that produced an offbeat rapport.

"What's with the hair?" he asked, pointing to the bleached spikes on her head.

"Remember that skinhead who passed us before the teds decided to fight?"

"The one that took the piss out of you!"

"Yeah, don't remind me!"

"What of him?" Joey asked, wondering if there was a problem.

"Well, he's me boyfriend now!"

"Oh, Floozie . . . Why deny the love you feel for me!" Joey said, taking on the mock attitude of a rejected school boy.

"Shut up you idiot!" Suzi said with a laugh.

"What's that got to do with your hair then?"

"Sshhh . . . Don't tell no one, but it's a disguise!" she whispered.

"Oh," he said raising his eyebrows then his voice. "IT'S A DISGUISE AND I'M NOT TO TELL ANYONE!"

Suzi slapped him on the shoulder. "Keep your voice down! You'll get me arrested if you don't!"

"In trouble?" he asked taking on a serious tone.

"I glassed a straight last night!"

"You're getting more like Sid every day!"

"What kind of compliment is that?" she asked with a grin.

Whatever kind it was, there was no time to find out as their conversation was disturbed by a young guy in a Fred Perry shirt, straight leg jeans rolled slightly at the ankle and Converse baseball boots. A camera was slung around his neck.

"Excuse me a minute!"

Both Suzi and Joey looked at him suspiciously. His hair was too long and straggly for him to be any kind of cop and a slight stubble gave him the air of an art student.

"I'm a freelance journalist working with several fashion magazines that focus on lifestyles."

"Our lifestyle?" Joey asked. It was obvious what the guy was after.

"Yeah . . . So how about it?"

"Hey, how do we know you're on the level?" complained Suzi.

"Sorry, you've lost me," the guy responded.

"There's been journalists hanging around before. They talk to us then go back to their little offices, get on their typewriters and produce more fertiliser than ICI!"

"Hey, that's not me!" the journalist said holding his hands up in a gesture of openness. "I'm after the real story, the way you see it, you know?"

"Heard it before son!" Joey pointed out, obviously unimpressed and fast getting bored with the intrusion.

"Yeah, I don't doubt that you have . . . " Realising he had to do something to rescue the situation, stretching his expense claim to include "entertaining" could well produce the lifeline his intended feature was in desperate need of. "Tell you what, to show I'm sincere we can adjourn to the nearest pub and I'll get the drinks in. Then if nothing else you'll get a free session out of it!"

That was all the arm-twisting that was needed and in the public house the trio took over a snug at the far end of the bar. The hack had introduced himself as Paul Yates and was soon up at the bar buying the first round.

"Fucking pleb!" Joey grinned, watching him from the table.

Suzi nodded. He was a strange one all right, yet with a certain spark of charm. They watched as he had a discussion with first the barman and then the owner.

"I don't think we're wanted here!" Suzi voiced what Joey was thinking, but, surprise surprise, Paul returned with a tray of drinks and a triumphant look on his face.

"Didn't think they were going to accept us!" Suzi said.

Paul glanced back at the bar. "I told them I was doing a feature on punk and would mention the place as one that won't tolerate punks!"

"That changed their minds?" Joey asked over the brim of his lager and light.

"Not quite. I mistook those two gents over there for teddy boys and asked if it was a rock 'n' roll pub. The manager said he would serve us if I don't mention the pub at all!"

The three of them laughed together. Suzi liked the way the guy handled himself. There was a large slice of cheek to his professional approach and he struck her as one of those people who couldn't take life seriously yet were blessed by being natural hustlers.

He caught the look in her eye and smiled back. Then deciding to get on with the job in hand, he unzipped the holdall he had been carrying and reached inside for his cassette recorder. Placing it on the table between them, he pressed the record and play buttons in unison. "Testing . . . Testing . . . one - two - three . . . "

Joey laughed and infected Suzi into sniggering.

"All right, insult my professionalism if you will!" Paul said as he rewound to check the sound level.

84

"Hey, it's a good job if you can get the work!" Joey retorted, leaning over the cassette recorder and speaking into its microphone, "Testing, testing . . . one - two - three . . . "

Suzi laughed as the cassette responded, "Testing . . . Testing . . . one - two - three."

Paul didn't care that they were having a joke at his expense. At least they were open and receptive to his presence. Which was more than could be said for the gang of bikers the editor had sent him along to interview last week.

"Okay, you've bought the drinks," Suzi said. "What do you wanna know?" She leant back in her chair and regarded Paul with a cool appraising look.

"Can you state your names first?"

Suzi looked at Joey who gave her the go ahead to answer first. "I'm Suzi . . . "

"Suzi the Floozie!" Joey said, using her full street name and laughing at her grimace. "I'm Joey Jesus!"

"Why Jesus, is that something of religious significance?"

"No, I'd piss on the church! They call me Jesus cos I'm always winding people up. 'Jesus Joey, get the fuck outta my face', you know?"

"I see . . . " Paul acknowledged with a smile. "You don't like the church though?"

"No not really. I mean they're part of the corruption ain't they?"

"What corruption?" Paul was encouraging a more expansive response from the young punk.

"It's all to do with exploitation. They wanna keep us down, keep us stupid. The church is merely an extension of political rule!"

"Some would say the church does a lot of good though."

Joey looked at him momentarily. "Yeah, mostly for themselves!"

"That's a very cynical attitude don't you think?" As he spoke, Paul glanced at the level needle to see that it wasn't going into the red band.

"Well the attitude fits the times don't it? Don't you think the church is more concerned with money these days than representing the Holy One? I mean, the only reason them and the politicians are bad mouthing punk rock, is because they're scared that we're gonna derail their gravy train!"

"Why's that?"

"Cos then they'll have to get a proper job!" Suzi declared, feeling it was about time she had a say too.

"You think they feel threatened by punk rock?" Paul asked switching his attention to Suzi.

"Yeah, cos we don't want to be part of their scam! We represent an awakening - an uprising if you like!" Suzi was warming to the task of presenting her personal views. "That's what has them panicking. I guess they have this Victorian image of anarchists as clock and dagger figures carrying fizzing black balls with 'bomb' written on them!"

"So, you feel you've been misrepresented?"

"Hey, given the chance, we'll fuck 'em!" cut in Joey. He felt passionately about the shortcomings of the way things were.

"Yes and no," Suzi continued. "We're being misrepresented because we're supposed to be living under a democracy, but we're only free to do what we're told! I mean, all that talk about the rule of law by mutual consent - what the hell is that supposed to mean?"

Joey smiled and sarcastically added, "I've been nicked loads of times and never consented once!"

They laughed together. Suzi carried on talking when they had regained their composure. "During that Vietnam war, there was that famous poster - Suppose they gave a war and nobody came - you know the one . . . "

Paul nodded. "Yeah!"

"It's the same for the politicians, the church, money, the whole fucking thing. Take money - if a law was passed tomorrow that outlawed money all you'd have is a wallet full of wastepaper. Society is a false idol, a shared dream state. The reason why they seek to oppress us is because we represent their greatest fear. Suppose there were leaders that nobody would follow?"

"So punk has a political role to play?" Paul was feeling pleased with his approach. He already had enough to piss all over the previous summaries of the movement.

"If it wakes up the closets to the fact people are getting fed up, then it has performed a political role. But for me, anarchy is about personal freedom - being able to do what you wanna do. Maybe this is what they fear. If enough of us adopt the same attitude then they've no control over us!" Suzi found it strange talking to an outsider as she tried to make a lot of disjointed perceptions form a clearer understanding.

"What about the violence connected with the cult?" the journalist asked.

"It's all right for kicks!" Joey said with a laugh. What did the guy want to hear? A rebuttal? Get real!

86

"You approve of violence then?"

"Yeah, course I do - World War One, World War Two, Suez, Korea - get my drift?"

"I think so!"

"Well, what I'm saying is today they'll jail you for being violent," Joey explained. "When there's a war they'll shoot you if you ain't violent . . . "

"We fight because we've no choice . . . cos we've been set up by the newspapers as something to be opposed and put down," Suzi murmured, thinking of the straight in the Wellington.

"That's an interesting perspective," Paul said.

Her words had obviously captured his attention and suddenly she felt shied by his inquisitive gaze. It had only been an off the cuff comment, something she had said first and only considered afterwards. With a malicious glint, she regained her composure and retorted, "Yeah, I guess the truth must be an alien concept in your trade!"

She rocked with laughter at the gall of her own sense of humour. Joey and even Paul joined in. It might have belittled his profession, but it was hard to take it badly.

"No, seriously though," Suzi declared, knowing there was an element of truth in what she had said. "Fleet Street has a habit of creating tomorrow's news by the way they present today's - if that makes proper sense!"

"Sort of . . . can you give an example?" In fact, it had made sense to Paul. The gutter press were the butt of more journalist's jokes than the two punks would ever have credited.

"Okay, what can I say?" Suzi searched her mind for an example. "Take this war with the teds."

"Yeah."

"You know how it started?" she asked him in earnest, her eyes fluttering from the intensity she felt.

"Because the teds resent the presence of a new cult as it threatens their own revival," came Paul's reply.

"That's what the 'papers say to keep it going. Nah, the real reason was they were bitching about Malcolm. He had been running a rock 'n' roll shop before, and they got the hump when he changed over to sex clobber. So they targeted the shop and trashed it. It was a personal vendetta, not a tribal war!"

"So you're saying . . . " murmured Paul.

"Look, what I'm saying," Suzi snapped, "Is what have you got now? War on the streets because that's the way it was reported. That's what they wanted the public to believe! The public believed it and so do the teds. So now you have a continuing situation from an event that never happened and a perception that didn't exist! Fucking crazy ain't it?"

Sitting back heavily, Suzi was agitated and nervous. A fuming expression had formed on her face from her attempts to stifle the rising emotion that threatened to burst forth as violent energy.

"Hey, I didn't mean to upset you!" Paul said, leaning forward and placing a reassuring hand on her forearm.

She felt a stirring from his touch, as if the frustration had been rechannelled to her sexual responses. The tingling sensation was both desirable and yet unwanted, and it shocked her into pulling away. "Don't touch me!" she pleaded, holding both hands back out of reach.

Paul looked at her with concern. He was a sensitive kind of guy and didn't like to feel responsible for putting on people. Though what he had done to cause this was beyond him. It bothered him more than usual because he found the girl interesting with a good mind. The sort of girl . . . Well what did it matter now?

"I'd better go!" Suzi said, ignoring the surprised look on the journalist's face. She was angry at herself, angry because her desire was so strong and without any real reason. It threatened to break free and stifle her and like a panicked claustrophobic, she only wanted out.

Her friend Joey watched her flight as opened mouth as the young journalist. He couldn't understand what had got into Suzi either. "Women . . . Who can understand them?"

Paul chuckled at Joey's words. In spite of the middle class perception that gangs and street culture were an alien existence, the statement proved that the trials and tribulations of life transcended the divisions people set up.

Breathing more easier once she was back on the Kings Road, the trembling Suzi felt began to subside. "Jesus," she breathed. "What the hell happened there?"

* * *

Howard checked he wasn't being followed as he went to meet the NF official in the small Knightsbridge wine bar. He was all too aware of the fact that security mattered if the affair was to remain a clandestine one. Nothing could be taken for granted now that the plan was being put into affect.

Simon had phoned to say that he had drafted in some help to fly poster the GBP across the borough. Howard was pleased by the way the skinhead was shaping up. He had recognised the qualities of a leader in him and knew that he'd made the ideal choice.

Simon had also told him another bit of good news. Ralph had given him free reign to live in the office. Ralph obviously was happy to have the 24 hour security Simon's presence would provide, and with no rent to pay, things couldn't have been sweeter for the ex-mercenary. For Howard, it meant his man on the inside wouldn't miss a trick.

Vivaldi played in mellow harmony with the American's mood as he nestled the Rover into the parking zone a hundred yards or so from Zen's wine bar. Stepping out on to the pavement, he slammed the door shut and after ensuring that it was locked, he poked a few ten pence pieces into the meter.

Inside the bar, things were quiet with only a few people from the upper echelons of the office world and the awaiting official from the Front to be seen. The man from the NF blended perfectly with the surroundings and its people and this intrigued Howard. The guy was obviously working below his station within the party structure.

"Aaah!" said Hubert Crawford, stirring the cream on the top of his iced coffee and brandy before sipping it. "I'm like you Howard. My position prevents me from becoming too openly involved. You do know who I am?" It had just occurred to him that the American might not understand the implications of possessing a family title.

"Yes, I know your father is an Earl," Howard responded.

"Well, it wouldn't do to be seen courting the fascists. It nearly brought down the royal family the last time which is why they changed their name to Windsor and ignored their German heritage."

"Thanks for the lesson, but I know my history!" Howard was being abrupt without being offensive.

"Drink?" Hubert asked the American.

Howard nodded in response. "Straight Bourbon."

Turning to face the barman, the NF man called him with a curt, "Mario", accompanied by a snapping of his fingers.

"Yes sir?" the barman responded with the respectful precision required in a high class joint.

"A Bourbon for my American friend if you please!"

"Certainly sir!" Without further ado, Mario selected a measure of Ambassador, an imported bourbon cultivated in the American Mid-west rather than the more usual Kentucky or Texan varieties.

Once the additional drink had been bought and paid for, the two men took themselves outside and sat at a table in the cordoned off pavement garden. Howard chose a table that provided a wall of vine behind him where he felt he could discreetly conduct the business at hand, while watching out for any indication of them being listened to.

"Nice," Howard said as he tasted the strength of the dark amber liquid.

"Okay Howard. I'll be acting as your go between in this matter purely for the reason that there should be nothing unusual about people of our stature meeting in public like this."

"Shrewd move!" agreed Howard.

"Okay," Hubert said as he placed his briefcase on the table and retrieved a buff coloured file which he handed to the American. As Howard opened it and eyed the contents, he continued. "The first page details the individuals we want harassed. Thereafter is a list of addresses of mail order establishments, office premises and commercial fronts for the undesirables. The third page contains a short list of individuals within the ranks of the Front who have the dubious honour of establishing our party's credibility."

The names meant very little to Howard. "How were these people selected?"

"You know how it goes. Some are expendable, others need to be brought down a peg or two . . . "

Howard placed the file down. "So why does a man like you want to get involved in all this?"

The young noble smiled. "Boredom I guess. Most young people rebel because they have nothing whereas I'm forced to rebel because I have everything. It makes life predictable and dreadfully dull."

"Seems like a dangerous way to get your kicks," Howard said, aware of the kind of repercussions that would come from a revealing investigation.

"Where's the excitement without the risk?" Hubert responded and Howard had to concede the point.

Finishing his drink, Hubert concluded their business by handing him a building society account book made out in Simon's name. "Tell your man that his money will be paid in every Thursday!"

Howard nodded and after shaking hands with the man, he departed.

* * *

"You want a cup of tea love?" Derek's mother called from the foot of the stairs.

Del had gone straight to his room after returning from work. Sometimes she worried about him. Life hadn't looked down too kindly on her family what with Derek's father running off with that old tart who had worked at the bakery on Sycamore Road, and then that day the police turned up with the news that her eldest son Graham had been killed in a fight.

"Yes please, Mum!" Derek called back.

As he looked around his room there were 45s and LPs everywhere. Scattered on the floor, in a heap on his bed and in several collapsed stacks against the sideboard.

Shit, what a mess.

Obviously a tidy up was in order, but first there was the tune he held in his hand that needed to be played. Gingerly picking his way through the waxes on the floor, he dropped the disc on the turntable. It was a Dandy Livingstone track from the defunct Giant label and soon the room was full of the unmistakable Jamaican voice, singing, "People get ready, let's do rocksteady, ah ha, ah ha!"

Frantically Del attempted to create some kind of order out of the chaos that surrounded him. He thought he had things pretty well sorted by the time the cup of tea arrived, but his Mum soon put an end to that illusion.

"Oh! Look at the mess! I hope you're going to tidy it away once you've finished!"

"Yes, Mum!"

She gave him a stern look to underline the fact that she meant tidy up properly and not just put everything into a single heap as he usually did. Satisfied that the message had got through she left him to it.

Del glanced at the small stack of records on the pillow along with a few sheets of paper and a pen that had been keeping tally of the selections. *Grooving Out on Life* - Hopeton Lewis, *DJ's Choice* - Winston Wright, *Riot Inna Notting Hill* - The Pioneers, *Double Barrel* - Dave & Ansell Collins, *More Axe* - Dave Barker & The Upsetters, *Swan Lake* - The Cats, *Seven Wonders Of The World* - Prince Buster Allstars, *Prince Royal* - Buster's Allstars, *Ride On* - Dennis Brown & Big Youth, *Too Experienced* - Owen Gray, *Stop That Train* - Keith & Enid.

Another half a dozen titles and that'll be it, he told himself.

I'm a fascist dictator, baby, that's what I am,
I'm a fascist dictator - I'm like no other man!
FASCIST DICTATOR - THE CORTINAS (1977)

CHAPTER SEVEN

THE hall above the library had been made ready during the afternoon by several volunteers acting under Greta's directions. Looking around, Simon found himself impressed by the aura she had created. Chairs had been organised and lined up in several blocks, with aisles created between them to allow access to the stage area. The screen printed flag and the other banners on the stage lent a spirit of Teutonic splendour to what was normally a large, basic and cold room.

"Simon . . . " Greta said.

"Yeah girl?" It had taken only a few days of being in the office together to break the ice and adopt an air of familiarity in their relationship.

"Did Ralph mention the uniform he wants you to wear?"

Simon nodded. He felt the uniform was gross and more in line with a fetish than a public meeting, but despite his personal misgivings, he knew he had a role to fulfil and had to maintain Ralph's total confidence. Even so, he had already promised himself that if any of the skinheads who turned up took the piss, he was going to give them a thick ear.

"Okay, when you're ready, it's laid out in the back room," she said before disappearing into the kitchen to fix some drinks for the helpers.

Simon dreamily watched her rear end as she walked away. The shin-length skirt swished from side to side, accentuating the wiggle she put into her walk. Smiling, a wicked thought crossed his mind. He knew what he'd rather have laid out in the back room waiting for him.

There was half an hour before the doors opened. At the back of the hall three party workers were preparing the display table with pamphlets and books that were to be given away free or for a nominal charge. Calling out to one of the men, Simon said he was going to be in the back if anyone needed him and the guy waved his acknowledgement.

The uniform lay on the table in the middle of what was ambitiously described by the council as a dressing room. He could see it was based on surplus items from the L.A.P.D. with the inclusion of shoulder flashes to denote his rank as Sergeant In Arms.

Oh Well! They do say the girls like a man in uniform!

Unlacing his boots, he sat down to remove them as he methodically began to change his attire. Unbeknown to him, Greta had emerged from the kitchen just in time to see him go into the changing room. She had then waited for a minute or so to pass before barging in, catching him 'by accident" in just his grey boxer shorts.

Startled, he looked up, then smiled not even attempting to be modest. Greta started to apologise for the intrusion, but all the time her eyes were sweeping over his body. His face, his lips, his torso, his biceps, his groin, his stomach, his groin, back to his face.

Once she had taken a good long look, she pointed to behind herself and said, "I'll see you when you're dressed, okay?"

"Yeah, sure!" he answered, slipping the black shirt over his head. Then taking the trousers, he pulled them on as well. As a final military touch, Ralph had also provided a thick belt with shoulder straps. Simon realised immediately that it was the webbing from a shoulder holster, only minus the actual holster.

Simon returned to the hall just as Ralph arrived. "Ah, Simon! How do you feel?" he said, beaming a smile.

"Okay, I guess," Simon answered as he came to stand next to him.

Ralph took off his raincoat to reveal a uniform of his own. He handed the coat to Greta who silently took it away to be stored in the room behind the stage.

"Well, tonight's the night that we begin our historic rise!" boomed Ralph.

"How many are you expecting?" Simon asked. He knew the leaflets had been handed out, but there was a difference between that and parking arses on seats.

"I'd anticipate in the region of a hundred and fifty, maybe more," Ralph replied confidently. "Don't forget that many people are sympathetic to our cause!"

Simon wondered if the assessment was just a bit over zealous, but within twenty minutes of the doors opening, he was surprised to see around a hundred faces in the audience.

As everyone waited for the meeting to begin, Simon positioned himself just to the left of the dais which was centre stage. He stood there with folded arms and the grimly set jaw that he had been made to rehearse under Ralph's critical eye. Behind him, on the stage, Greta and a few of the party's leading figures sat on a backline of chairs.

Ralph made his entrance from the door at the back of the stage with sheaves of paper in his hand. Quite deliberately, he adjusted his tie and glanced around the hall, before striding up to the podium. Although the hall wasn't overly large, Ralph had arranged for a small public address system to be rigged up. As he had explained, you cannot project an image of power if you are feeling and sounding hoarse. It was a question of inspiring awe.

Resting his papers on the angled top, he gripped the sides of it in both hands and stared into the audience of football lads, skinheads, old soldiers and a surprising amount of ordinary looking people.

"Good evening friends!"

The speakers blasted out the words then whistled as the inexperienced sound engineer fought to control the warbling. Simon wanted to laugh and had to bite his lip to stop himself.

Giving the sound man a stern look, Ralph referred back to his notes for his lead. "By coming here tonight, you have shown an interest in the fate of your country, your people, your families!"

He glanced at the gathering and could see that he was having the desired effect. The P.A. joke was over and they were listening to him with serious intent. There were nods of approval from some of the older faces, while the younger ones present looked as if they were waiting to hear something they could fully relate to.

"The problems we face as a society today are inherent of the corruption that our government endorses. They embrace the Jewish philosophy of Capitalism with a zeal that is obscene.

"Take the firemen. They are striking because they are not being paid enough for the risks they take, while Parliamentary fat cats collect four times as much for parking their obese behinds on wooden benches and say you cannot have any more!

"Why not, I say! If we cut off the Lend Lease Reparations to Uncle Sam, we could ensure the public sector were getting a fairer deal. After all, what does that debt represent, but the price of defending the star spangled banner from the swastika and the rising sun! The war could have ended for us in 1941, when Rudolph Hess landed in Scotland with peace proposals, but because of our illustrious puppet leader Churchill, we were committed to prolonging the fight for a further three years.

"And for what? I'll tell you. So we could increase the national debt both in terms of finance and human life. What did we gain from those further three years? Absolutely nothing."

There was a murmuring among the old soldiers, something that Ralph was forced to take note of and direct his attention to. "That's not to demean the bravery of our fighting men who gallantly defended this great nation of ours from a foreign power. The decision was not yours to make - it was those in charge that must bear the responsibility for making this a mercenary nation at the beck and call of the Americans."

It was obvious to anyone in the hall that this was a subject Ralph felt passionately about as he worked himself up to a virulent rant.

"May I point out that I'm not advocating an anti-American stance. Their presence as an anti-Communist power is desirable to the stability of world politics. But they were the only ones to benefit from the extension of conflict in Europe. We kept the Reich busy so the Americans could concentrate on ensuring that the Japanese didn't extend their influence throughout the Pacific with the support of their Axis allies - as would have been the case if we had accepted the Hitler's peace proposals.

"So why should we be made to pay for the privilege of fighting a diversionary action on behalf of another power. Surely they should be paying us?"

A couple of the old soldiers got up and walked out in disgust, but others stayed and nodded in agreement. Simon found himself being impressed with the way Ralph was handling things. He wasn't as clued up on the details as the party leader, but it had sounded a well reasoned argument.

"While the Americans enjoy a moderate income tax levy, we are paying thirty percent, yet not feeling the benefit of the accumulated funds because they are being absorbed by the national debt. Why should our once glorious nation be forced to go cap in hand to the IMF like a street beggar?

"And what of our young? They have to suffer the prospect of unemployment as they jostle with Third World immigrants for underpaid positions. The industrialists, shareholders and the Treasury meanwhile get fat off the backs of a mistreated people. We advocate that all immigrants are repatriated to their countries of origin, as they represent an excess labour force that this country's rising unemployment figures show we no longer require!"

Pausing to catch his breath, he gauged the correct amount of silence before raising his voice.

"NO MORE!

"The time has come for action! This country is fast becoming a hotbed of corruption - political, financial and social. Join with the Great Britain Party and be part of the new broom that sweeps this filth and deprivation from all levels of what should be a proud British nation!"

At the instigation of the officials sitting behind Ralph, clapping began and the applause went around the hall with the speed of a bush fire. Simon noted that several of the skinheads he had invited were getting into the spirit of things, and in a perverse way he felt it was quite a self-satisfactory reward for his efforts.

"The full manifesto of the GBP is available free of charge from the table at the end of the hall!" Ralph said, pointing to the manned merchandise stall.

"In brief, we stand for the resurrection of British pride. An end to the Jewish conspiracy of international finance and control. An end to excessive profiteering from the labours of the British people. We want a nation that's one hundred percent for its people. Only then can any government expect the people to be one hundred percent behind the nation!"

Another round of applause rippled through the hall.

"I'll stand down, so that my distinguished colleague Greta Kleine can speak to you on the aims of the GBP Youth League. Please give her a big welcome!"

Stepping back from the dais, he held out a hand to Greta who stood up from her seat smiling. The simple fact that she was young and beautiful generated a wild response from the teenage element in the audience, something Ralph had anticipated when he had appointed her speaker for the party's youth wing. Under Simon's guidance, Ralph saw the youth as the stormtroopers of the new party who would take it on from today to a great future.

* * *

After knocking on the door, Suzi waited while the sound of muffled movement meant the latch was cocked back and the door was about to open. It came as a surprise to see Clive standing there instead of Gillian, but Suzi didn't say anything.

"Ah, my favourite zombie!" declared Clive.

Suzi gave him the one fingered salute as she pushed past. There was no need to take offence - it was a game of insults that they often played.

"Gillian's in the kitchen," said Clive grinning and brushing back his black hair. Not that it needed it since it was held in place by hot oil treatment, but it was a habit of his that had evolved over years of being vain.

Gillian was back to her happier self, which pleased Suzi greatly. "Hello smiler!" she said.

"Suzi! Alright?"

"Yeah, not too bad you know."

"Where's the boyfriend tonight, then?" Gillian asked, noticing that Del was absent.

"Got a new boyfriend have you?" Clive asked as he joined them in the kitchen.

"Yeah, his name's Del."

"Where is this guy then?" asked Clive. "You gotta keep him satisfied or he's going to wander!"

"You'd know all about that!" Gillian said with a bitter irony.

Clive realised too late that he had condemned himself with his own mouth. "Hey! Hold fire baby. You know my business is unpredictable!"

"So get a proper job!" Gillian answered back.

"Clive in a proper job?" Suzi exclaimed. "Impossible! Face it Gill, your old man's a villain. He was never meant to be a Joey Worker!"

"Hey, less of the villain if you please," smiled Clive. "I'm a self-employed businessman!"

"Businessmen pay taxes, keep books and have records," Suzi pointed out.

"I've got records." Clive acted as if he had been insulted before adding, "Mott The Hoople, Eric Clapton . . . loads of records don't you know!"

Gillian took it upon herself to set up three cups of coffee, while Suzi and Clive sat at the table.

Suzi got the money from her pocket and said, "I've got that money, Gill!"

"Give it to the lord and master . . . After all, you don't want to mess up his business records do you!"

"Here . . . The return on sixty blues!" Suzi said, dropping the plastic bag into Clive's outstretched hand.

He was fun as a friend, but it amazed Suzi to see the sudden transition when money and repayments were due. All sense of warmth disappeared and only came back when returns versus dues balanced. It wasn't a front, just a part of the young villain's character. Suzi had been present when a bloke from Harlesden had tried to short change him on a large deal.

Clive had been helping Gillian prepare the dinner, and had listened quietly to the pusher's excuses as he carved the joint. "Hey, don't worry man," he had said to the guy, "If you can't pay me in cash, pay me in blood!" The cook's knife he had been cutting the meat with entered the guy's thigh point down and went straight through it into the wooden seat.

It had been a shock for Suzi, while Gillian was more concerned that Clive was going to kill the now screaming pusher. What frightened Suzi most was the blood lust in Clive's eyes - it was the first and only time she had witnessed that side of him. In fact, Clive had only let the man go when he promised to telephone his brother to bring the money over, and even then Clive had started flashing a shotgun around by the time the brother turned up.

"Spot on," Clive declared, snapping Suzi back from her daydream as he finished counting her money. "Do you want some more?"

She barely hesitated. "Same again!"

* * *

Greta's speech had been more basic than Ralph's. She relied heavily on working class terminology such as niggers, pakis and yids as she advocated a strong line of resolve when faced with "the fight ahead".

It was strange to see how the younger elements of the audience reacted to her brazen incitement. It was such blatant manipulation, yet it was laced with enough partial truths to evoke a sense of justification for directing hate against other races.

During her speech, Ralph had come down from the stage and had spoken quietly in Simon's ear. "Afterwards, do you think you can arrange a little taster of what we mean by purging? I think they'll appreciate the opportunity to burn off some of their youthful exuberance in a constructive way - don't you?"

Simon just grinned. He knew exactly what was required of him. There was an Indian restaurant on the main road that would suit their needs perfectly.

After changing out of his uniform, Simon returned to the hall to spread the word around that he was going for a drink at The Musketeer and the rest of them were welcome to join him. By the time they reached the street below the meeting hall, there was a fair sized crew of about forty skinheads and bootboys in tow.

Simon was doing his bit as a GBP representative, answering questions about the party and extolling the virtues of its leadership - although it was obvious Greta had already fuelled enough fantasies to heat the East End for the next decade or more.

As they began to walk off in the direction of the pub, the atmosphere was boisterous and volatile. All it needed was for someone to provide the match and the group were going to explode. As they drew nearer the Indian eating house, Simon called out, "Who's ready to fight for the cause?"

"You mean . . . ?" asked a bootboy from Bethnal Green, pointing to the shop front with its frilly canopies over circular windows.

"Why not? They've got no right to be in this country!"

"True! Okay, let's do it!"

The clientele and restaurant staff were not prepared for the unannounced assault. The peaceful and intimate setting for a night out, with its subdued light levels, discreet waiters and taped Sitar music fluttering lightly in the air, was about to be given a rude awakening.

In an instant, the calm was replaced by mayhem as the front door lost its frosted glass and the windows began exploding in unison. Diners rose in panic and several women started screaming, as what remained of the front door was kicked open and eight thugs with football scarves over their faces charged in. Tables were kicked over, as the marauders shouted abuse and attacked anyone who got in their way.

Simon made it to the bar area which also served as a takeaway counter. He laughed as he threw an ashtray against the optics and saw the bottles and their contents cascading down on the screaming Asian girl who was hiding in a frightened huddle on the bar floor.

From the door at the side of the bar, an irate Indian chef appeared holding a meat cleaver and attempted to pole axe Simon. The skinhead dropped low, feeling the swish of air as the cleaver just missed his head. Realising that his luck was holding, Simon's fist struck out and found the man's stomach, making the Indian gasp as the wind was knocked out of him.

Newhart, the Bethnal Green bootboy, had come over to aid Simon and he knocked the struggling chef to the floor with a wine bottle. As the chef lay there groaning, Simon gave him several kicks with his heavy steel toe-capped DMs. It was the least he deserved for daring to try and kill him.

The rest of the restaurant's staff were already beaten into submission, and with the customers fled, the place resembled a bomb site. Tables and chairs were turned over and smashed, while others helped themselves to several bottles of spirits and hundreds of cigarettes from behind the bar. As he joined in the pillaging, Newhart couldn't resist slamming his boot into the girl curled up in a protective ball beneath the bar. Someone else had sprayed PAKIS OUT! on the picture of the Taj Mahal and GBP on the toilet door.

"Okay," shouted Simon, "Let's quit this joint before the pigs get here!"

They ran from the restaurant and wormed their way through the service roads before coming out on the road behind the commercial block. Scarves had been stashed by then and the group started walking along the road as if they didn't have a care in the world.

Simon was pleased with the way he had organised everything. The confrontation had been brief and effective, using only those who had some method of disguise for the direct assault. It left him with a confidence that there would be no repercussions of any real consequence.

"Fucking brilliant!" called one of his compatriots.

Yeah, fucking brilliant! Simon thought in self-congratulation. He was finding that buzz again.

Howard was waiting for Simon as he returned to the office after the promised drink with the boys. The police had already been and gone, asking if anyone knew anything about a fight at an Indian takeaway. The mixture of denials and jokey replies soon had the Old Bill realising that there wouldn't be any profit in pursuing the point.

Simon told a pleased Howard about the attack and how the mob had fallen in with his leadership. "Want a drink?" Simon asked, knowing that Ralph kept a bottle somewhere in one of the filing cabinets.

Howard shook his head. "No thanks . . . And I think you should leave it out too. It would appear that you've already had enough for tonight!"

"Maybe you're right!" Simon agreed. "So what brings you out here in the middle of the night?"

"I've been asked to supply you with your provisional targets," he said removing a sheet of paper from an envelope. Passing it over, he carried on talking. "Target number one is a student union which is proving to be a hotbed of communist subversion. The second is a Front official who was selected for his close proximity to the city centre. You'll see it's on the Queensway. Then two establishments. The Workers Printshop Initiative which masquerades as a commercial business in Deptford and the Front's mail order lockup. These two are to be torched!"

Simon nodded. He knew arson was a heavy charge, but for him, the odd act of pyromania wasn't as serious an undertaking as the law tried to assume. "Okay!"

Howard then handed him the envelope. "In there you'll find a campus layout map and photocopied pages from the A-Z for the other targets."

"Cheers Howard," said Simon. "Leave it with me and it'll be done!"

I am nineteen and I'm mad
I am nineteen, getting it bad
I am nineteen, don't know what to do,
I won't reach twenty and I don't want to!
NINETEEN AND MAD - THE LEYTON BUZZARDS (1977)

CHAPTER EIGHT

THE flow of the market crowd was in a multitude of directions. Everywhere sales were being made as traders shouted their wares. In the middle of this bedlam, Simon and Greta were overlooking the half a dozen selected members who would be taking on Notting Hill as their recruitment patch. A Union Jack and the GBP flag were wedged against the wall behind them to provide a backdrop for their recruitment drive.

"I would have liked to have been there," Greta told Simon, referring to the attack on the Indian restaurant. It had caused quite a splash in the local paper and even *The Evening Standard* carried the story over half of page seven.

"Next time Greta, eh?" Simon replied.

The girl was a strange one all right. One hundred per cent woman for sure, but there was something about the way she craved aggression that made Simon wonder. Perhaps she was into sado-masochism. Not that he could say with any certainty, but it just seemed that way.

Turning his attention to the rest of the group, Simon gave the signal to begin the pitch to the few curious souls who had looked on in wonderment at what they were up to.

"GBP - the white man's voice! Read all about it! GBP - the white man's voice!" cried Tom, a young skinhead who stepped forward to hold a copy of the manifesto dramatically above his head. He had been roped into the job by Newhart by virtue of living on the same street as him.

"Told you he'd be good!" Newhart said enthusiastically to Simon.

Simon looked at him with an approving grin. "A real pro!" he said, which was indeed the case because Tom worked a pitch for the *Standard* during the week at a news-stand in Piccadilly Circus.

As was to be expected, the distribution of the GBP leaflets was a hit and miss affair. Occasionally someone willingly sort one out, but generally the leaflets were accepted, stared at blankly and thrown to the ground by passers-by. Newhart wasn't making things any easier with his knack of attracting trouble like manure pulls in the flies.

First, an irate student started screaming "Fascist!" at him, and Simon was disgusted when Newhart had just stood there lamely. With everyone looking on, Simon felt Newhart should have turned the situation around, and walked over to tell him so. "What the fucking hell are you doing Newhart?" he demanded angrily.

The skinhead looked at him not really knowing what he was supposed to be doing.

Simon looked straight at the student with his scraggly hair and tea cosy for a woolly hat. "Alright, fuck off Castro!"

"Fucking fascists!" replied the newly named revolutionary waving two Vs in their faces.

Simon wasn't in the mood to take shit from one of life's leeches. Giving his private thoughts an agreeing nod, the punch came swift and sudden, smashing into the student's nose with the force of a baseball bat. The guy wasn't a fighter and he collapsed dazed on the floor.

"Oi! Leave 'im alone!" shouted a young black guy from the other side of the street.

"Fuck you, wog!" Newhart called, following Simon's lead.

"You're dead meat!" called back the black. As he moved towards the GBP stall, pushing market-goers aside, it became apparent that he wasn't as alone as it had first appeared. There were another fifteen or so mean looking blokes with him, all in their late teens and early twenties.

"Shit!" Newhart's surprise found voice. He had failed to see the guy's friends lurking beyond the crowded market stalls.

"Took the words right out of my mouth!" said Simon as he stepped forward into the open area that separated the two groups. From his pocket he took a cosh and held it back, using his forearm to hide it.

Simon had stepped off the pavement just as the black guy rushed out to attack. Using a rough variation of a judo throw, Simon hauled him off his feet and bashed him across the back of the head with the cosh. Then letting him drop, he was aware of the cry of outrage from the young black's friends.

Spinning to free himself from the slumped form, he whacked the next leading figure across the face with the cosh. Berserk and howling with fury, the rest of the coloured gang caused the crowds to scatter from around them. An assortment of knives and machetes appeared, and Simon quickly realised it was getting too hot to handle. "Run!" he called out to the others.

Newhart grabbed hold of Greta's forearm and broke for the cross-roads, swiftly followed by Tom who gripped the Union Jack standard. The GBP flag was picked up by one of the other volunteers, but piles of leaflets had to be abandoned in the hurry to escape.

Allowing them the chance to get a slight lead, Simon felt at liberty to join the dash for freedom. Unfortunately, one of the black guys now blocked his retreat. He stood there with a machete and a look of certain triumph.

Simon quickly realised he was being trapped, with the coloured gang moving in on him from all sides. The on-looking public were horrified, but not willing to get involved. Most were convinced they were about to witness a murder.

The skinhead also knew if he didn't do something quick he was going to be dead. With no time to formulate a great masterplan, Simon ran head down at the machete wielder. Surprised, the black's momentary hesitation cost him his only chance of hacking down the skinhead.

Crashing into him, Simon used the momentum of his charge to throw the guy bodily over an antique and bric-a-brac stall. Not stopping to see it all go crashing to the floor, Simon darted for the open space.

There was no need to look back anyway. He could hear the enemy's pounding steps and goading voices behind him as his legs worked like pistons, carrying him at breakneck speed, but Simon was beginning to revel in the situation. "Only by facing death can you truly feel alive!" was a philosophy that had seen him through Angola not to mention other tight situations back home.

He saw the other GBP members disappear around a fenced off football court and when he got there, he found Greta and Newhart had dropped back from their compatriots. "Hey, come on!" Simon shouted as he caught up with them.

They started running together, but Simon now had to slow down to Greta's speed. The chase continued along side the football courts, past a row of run down shops and across a piece of green. As he ran, Simon tipped several litter bins over in a bid to slow down their pursuers. After two more roads they emerged out on to a stretch of wasteland, and headed for the only visible cover, the garaging area of the local housing estate.

Greta decided enough was enough. Her throat was raw and on fire from panting, and sweat trickled freely from her brow and between her breasts. Simon tried to coax her on, but she could run no more. She leant against the wall with her hands placed on the top of her thighs for support.

"Shit!" snapped Newhart, punching a garage door, his lungs also fit to burst. Noticing a cut section of scaffold pole lying on the ground, he snatched it up - a lethal weapon for sure!

Together they waited, breathing heavily, each as nervous as the other. After about a minute and a half, they began to look at each other, wondering where their pursuers were. Suspecting a trick, but needing to know for sure, Simon went to the mouth of the garage complex and looked back across the green. All he could see was a couple of kids playing football. Incredible though it was, it looked like being their lucky day.

"It's okay, they've given up!"

The grin on Simon's face spoke the relief they all felt. When he got back to the office, he would have a bone to pick with Ralph. It was wishful thinking to believe they could operate a pitch at a market and come away unmolested. *Stupid fat git!* he fumed quietly to himself.

Greta threw her arms around Simon. "That was exhilarating!"

Newhart exchanged glances with Simon. Neither could believe the girl was for real. Excitement was one thing, having one foot in the grave another matter entirely.

Del was looking forward to seeing Suzi again. It had occurred to him over the last couple of days, that it might be a good idea to invite her along to the show. Leroy wouldn't mind and it would give them a chance to be together. Getting off the bus opposite the tube station, he started heading towards Suzi's.

As he approached the squat, he stopped and studied the dilapidated state of the house. From the rotten window frames on the upper floor to the peeling paint on the front door, it was obvious the house was in a poor state. The garden too was uncared for and had more foliage than Kew Gardens. *It wouldn't be such a bad place with a bit of work,* he thought to himself. Then, as the garden gate almost came off in his hands, he changed that to "a lot of work".

He knocked on the door, but when he got no reply he banged again, harder. "Come on . . . Where are ya?"

He was beginning to think Suzi wasn't going to be in when he heard her voice from the other side of the door. "Who is it?"

"What's up Suzi? Don't you recognise my voice? Jesus, it's only been a couple of days!"

Her apprehension fell away and she tore open the door. "Del!" she cried happily, jumping into his arms and wrapping her legs around his waist.

Staggering slightly, he regained his balance and returned the squeeze she was giving him. "You okay, girl?" he asked.

"Kiss me and I'll tell you!" she demanded, determined to have her own way.

Del conceded willingly. He had been anticipating the feel of her lips on his all morning.

"Yeah, I'm better now!" she said chirpily.

"Well, I have that affect on women!" Del boasted jokingly.

"Name them and I'll kill 'em!" promised Suzi, lifting the collar of his shirt out and blowing lightly on his neck.

Del shuddered as her hot breath triggered a sensation of unbearable pleasure to run through him. It became too much and he shied away by bringing his head and shoulder together. "Leave it out will ya?"

Suzi laughed and placed her feet down to give Del the opportunity to lower her gently to the ground. Pulling one of his arms around her waist, she guided him in through the front door. "I didn't think I was going to see you today. You've got that thing with Leroy tonight haven't you?"

"Yeah, that's right!" he answered as they climbed the stairs to her room at the back of the house. "I thought I'd come and see if you wanted to join us. It should be good for a laugh."

"Oh, sorry, I can't. I've got a bit of selling to do." Suzi was genuine with her guilt. She really did feel bad about turning him down.

"It was just an idea," he said, not bothering to hide the disappointment in his voice. "Can't you sell it there?" he asked.

"Show me a student who has money and I'll show you a dealer already working the patch," Suzi pointed out. It wasn't just that though. Students tended to buy hashish and her speed would be about as popular as a collection tin at the royal mint.

Derek was about to resort to an emotional blackmail ploy, but stopped himself before he voiced the "do it for me" pitch. If they couldn't spend the night together, at least there was the afternoon.

106

"You want a coffee or tea?" she asked him as she pushed her door wide open.

"What, you had the gas put on or something?"

"No," laughed Suzi. "I bought one of those camping stoves from a junk shop down Kentish Town way, didn't I?" Her finger pointed to the appliance sitting in the corner of the room by the window. A twin burner fed by a Calor gas bottle. Around it were some cooking utensils and tins of foods. "Got sick of having burgers and shit all the time."

Things were certainly looking up. "I'll have a coffee seeing as you offered," said Del flopping on to the bed.

Suzi squatted over the small stove and made the drinks. It might not have been much in the fitted kitchen stakes, but it did make the place more of a home for her.

"So what you been up to over the last couple of days?" he asked.

"I got interviewed by some journalist and I've been to see Gillian. Not a lot really!"

"What do you mean, not a lot?" Del said in disbelief. Talking to the press wasn't exactly what he had in mind when he said they should stay low for a few days.

"Sorry?" Suzi sensed she may have done something wrong in his eyes.

"The interview . . . Ain't exactly the brightest thing to do considering we may have the pigs looking out for us, is it?"

"No, s'pose not," she said, sniggering just enough to show that frankly she didn't really care if it had been prudent or not.

"So what was the interview about?"

"The usual on the punk scene. I kind of got bored and walked out half way through." It was obviously better to tell a white lie than to say the guy had turned her on. "Here's yours - two sugars?"

"Yeah, that's right!" he confirmed as he accepted the mug from her outstretched hand.

Settling herself next to him, they sat shoulder to shoulder with their backs propped against the wall.

"What about you?"

Del looked at her. "You mean what have I been doing?"

Suzi nodded as she raised the steaming mug to her lips with both hands, her eyes peering over the top of the rim at him.

"Bit of this, a bit of that I guess."

"Nothing in other words," challenged Suzi.

Del smiled. "Yeah, that's about the size of it. I've been having a right old time sorting out tonight's play list. Kind of got things sorted out, then changed my mind when I took a final look. Trouble was I changed it about ten times!"

"You happy with it now?" she said as she held his gaze.

"Dunno. I kinda gave up and said, fuck it, that'll do."

"Yeah, I get like that sometimes," Suzi said with knowing sympathy.

Derek nodded and accepted the hand that she slipped into his, acknowledging the light affectionate squeeze with one in return.

After the coffee, Suzi asked if he wanted to take a walk around the park. He grinned and replied, "I've heard it called many things in my time, but that takes the biscuit!"

Suzi pushed him over and pinned him down. "Your brains always been in your shorts?"

"Dunno, wanna find out?"

Sitting up again, she pleaded her case. "Come on, I wanna get out for a bit."

"What in full view of the public? I'd rather have a bit in here!"

Although Del wasn't keen on the idea, Suzi got her own way and they ended up arm in arm, heading for Regents Park. While there, Del had the crazy notion of going to the zoo. It was something he hadn't done since he was a kid and it seemed a bit more interesting than waltzing around the park. Serious or not, the idea appealed to her as well, and after queuing up for ten minutes, they were through the turnstiles and into the complex.

Del had to grin at the way she cooed over the chinchillas and the baby panda, especially when her maternal declarations were getting the strangest looks from the rest of the animal watchers. The cheekiness of the monkeys held the pair spellbound too, but it was the big cats that held the biggest attraction for Del.

Stopping at a refreshment hut, they bought a couple of hotdogs and two overpriced tins of Coke. As they sat with their purchases at one of the plastic tables with a parasol stretched out overhead, Suzi turned to Del and ventured. "Hasn't been a bad day, has it?"

"Nah, it's been all right!" he agreed before biting into the Westler roll.

"You know, that's what I like about you," Suzi said, leaning forward and propping herself up by her elbows on the table top.

"What's that?" he responded.

"The way you are . . . You know, when I first saw you I thought you was just another prick with legs . . . "

"Thanks a fucking lot!" Del was shocked and insulted, but was laughing all the same. It seemed such a bizarre thing to say.

"Nah, wait a minute . . . Let me explain. What I mean is I thought you was just another one of those guys who only see women as a fuck and that's it, but you're different."

"In what way?" Del asked.

"Don't know really, you're just different - it's like a friendship as well . . . You know, fun!"

"Okay girl, just keep having the therapy and you'll be all right!" joked Del.

"Don't take the piss . . . I mean it." She looked flustered, like it was an uncomfortable admission to make.

"Hey, I'm not knocking you, I just . . . " He froze, not too sure what he meant, then meekly he smiled and added, "Sorry!"

"That's all right, I forgive you!" she allowed.

"Can we kiss and make up now?" he blurted out, eyebrows raised in exaggerated enquiry.

Giving in to his idiosyncratic ways, she leant over and pressed her lips against his, allowing his tongue to play with hers.

They stayed in the zoo for another hour, then with time getting on, Del decided that it was time to leave. Walking back towards Camden Town, both were locked in their own private thoughts. Suzi was considering the way their relationship was in comparison to past affairs, while Del was thinking about the night ahead.

A parting kiss at the end of Suzi's road, and an arrangement to meet at a pub on Portobello Road tomorrow lunchtime, gave them both something to look forward to.

The University hall appeared massive to Del. It was as big as any West End club he had been to, that was for sure. Even though it was only eight o'clock, the place was already filling up nicely, mainly thanks to the discount bar prices that meant tanking up before hand was unnecessary.

Nursing a pint of lager, Del stood in the company of Stan, Alan, Robert and Rebel, who had been a bit disappointed that Suzi wasn't there. Rebel had joked that she'd like to have had a good chin wag with

Suzi about Del, and he'd answered back, "Why talk? Lose Rob for half an hour and find out first hand!"

She smiled quietly back while Alan and Stanley loudly compared the talent on offer. Alan was quite taken by a set of birds gathered around the pinball table, while Stan was more for a slip of a girl sitting with a friend by the corner of the stage.

Leroy was busy on the turntables. "Blood and fire, wickedness and dread. Dirty Babylon, I cut off thy head - This is the medusa!"

Del kind of liked this one. An I-Roy lyrical toast over a dreamy backing track featuring the saxophone talents of Tommy McCook, one-time member of the legendary Skatalites. The rhythm flowed like liquid mud, as the brass notes hauntingly fluttered in and out. I-Roy sounded stoned, his words riding through on an incessant hum.

"What you drinking?" Alan asked, turning to Del who had after all sorted them out free entry on The Ethiopian Express guest list. Not only that, Alan had seen a chance to get talking with the pinball princess.

"Make mine a lager!"

"Okay, a lager. Stan?" Rob asked.

"Same, mate!"

"Rebel?"

"Bacardi and Coke!"

After enlisting Stanley's help, the pair crossed the dance floor to the bar which stood in an alcove on the far side of the hall.

"When you on?" Rob asked Del.

"About nine or something like that. I've got an hour before the band goes on."

Rob nodded. All he knew about the band was they were an experimental white reggae band by the name of The Police. What that meant exactly, neither he or any of the others were quite sure.

"They're taking a while," Del said when Alan and Stan failed to return in good time.

Rob glanced through the crowd on the dance floor who were dancing lazily to *Guns Fever* by The Starjets. "It's no wonder, he's scored!" he exclaimed, catching sight of Alan with a bird.

Both Del and Rebel had to take a look for themselves. Sure enough, Alan was involved in a passionate embrace with the girl who had caught his eye. Stanley looked like he was still making preliminary small talk with the girl's friends.

Del saw the chance for a laugh and beckoned the others to follow him. Picking his way carefully through the crowd with Rob and Rebel behind him, he crept up on Alan. Stanley saw them coming, but held his silence when Del held a finger to his lips. From the table in front of him, Del fished an ice cube out of an emptied spirit glass and, holding it just above the nape of Alan's neck, he suddenly pinched the collar of his Ben Sherman and let it go.

Hot passion gave way to cold cursing as Alan reacted to the shock of an ice cube down his back. The girl wondered what the hell was going on as he swivelled round, trying to dislodge the damp rock. Rob, Rebel and Stan were laughing with Del, as their friend finally managed to free it.

"You bastard!" he cried, pushing Del who couldn't resist because he was laughing too much. "These people are my friends!" he told the girl who had recovered from the shock of his sudden convulsion.

"Hi," she responded.

Rob and Rebel acknowledged with the same while Del held out his hand. "Sorry about that girl, just a bit of fun," he said as they shook. "So where's these drinks you were getting then?" he called to Alan.

"Forgot 'em," Alan admitted, only just remembering why he had gone to the bar area in the first place.

"Kinda justifies waking you up a bit then, don't it?"

"Okay, okay. I'm sorting it now!" Alan said before turning to the girlfriend he had just acquired. "You want something, Alison?"

"Bacardi and Coke," she replied, gaining Rebel's immediate approval.

"That's right luv, us girls have gotta stick together," she said putting her arm around Alison's shoulders.

Alison could only nod weakly, not realising that Rebel was talking about the fact that they had ordered the same drink.

By the time Del was up for DJing, the hall was reaching capacity and had an oddball collection of different types in attendance. There were smatterings of bikers and hippy chicks, soul boys, art school punks, cliques of girls, the works.

"Okay, folks. A warm welcome please for my good friend, DJ Del Peterson. Here to hit them old revival sounds . . . "

Taking his cue, Del held the second microphone up to his mouth and spoke - weakly at first, but gaining strength with confidence. "Thanks, Leroy. Okay let's cut the chat and turn it back. Rewind to another time. Place the needle in the groove, grab your space and start

111

to move! This are Keith Poppins with a dub cut of *Longshot 'Im Kick De Bucket*!".

Apart from a gap of two or three seconds between the end of his intro and the start of the music, Del was quite pleased with his first effort. He was even more chuffed with himself when both Leroy and the roadies gave him the thumbs up. Rob, Stanley and Rebel were up and dancing just in front of the sound system which was set up on a low stage to the léft of the main one, and looking across the dance floor, Del could see the tune was getting a good reception.

As a dub, it was a good selection. No one could mistake it as the one made famous by The Pioneers so it had rarity value, but it still scored points by association with the people who recognised the tune. Leroy ad-libbed a toast over the track when it was about half-way through. "Dis horse has run its course! Now count the cost of what's been lost!"

Del was enjoying the experience tremendously, as he picked his way through the hour, dropping in a good mix of sounds. Reaching back to the ska tunes of Prince Buster, Bob Marley & The Wailers, and Andy And Joey, he then went into rocksteady with the original cut of *Stop That Train* by Keith And Ken followed by the more recent Scotty version. With a dedication to his friends, he also span *Reggae Fever* by The Pioneers, which attracted exuberant cheers and catcalls from Andy, Rob and Stan because the record, a cut of The Valentines' *Guns Fever* rhythm, had changed the lyrics to acknowledge the skinhead cult.

"Every time you read the *Mirror* or the *Sketch*,
Skinheads are always at their very best.
It's the fever, oh yeah,
Reggae fever."

The lyrics might have been simplistic, but the tune had a far greater harmonious feel to it than the Symarip anthem, *Skinhead Moonstomp* - itself a reworking of a tune called *Moonhop*.

All too soon the need to play out and allow the band to take to the stage had arrived. "Okay people! I say bye bye and finish off with this little tune from the Joe Gibbs stable - *No Bones For The Dogs.* It was a heavyweight dub with the Gibbs And Errol trademark stamped all over it. Rolling echo and sudden drop outs where lead vocals became distant harmony behind the bass throb.

The band took to the stage with the cheers of the audience ringing around the hall. Del dropped the volume by fifty percent and waited for the sound engineer to switch from auxiliary to all lines in. Once the transfer had been made, he took the last disc from the turntable, placed it into the record box and stepped off the podium.

Stanley gave him a hearty slap on the back. "Good session!"

"Thanks!" replied Del.

Together they turned their attention to the band who were blasting the hall with a racey song called *So Lonely*. The gig wasn't bad for the skinheads, with songs like the power pop of *Roxanne*, with its skanking guitar segment, and out and out reggae sounds like *Walking On The Moon*, giving them a chance to display their dancing prowess.

After the band had finished their set, Leroy and his number two went through a DJ battle sequence. With a deck each, they tried to outbid each other, playing multiple versions and going for dub counter attacks. The verbal banter between them added to the fun of the occasion.

The bar closed at half past eleven, which was just as well because Del and his friends were beginning to look a bit worse for wear. Not totally slaughtered, but two-thirds pissed nevertheless.

On the drive back, Del insisted on stopping the van when he thought he was going to be sick. Leroy was taking the piss by offering Del a large spliff as he propped himself against a bus stop sign, waiting for things to take their course.

"Leave it out Leroy," he pleaded weakly. "Fuck, I feel like shit!"

The rasta laughed. It was getting late and it seemed like a good idea to shift Colin, one of the security guys, from the front of the transit to the rear, so that they could get on their way and Del could hang out of the window if he had to chuck up.

As it happened, the cold night air on his face brought him back from the edge of despair and by the time they arrived at Leroy's place, he had recovered quite considerably. Even before the van had emptied out its human cargo, Leroy's woman, Jennifer, came down the garden path to meet them.

"Something wrong?" Leroy asked as he got out of the driver's door. She didn't usually come out like that.

"Uh, huh . . . Del, you want to go into the house. Suzi's been beaten up!"

"Beaten up?" Del exclaimed, tearing the passenger door open and jumping out. He didn't wait for the others, but followed Jennifer's lead in rushing up the garden path. All sorts of things were going through his head.

He found Suzi in the kitchen being consoled by a couple of Jennifer's friends. Her face was a mass of bruising, one eye was closed and her lips bulged out at the corner by her left nostril.

"Del . . . " She rose shakily, moved weakly towards him and fell sobbing into his arms.

Holding her tightly, he let her cry for a bit. The tremors that racked her body were echoed by the anger that gnawed at the pit of his stomach. The others soon joined them in the kitchen, and Rebel gently lifted Suzi's head off Del's shoulder. "Suzi, it's me, Rebel."

"Who the fucking hell done that?" exclaimed Rob.

"Keep your hair on," snapped Rebel. She knew that the last thing Suzi needed was being talked to in an aggressive way.

Gesturing to Suzi, she held out her hands. "Come here girl, let's get you cleaned up." Taking the responsibility for comforting her from Del, she turned to speak to Leroy, but he had already anticipated the question.

"It's up the top of the stairs on the right. There's cotton wool in the cabinet."

Del touched Rebel on the forearm and mouthed silently for her to find out who did it. While she and Suzi went up to the bathroom, Del stood there, making and unmaking a clenched fist. The suppressed rage made him look fit to explode.

Colin broke the silence first. "Del, you want we should do some ting about this?"

Del looked at the stocky black guy and then at each of the skinheads in turn. "Yeah, we're gonna do something . . . Find out who it was and fucking kill 'em!"

"Smoke this," Leroy said, passing him the joint. Del accepted, but only took one draw. Enough to take the edge off the feeling he was going to erupt.

Rebel returned to the kitchen alone.

"Well, who was it?" several of them asked at once.

Looking at Del, she explained what she had been told. "Suzi said it was the other people at the squat. She had found her room broken into when she went back this afternoon. She waited for them to return to have it out with them and they beat her up. That's basically it!"

"Where is this place?" Leroy asked, turning to Del.

"Camden Town!"

"Okay, let's take the Transit and deal out some biblical justice."

"An eye for an eye, a tooth for a tooth," grinned Colin knowingly.

"Yeah, let's go," Del agreed.

"Stay here and look after Suzi," Rob told Rebel.

Much as she liked mixing it herself, she knew he was right. Suzi needed someone to be with her. Nodding, she pecked him on the cheek. "Watch yourself."

"Yeah, sure," Rob acknowledged.

The drive to the squat was taken up with Del answering questions about the type of place it was, who was likely to be there and so on. Del tried to answer them the best he could, but his only aim was to cause as much pain as possible.

Parking just down the road from the squat's front gate, the group assembled by the van before moving off together. Stepping on to the garden path, they bunched around the front door. The sound of music told them that at least some of the people they were after were in the front room.

"Ready?" Colin asked. He had equipped himself with a baseball bat from Leroy's place, one used to sort out any door disputes during the yard gigs.

Rob gave Del a thumbs up sign, and fought to control the grin that wanted to appear on his face.

"Okay, let's go!" Colin whispered before raising the bat and punching out one of the door's glass panels. Then groping inside for the catch, he forced the door open.

In the hallway, the punks were emerging from the living room with chair legs and other implements to see what the noise was, but the sight of Colin and Del robbed them of any confidence for a stand up fight.

As the mob charged in, Colin went straight for the leading punk, a gangly young bloke in black strides, shirt and biker's jacket. Even though he was armed with an iron rod, he made no attempt to use it or dodge the blow from the baseball bat that Colin slammed down over his head. Once in the living room, pandemonium broke out.

There were more punks than usual, as if they were partying on Suzi's supply of speed. Del was staggered by a blow from a bulky wooden leg that had once been on a snooker table. Meant for the head, the blow had caught Del on the upper shoulder and pushed him over a kitchen chair. Luckily, the guy didn't get the chance to take advantage of him because Alan, sporting a brass knuckle duster he had fashioned one idle afternoon, punched Del's attacker square in the face. His club flew out of his hand as he staggered back, totally stunned and his nose a mess of blood.

Del found his feet, picked up the chair and threw it at three punks huddled in the far corner of the room. Colin went around the back of the sofa towards them just as Leroy, Stan, Alan and Rob appeared. Rob didn't wait for an invitation and went steaming into the remaining combatants, headbutting one while trying to kick out at another.

Everyone went for them at once and only Stanley fell back, his lips pulped by a lump of four by four he had failed to notice swinging at him. Apart from that, resistance was minimal and the fight quickly ended. Most of the punks were out for the count, while the only coherent one was huddled into a corner, with his hands waving about in a pathetic attempt at blocking any further blows. The guy was frightened witless. "No more, please no more!"

Del walked up to him with deliberate intent, drew back his foot and kicked him in the head. "Fuck you!"

As the punk rolled over, Del repeatedly kicked him, his mind full of pictures of the state Suzi's face was in.

"Hey, we gotta quit before the law gets here!" Colin said, resting a hand on Del's shoulder.

Del shrugged it off in anger, and it looked for a moment like he wasn't going to stop until he had killed the guy. Fortunately for the punk, Colin wasn't the sort of bloke who was going to ask politely twice. Giving the baseball bat to Leroy, he got the skinhead in a bear hug and picked his feet off the floor. "Let's go," he said, marching to the door with Del struggling to break free.

"All right!" growled Del. "I'm alright! Fucking let me go!"

"You sure?" Colin whispered in his ear.

"Just said it, didn't I? Look, I wanna see if there's any of Suzi's stuff still here."

"Okay, but be quick," Colin said, releasing him.

Del bounded up the stairs, while the others filed out of the house. Suzi's room had been wrecked. The mattress had been slashed and its guts strewn across the room. All her posters hung in tatters from their cellotape. A lot of her clothes had been ripped up and others were covered in a sludge of instant coffee and water, and it didn't take a trained eye to see that a lot of things were missing.

It was obvious there was nothing worth salvaging. Giving up, Del walked out of the room and down the stairs. The unconscious punk Colin had floored when they had first entered the squat, was still sprawled out in the hallway. Maliciously, Del gave him a heavy kick to the stomach and then left.

What the hell is wrong with me?
I'm not the person I ought to be.
WHAT'S MY NAME? - THE CLASH (1977)

CHAPTER NINE

FOR the next couple of days, Suzi stayed with Jennifer and Jennifer's baby son from a previous relationship. The beating had left Suzi feeling withdrawn and for days she didn't want to leave the house, no matter how much Del and Jennifer tried to coax her. Jennifer had finally brought Suzi back to her senses by being cruel to be kind. One morning, when Suzi was playing with her little boy, Jennifer marched in on them and threw a towel at Suzi. "Okay, strip your things off and I'll wash your clothes for you!"

The punk girl had looked at her blankly.

"Come on," demanded Jennifer, showing she wasn't going to take any more bullshit. "If you stay here, I'd appreciate you not smelling."

It was brutal, but having to sit around in a towel all afternoon with those words ringing in her ears did the trick. And the following day, Del was happy to see that she wanted him to escort her to the Oxfam shop in Brixton High Street.

Her face was still swollen and when she had looked in the mirror just before venturing out with Del, she had had second thoughts. Still, what did she care what people thought of her and she was determined not to become a prisoner in a council flat for the rest of her life just because of the attack.

The High Street was quite a busy thoroughfare and people did seem to be taking a second look at Suzi as they passed, but she knew it was probably due to the clothes she was wearing as much as the nature of her facial injuries.

The charity shop was situated at the far end of the street, amongst the less desirable and therefore cheaper to rent properties. Inside, there was a wealth of old clothes that had great potential as fashion items in the punkette's eyes. First she found a lightweight semi-transparent plastic mac on the coat rack nearest the window, and from the heaps of clothing on the table she managed to retrieve a bus driver's jacket.

In her mind's eye she was already making alterations to the jacket. The perfunctory slogans were a must, as were safety-pins and chains. The idea of creating a web of chains connecting the arm to the body of

117

the jacket, with just enough slack to allow movement, also began to seem feasible. From there she had the idea of getting one of the men's shirts and cutting the sleeves into one inch hoops, then reattaching them using safety pins or cloth tape sown in as a skeleton, making it possible to miss out each alternate piece.

Having found several items that intrigued her, there was one problem that she hadn't considered before. Sheepishly, and in a low voice she called Derek over.

"What?" he asked, turning his attention away from the football comic he was flicking through.

"I've just realised - I haven't got any money!"

"Hey, no problem girl. I'll treat ya."

"Thanks!" she said, smiling for what seemed like the first time in ages. It was what she had hoped he would say.

The damage to her face caused some comment between the two old women standing behind the counter. Del realised they were attributing the beating to him, and so as not to disappoint them, he quietly explained, "She forgot to put sugar in my coffee!"

Del was enjoying the shocked looks he had inspired when Suzi hissed, "What d'you wanna tell them that for?"

Del glanced at her and lowered his voice. "You think they'd believe it wasn't me?"

Suzi shrugged, still feeling it was inconsiderate of him to exploit her problems for fun. Still, she wasn't complaining when it came to paying for the goods. The two old dears obviously felt sorry for her and they couldn't price the clothes cheap enough. By the time she left, Suzi had two large carrier bags full of clothes and had only spent two pounds of Derek's money

"That was a result!" he declared as they joined the crowds back out on the High Street.

"See the looks on their faces when you said it was over coffee! They were shocked, man!" Suzi found she could laugh about it now. Why she had become so withdrawn she didn't know. Perhaps it was a residue of the mentality that said a woman should feel ashamed to be seen in public with her face in that state. Yet wasn't the punk ethic about breaking with normal convention? All things considered, she decided that perhaps she had let her mind stray from its stand. *Never again*, she promised herself.

Popping into the local Wimpy, Del bought a couple of coffees and treated Suzi to a banana sundae. As they sat there, Del sensed that there was still something on Suzi's mind.

"What's up girl? I thought you was straightening out?" He stared across into her eyes.

"Nothing," she replied unconvincingly.

"Don't lie, girl I know when something's bothering you."

Looking down at her dessert as if it commanded all her attention, she said, "It's not your problem!"

"Hey, don't be like that. If I can help you, I will."

"I know you will!" she said looking up at him. "Just it don't seem right, you know."

"Let me decided that! What's the problem?"

Sighing, she decided to let go. "I don't know how to tell Gillian I was ripped off!" It was nearly the truth because it was her old man, Clive, she was really worried about. The idea of having him upset with her was making her nervous.

"I'll go round and explain what's taken place, all right?" Del offered, hoping it would ease her mind.

Suzi looked at him. It would save her facing up to her worries, but she didn't know whether it was fair putting Del in the middle like that. "Would you?" she asked, still undecided.

"I said I would didn't I?"

"Be careful of her husband, he can be a bit funny!"

"Hey, no problem!"

"No seriously Del, he ain't nobody's fool. Look, tell them I'll try and sort out the cost of what got stolen, okay?"

"How much is that?"

"Fifteen quid," she replied. It seemed like a lot of money when there was nothing in her pockets. The dole only paid just below thirteen pounds and that wasn't due until the following Thursday.

It occurred to Del that he could help bail her out if necessary as there was twenty five pounds in his Post Office account, but he would see if a deal could be worked out first. "Okay, I'll do it this afternoon, all right?"

"Thanks Del, you're a diamond!"

"What you gonna do?" he asked her as he finished off the bitty dregs of his coffee.

"Sort out my wardrobe, I guess!" she said, patting the bags that leant against her chair legs.

After Suzi had stolen a packet of markers from W.H. Smith's, she went back to Jennifer's flat and Del headed for the tube station and the fun and games of changing at The Elephant And Castle, and then again at Euston to track back one stop to Camden Town.

Out on the streets, Del kept watch for the squat punks. He skirted their street by taking an earlier turning, but he didn't fully relax until he found himself on the path leading up to Gillian's front door. Pressing the doorbell, he heard it ring and waited for an answer. Seconds later the door swung open and Gillian's face appeared in the gap.

"Hello Del!" she said, noticing he was alone. "Where's Suzi?"

"That's what I've come to see you about. Can I come in?"

"Yeah sure," she responded, opening the door.

Del could see she was still wearing a dressing gown. "Late night?" he asked as he closed the door behind him and following her into the kitchen.

"Yeah, me old man was back for a couple of days!"

"Was?" Del repeated her choice of word.

"Said he had some business up north . . . So I guess I'll see him when I see him!"

"Sounds like you're not happy with it," Del suggested, sensing and playing up to her mood.

"I married him so it's me own fault," she said with a philosophical flair. Sometimes she felt like it was too much and she wanted to walk out, but there was something that kept her hanging on. Quite what it was she didn't know, although sometimes she suspected that it was merely the challenge of trying to curb his wandering tendencies. "So what's happened to Suzi then? I spoke to the guy at the paper shop and she hasn't been there for a few days. She's not ill is she?"

"Ain't you gonna offer me a coffee?" Del said, changing the subject with the intent of buying a little bit more time to formulate a response.

"Oh, sorry," Gillian said, apologising for her lack of hospitality. "It was a late night and I'm still not with it!"

"Hey, no problem!"

While Gillian filled the kettle and plugged it in, Del decided it was time to lay the cards on the table. "Nah, the reason I came was Suzi was scared to come herself."

"Why?" Gillian asked.

"She lost the pills you gave her!"

"What do you mean, lost them? How?" Gillian was immediately suspicious.

Derek reacted to counter the idea of wrong-doing. "Hey, it's not a rip-off if that's what you're thinking. She's been straight with you all the time ain't she?" he pointed out.

Gillian reacted with equal hostility. "Until now!"

"She got robbed and beaten up," Del stated flatly.

"Who by?" Gillian's voice had softened slightly.

"Those toe-rags she shared the squat with!"

"That explains the ambulance," Gillian said, looking to the ceiling with sudden realisation.

"Pardon?" asked Del catching her gaze.

"Was she taken to hospital last night? I heard a couple of the neighbours talking about a disturbance up her road. I didn't pay it much attention, but there was something mentioned about an ambulance turning up."

"Nah, that probably turned up for them!"

"A pay back?" Gillian asked.

"Paid in full!" he confirmed with a thin smile.

Allowing her cold attitude to drop, Gillian asked, "How is she then?"

"She's took a right battering, cos there was three of 'em having a go."

"Jesus . . . I knew they didn't get on, I just didn't know it was getting that bad."

The kettle was boiling, so she turned it off at the power point and filled the cups. Taking a bottle of milk from the fridge, she finished off the preparations and placed a cup in front of Del. "So how is she now?" Gillian asked as she sat down next to him.

"Oh, she's getting better. She got right depressed about it cos they trashed everything she had as well as taking the gear."

"I take it she hasn't got the money to pay back the short fall then?"

Del looked at her and decided there was no point in not being straight. "That's about the size of it."

Gillian sat silently considering the problem and after weighing things up, she turned to Del and spoke. "Look, tell her not to worry. I can tell the old man she paid up. He's got no idea how much money's coming in from the speed - so he'll never suss it."

"Great!" said Del. "Is there anything I can do in return?"

"Nah, the old man came back just in time. Maybe later?"

"Saucy!" replied Del, picking up the meaning of her words straight away. Teasing was her favourite game.

"Serious!" she said, leaving him with the realisation that she meant what she had said.

Bloody hell, Del thought to himself. His mind was divided between thinking about Suzi and wondering what Gillian would be like in his arms.

She could see he was struggling with his thoughts. Smiling, she noted the fact for later use, and let him down gently. "Look, tell Suzi everything's okay. If she wants to carry on, tell her to come around and see me."

"Thanks, Gill."

"Think nothing of it!" She lent over and kissed him lightly on the lips. A sign of friendship and a promise of much more.

The student union was an old converted dining room and the old serving hatch now functioned as a bar. Tables had been arranged in conference style and were playing host to thirty people who were taking part in a meeting between students and members of the Socialist Workers Party.

Tom Watts, the head of the student committee, had been working up support for his idea of a firm commitment against the rising tide of racism. He was concerned not only about several minor incidents involving Asian students, but beyond higher education too, where the alarming rise of the National Front posed a very real threat to his sensibilities.

"If I can address the chair?"

Tom and the others looked to Sarah Campbell, a pretty Scottish girl who was on a Humanities course in London because of the lack of places in Edinburgh. "Yes, Miss Campbell?"

"Why were the two SWP representatives invited to this meeting when no firm decision was taken by this committee on requisite action?" Looking down at her notes, she paused to digest her next point before talking directly to Tom. "Inviting these guests now indicates the chairman has presumed the result of a ballot, and so compromises the neutrality of his position and the freedom of choice for all of us to vote as we see fit."

Her statement drew some barracking from those who thought she was just being pedantic at the expense of a serious problem. Their ridicule caused Tom to stand up in her defence. Holding his hands up to calm the meeting down, he told the committee members, "It's a valid question and one I intend to answer . . . "

Looking at her peering from behind her spectacles, with her black glossy curls flowing around her soft cheeks, he stuck his hand in his trouser pocket. Then rubbing his nose thoughtfully with his other hand, he said, "Miss Campbell, I am fully aware of my responsibilities to this committee and the student body. Yet I contend that the presence of the two honourable guests constitutes no breach of confidence. They are here merely as observers and will take no active part in the proceedings.

"If however the committee does decide that it wishes to join a unified campaign, I thought the nature of the problem being of the utmost urgency, would benefit from being able to be addressed immediately. If this constitutes a breach of confidence, then I can only apologise."

His response received a round of applause from those who felt he had circumvented her objections well. Knowing that her point wasn't going to receive any sympathy and not wishing to alienate herself, she conceded the point. "Mr Chairman, I withdraw my opposition to the invited guests."

"Thank you, Miss Campbell . . . Now if you've all read the contents of the report concerning the number of racial incidents recorded within the universities and colleges of Greater London, I think you'll agree with me that the rise in incidents over the last three years is alarming, and something must be done about it!"

Prompted by Tom's point, Michelle Dunbar stood up to address the committee. "I think it is also worth pointing out that a large number of these incidents are at technical colleges that teach trade apprentices as well as intellectual students."

Sarah thought the girl's comment smacked of class prejudice, but held her silence.

"Point duly noted, Miss Dunbar," Tom responded, checking that the girl next to him had jotted it down in short hand. "Anyone have any suggestions as to how we tackle this particular aspect?"

A young Asian student sitting at the far end of the conference table held his hand up.

"Yes, Mr Choudhary!" Tom gave him permission to address the meeting.

"I suggest we start an awareness campaign!"

"What sort of format do you have in mind?" Tom asked.

"A poster and magazine campaign, possibly backed up with an events itinerary to provide focal points to attract and consolidate long-term support . . . "

"Yes, I do like that." There was a quality of the mountain to Mohammed parable in Tariq Choudhary's thinking. It answered the problem of how to make the public not only aware, but become actively involved too. "With the committee's permission, I would like to call for a vote to confirm that we are to take concerted measures to stamp out this wave of fascism."

Looking around, Tom noted that there weren't any objections and several nodding heads. "Okay, voting is by a show of hands. Those in favour?"

With satisfaction he noted that the majority were with him.

"Those against?"

No hands went up so those who hadn't voted were intent on abstaining rather than objecting.

Glancing at the secretary's notes for confirmation, Tom said, "That's twenty-five votes in favour and three abstentions. Motion carried in favour of taking appropriate action. Now I'd like to . . . "

Whatever it was that Tom would have liked to do, it was lost in the commotion coming from the hallway. Shouting and hollering was accompanied by the sound of breaking glass. Bewildered, several committee members rose from their seats as the double doors burst forth and spewed an angry mob into the meeting.

A chair to the left of the door went sailing through the air and knocked one of the standing committee members to the ground. The meeting erupted in chaos as the attackers swept through the room, punching and kicking at all and sundry.

Simon had one of the SWP supporters pinned to the table and was methodically seeking clear punches to the head. Sarah Campbell screamed as someone pulled at her hair, and as she fell backwards, she wanted to vomit as the toe of a boot drove into her side, winding her. A couple of the students attempted to defend themselves, but it was too little too late.

Letting go of his hold on the bloke's collar, Simon hit him one more time, then stepped back and looked around the hall. There were a couple of fights still in progress and the Upton Park bootboys were obviously making a field day of it, but by and large, he realised the enemy had been defeated by the suddenness of the assault. Mindful of the fact that time was limited, he shouted over the commotion, "Okay, pull out!"

As unified as an automaton, all fighting stopped and the GBP members backed towards the door, still facing their enemies. Tom, who was propped against an overturned table, felt too weak to move. He was only dimly aware of the blood that trickled warmly down his face. Blankly he watched a large skinhead scatter some leaflets as he followed his friends out of the room.

It was as if a tempest had burst into their midst, leaving the place turned totally upside down. Forcing himself to his feet, Tom staggered weakly to pick up one of the calling cards. Looking down at the piece of paper, he saw it was a call to arms by the Great Britain Party.

Who the bloody hell were they?

Tariq called out to him. "I've called the police and ambulance service." He shuffled uncomfortably, the result of a steel toe-cap striking him on the upper thigh.

Strangely enough, Tom was beginning to think that the attack was a godsend. *No one's going to object to any of the proposals now!* he told himself, forgetting the price that had been paid.

"Showed those commie bastards didn't we?" said Dave, slapping Simon on the back with glee.

"Yeah, we did," Simon agreed.

At the bottom of the road, the forty strong group dissolved into fours and fives and headed out in all different directions.

"You going down the pub?" Dave asked Simon before they each went their own way.

"Gotta see someone first," replied Simon. "If I get away in time, I'll see you there, okay?"

Dave nodded and departed with his group. Simon set out alone, intent on calling on Howard to appraise him of the attack. Dropping the leaflets had been designed to increase the GBP's profile. The next move was to send out some boys to turn over a few Front Members to maintain the GBP's independence. Things were going well as far as the plot was concerned.

Stanley and Alan were in the Carpenter's Arms in Hackney and Stan was taking the piss out of his mate. They had travelled to the East End because of some girl that Alan thought he was well in with, but with the time now at nine-thirty, it was looking increasingly like lover boy had been stood up.

Dave entered the bar in the company of ten others and called out their orders to the barman. Alan watched them idly, sensing a strange strained atmosphere about the newcomers.

Dave watched the pair silently. He recognised Alan's face, but the black guy? He hadn't been aware of black skinheads before. There certainly weren't any in the East End.

Ferret, a skinny sixteen year old, moved to his side. "What's the fucking nigger doing dressed as a skinhead?"

"I think we've got trouble!" Alan said to Stan.

Ferret's comment had been heard by the pair of them. Stan nodded and slid off the bar stool to stand on his feet. "You got a problem?" he called to Ferret.

Alan got to his feet too. It didn't look good. They were badly out-numbered and he sensed the likelihood of walking out of there in one piece was minimal. Fear, adrenaline and indignation combined into a nervous charge that both goaded a reaction and repressed it at the same time.

"Yeah, I have," said Ferret. Assured of support, he found it easy to feel in command of the situation. As he moved forward, the others spread out and pressed on behind him.

"Do 'im Ferret!" said one of his friends with a malicious glint aimed at Stan.

Alan moved to side with Stan. "This ain't a good idea lads!" he said to them, hoping there was some way of turning back the situation.

"Fuck you!" said Dave as he planted a fist in Alan's face.

"Fuck!" cried Alan as the painful blow jarred back his head. He tried pulling away, but only got as far as Dave's restraining grip on his collar would allow.

Knowing the game was up, Stan helped Ferret finish his advance by hauling him towards him forcibly by the collar where he could headbut him. The crunch of his forehead on the nose of the mouthy little sod gave him a real sense of satisfaction. If he did nothing else at least he'd done him.

Alan never even got the chance to react. Groggy from the initial blow, he disappeared under a further hail of blows as others fought to join in. Stan managed to grab his next attacker and take him to the floor, but as he raised his fist, a steel toe cap bashed against his temple and shook up his senses. Another kick rushed into sight briefly as Stan fought to regain control over his limbs. It connected with his nose with a blinding flash of noise and pain. What happened after that became a dim awareness. The blows from a dozen boots rained in as he struggle to remain conscious.

"I've called the police!" screamed the manager above the din, hoping it would frighten them off before the beatings went too far.

"Leave 'em," Dave ordered, backing off.

Alan lay unconscious, partially jammed under one of the benches that surrounded the tables. Stan twitched and groaned beside him, unable to open his eyes or co-ordinate himself properly. The attackers were breathing heavily as they let up.

Dave looked at the manager. "You didn't see nothing pal, understand?" He held the man's eyes in his glare, and meekly the man nodded. "Okay, let's go!" Dave wheeled for the door and the rest of his gang followed.

I think I'd better warn ya about the kids on the corner tonight!
Cos it's a human jungle, that'll see some rumble tonight . . .
TONIGHT - THE BOYS (1977)

CHAPTER TEN

"YOU can go in now!" said the young nurse, approaching the bench that Del and Suzi were sitting on. Rob and Rebel pushed themselves off the wall that they were lounging against on hearing her words.

It had been a shock to find out that Stan and Alan had been hospitalised. They still weren't any the wiser about who had jumped them, but they were about to get the opportunity to find out. Following the nurse, they found Alan and Stan billeted next to each other in the middle of the ward.

"Alright Stan, brought you something!" Del said placing a Waitrose carrier bag on the bed.

Peering inside, Stan saw the shiny tin lids of a four pack. "Cheers, Del. Could do with it - things is fucking boring here!"

"Don't doubt it!" Del responded, noticing the aged patient in the next bed. The tubes running from his nostrils made the old boy look like some life after death experiment.

Stan was feeling okay now. A bit sore perhaps, but nothing he couldn't live with. The twenty-four hour observation thing seemed bloody pointless to him. Alan on the other hand had needed an operation to rewire his jaw. It had been shattered by a heavy kick from someone's steelies.

Rob was trying to speak with Alan. Although he was pleased to see his friends, the effects of a general anaesthetic kept swamping him, making it hard to think straight and stay with it. Talking was even harder, as his words were strangled by the brace he was wearing and fuzzed out from the drugs.

"I doubt if he's gonna make much sense!" Stan told Rob. "He's just come back from theatre. They couldn't operate on him last night cos of all the alcohol he had drunk!"

"So what happened?" Del demanded. He had heard they were bashed over the East End, but that was about it.

"When they letting you out Stan?" Rebel called across from the other side of Alan's bed.

"Don't know . . . Tonight or tomorrow morning I guess!"

"Who was it?" Rob asked.

"Some skinheads who didn't like my colour!"

"Skinheads?" Del said. "Shit!"

One thing about the skinhead scene had been the cross London unity and now, in one instance, it was obviously a thing of the past.

"Does it matter who it was?" asked Rebel, taking Del's reaction for indecision. "We gotta show 'em they can't mess with us, guy!"

"Goes without saying!" Rob agreed.

Del looked at the group and Stan looked at him. "Okay," Del said, "Pass the word around that I want the whole gang together - and that includes those hiding away with their bits of fluff!" Then to Stan he said, "You feel up to going hunting tomorrow night?"

Stan nodded. "There was something that might help narrow down the hunt. I heard a couple of names mentioned before we got clobbered. One was Ferret and the other was Dave something or other."

"Dave Shepperton!" Del made the connection via the mention of Ferret. That little rat-faced fuck was always stirring things up! It came as no real surprise to find out he was at the bottom of the rumble. He'd seen him wind up a party argument over a girl called Chrissie until it had blown into a household riot that spilled out into the street with soul boys and skinheads slugging it out until the law arrived.

"You know him then?" Rob asked.

"Met him on the Kings Road a few times. He's a Hammers supporter . . . His mob comes from Hackney and Bow!"

"How many bodies?"

"Don't know for sure, fifteen or twenty!"

"Kind of makes things even I guess!" Rob said, knowing their full compliment was twenty five. Still, it was going to take some leg work to get them all out. Some of them hadn't been about for weeks.

"Look, Stan. Much as I wanna stick around, I haven't had chance to even change out of me work togs!" Del wanted to make a move, but felt obliged to underline his reasons. He was starving, having turned down the chance of a lunchtime pie in the pub.

"Hey no problem, man. I'll see you when I get out okay?"

"Sure. Rob, do me a favour. Arrange the meet at the Dragon for seven-thirty. I've got an idea where we can find these people."

"See ya!" Stan called.

"Likewise mate," Del answered, placing an arm around Suzi's waist. "Let's go, girl!"

"Sure" Suzi responded, giving a casual wave to the two in bed.

For the final half mile walk to Jennifer's place, Suzi had watched Del brood in silence. It was obvious to her that something about the whole thing was on his mind.

"Problem?" she asked as they entered the estate with its grey concrete towers looming over the lower blocks.

"With getting even?"

Her agreeing look encouraged him to carry on.

"No, no problem with that. We're bonded by who and what we are!"

"So what's the problem?" she asked as they turned from the footpath that cut across the grassy verges towards the road with Jenny's block in it.

"I guess I feel a bit down about the fact it's skinheads against skinheads this time. For the last two years, it was like all London skins were in it together. Us versus them kind of thing!"

"It was bound to change, sooner or later," Suzi pointed out.

"Yeah, I guess I knew that, but it definitely ain't for the better, is it?"

Suzi stopped walking and restrained him from carrying on. Looking into his eyes she gave him the benefit of her perception. "Hey, good or bad don't enter into it. Things change and all you can do is make the best of the way they are!"

Del sighed. Knowing she was right, he tried to put it to the back of his mind. Together they began walking again, but only got a few paces before they were halted by Leroy shouting Derek's name from behind them. Looking back, they saw him bounding the hundred yards or so to catch up.

Del held out his hand and exchanged a slapping of palms with the rasta.

"Where you been people?" he asked, heaving slightly from the sudden burst of energy.

"Hospital!" Del responded.

"You got a young Del cooking?" joked Leroy, laying a hand on Suzi's midriff as if searching for the maternal bulge.

Suzi pushed his hand away declaring there was no way she would have a kid. "I'm still a kid meself!"

"Nothing like that mate. A couple of friends got turned over last night." Del told him what he knew of the situation as they headed for

130

Jenny's together. Finishing the narrative, he watched Leroy for his response.

"Ain't no different from when I was a skinhead, man. We use to fight like crazy with the Balham boys. They couldn't take being lower league to a mixed gang. You'll always find people who think like that, man - it's the facts of life you know?"

"Yeah, I guess so."

"Hey, I know you liked the alliance you had between the gangs, but it was something we never had back then. There was always a dispute of one sort or another. A personal fight from the week before became a gang rumble of the next weekend. Just take it as conformation that the skinhead thing is growing again!"

"Didn't think of it like that," agreed Del, suddenly feeling a lot more convinced that he wasn't about to do anything wrong to the cult he loved.

Once inside Jenny's, Leroy joined her in a loud discussion in the kitchen about a showing of African Art at the Community Hall. Suzi and Derek overheard him nominating them as baby-sitters if Jenny would go with him.

Suzi tossed the newspaper from the armchair and sat down. Then realising she had forgot to put the television on, she got up again and crossed over to the old black and white Pye set, with its once proud white plastic case now discoloured and marred.

Pressing the stems of the channel selectors, she flicked between all three channels, before settling on ITV and *The Tomorrow People*, a favourite of the generation brought up on the Sixties' science fiction boom of programmes like *Dr. Who*, *The Time Tunnel*, *Timeslip*, *Lost In Space* and the whole array of Gerry Anderson productions.

Del picked up the 'paper which Suzi had so carelessly discarded before settling down on the sofa. Half watching the programme and half reading the *Evening Standard*, he found that neither was of any great interest to him.

The programme had something to do with a batch of sonic devices planted around the country that when activated would cause the people to forget all about self-control and descend into the anarchy of mob rule. The story he was reading in the 'paper wasn't all that different. It was a two page spread on the power blackout in New York, and the crime wave and three and a half thousand arrests that had followed.

Jesus, Del thought, wondering what it would be like if the same happened in London.

131

Turning to the next page, he saw a story that drew his attention away from the television set completely. SKINHEAD RIOT IN COLLEGE GROUNDS! screamed the headline.

"What the fuck?!" Del exclaimed, causing Suzi to look over in his direction. "Something in here about skinheads!" Del then explained as he scanned the photo of a row of smashed windows next to the one of an Asian girl with a bruised and battered face.

"Read it out to me!" Suzi said, showing a bit of interest.

"Like a spectre from the past, the skinhead cult is re-emerging on the streets of Britain. In the past, these shaven headed thugs brought violence to the terraces of English football clubs. The new breed of skinhead has increased its appetite for aggro by becoming a rent-a-mob for the lunatic fringe of English fascism, as shown so graphically last night by the attack on a meeting of Student Union leaders. A meeting that had ironically been called to discuss student policy towards the extreme right wing.

"Professor Mowatt, Head of Sociology, witnessed the ferocity of the attack from his study window. 'I can only liken it to the archive footage of Hitler's followers at work in the Jewish Quarter of Berlin in the Thirties. For over five minutes, sheer mayhem reigned, and the screams of the victims of these modern day stormtroopers could be heard above the crash of window panes being smashed throughout the building.

"It was incredible that more people weren't injured. Student Ashley Goodge had his nose broken in the attack. 'It was really scary. One minute we were conducting our business, then the next it was as if a bomb had gone off. Tables and chairs went flying as these morons beat up everyone in sight."

"After the attack, right-wing pamphlets were recovered from the scene by the police. They featured a policy statement by a group calling itself the GBP (Great Britain Party), who unashamedly advocate a hardcore right-wing stance - and a thinly veiled incitement to violence.

"The National Front's press officer claimed to know nothing about the GBP or its aims and would not make any statement last night. It can be revealed however that the self-styled leader of the GBP is Ralph McLare, a one-time campaign official of the NF. Sources inside the NF said last night that Mr McLare was expelled after making an inflammatory 'Hitler had the right idea' speech at the Bermondsey by-election of '73 that cost the Front its deposit.

"The GBP may be newer and smaller than the Front, but its ready use of violence could pose a far greater danger in the long term. Certainly it is disturbing to witness the GBP's skinhead following at work as they bring back the horrors of so-called 'paki-bashing', a popular pastime of skinheads in the early Seventies."

Suzi could see Del was struggling with an anger that had built up from the first paragraph. Trying to make light of it, she joked, "Now would be a good time to buy into British Gas!"

"Don't take the piss!" snapped Del. Throwing the newspaper at her, he got up and walked around in an aimless manner, trying to contain his anger. He wanted to lash out at something, especially those responsible for the article that dragged the skinhead name through the mud.

Leroy and Jennifer had come in from the kitchen. "What's up man?" Leroy asked, drawing Del back to the real world.

Suzi had taken offence at her treatment, but seeing that an explanation for the raised voices was needed, she straightened up the 'paper and found the story for Leroy. "That's upset him!"

Leroy read the feature, with Jenny leaning on his shoulder to see what was so important. When Leroy looked up he said, "Them Nazis are getting very rude these days!"

Del did what he could to moderate the anger in his voice. "That's not the point. The way it's presented makes it look like we're just a fucking puppet movement." Realising his slip of the tongue, he added, "Sorry Jenny."

"Don't do it again!" Jennifer ordered, smiling to show her reprimand was a joke intended to defuse the situation.

"Hey don't worry about it, man," Leroy said. "The guy's a jerk! The paki-bashing ting were just a trend in certain areas. Not everyone got the pakis inna yard you know?"

"What you saying?" Del asked.

"Just this, man. These people don't see it like it is, they adopt ideas like coloured lenses. You know the ting about coloured lenses? Dem only let in certain colours of light. You wear red lenses then everything red isn't it, there you know? Same for these people. They see things only one way. Anything that don't fit with what they wanna see, what they wanna understand, then man, them a don't see it! If I believed what this 'paper say about the skinhead, then I must be first the black Nazi in history!"

133

"You mean . . . ?" asked Del, unsure if it was his place to voice his understanding of what Leroy was getting at.

"Yeah, me, your brother, all of us, we fight with a Pakistani. Hey, them a soft target like the hippy! You know? Jez, I fight everyone who wasn't in our gang - other skinheads, greasers, all of dem. You was expected to defend your reputation against everyone - it were a mark of commitment, you know?"

Pausing slightly, the rasta allowed Del time to digest the meaning of his words before bringing it up to date. "Look, I don't like them that call themselves Nazis in these times. "I'm black - them a make me their enemy, whether I care to fight them or not. No matter, I'm their Babylon! They have decided this without consultation - therefore I will fight them because they wanna fight me. Whether this is according to the teachings of Jah is between me and my God. But the Testaments a tell of the way of justice. So as far as my own mind, my conscience is clear and in harmony with my beliefs!"

"What's this got to do with that?" Del asked, pointing at the 'paper.

"Everybody got their own beliefs - always had, always will!"

Jesus Leroy, you're becoming a fucking freak, Del thought to himself. He preferred him when he was an uppity black guy with a lip you wouldn't believe. At least they were talking the same language then.

"Hey man, get this. The skinhead ting it came through as a class identity. The mod scene - I was there, I know - was taken over by them from the middle class. Dem a mix it with the hippies and make this psychedelic idea. It were a bad time for us. This were our ting and dem had come and taken it from us and made it some ting it would have never become by itself or through us. Dem a bad breed. When we start the mod ting, them not mod. No man! Them like the parents, them a junior jazzniks you know? Dem come and take our ting, so we make the difference between us and dem known - the borstal clip . . . You know, the peanut? Yeah, well that become our symbol. The only way to show we were completely opposed to these people with their long-haired look.

"Dem talk about skinhead fashion . . . There were no fashion - it were anti-fashion! None of dem boutiques and such places sold anything we could wear without looking like them we despised. This is what I'm saying, and get this, okay? There are always two versions of the truth. One is the real truth and the other is the truth that supports individual ideas. Sometimes they are the same, then at other times they are not - this is the point to bear in mind. Everybody got their own beliefs, everybody got their own version of the truth. Sometimes the people lie deliberately. Then sometimes dem believe what they say because dem don't know any better and don't care to find out. So you just keep the truth here . . . "

With his index finger, Leroy touched his forehead. "Then what's it matter what other people say? You know where you're at!"

"Yeah, but Leroy, they're rubbishing us," said Del, pointing to himself, "Rubbishing me! There's gonna be people who believe this without question!"

"So what? When was the skinhead ting ever interested in public acceptance? It's not the boy scouts, you know!"

Leroy's offbeat humour shattered Del's morose mood. Like a ray of genius, wisdom always seemed more profound when tempered with wit.

"Forget it, bro!" Del said, sitting down.

"Hey Del, don't forget that the music of the skinhead is black - them that lose sight of that, lose sight of what they are!"

"Yeah, sure . . . "

Jennifer took it that the subject was over and decided to ask for the favour on Leroy's behalf. "Now that's sorted, would you two look after little Stephen tonight? Me and Leroy wanna go to the Community Hall."

For Suzi it was the least she could do after Jenny had been so good to her since the aggro with the other squatters. "Yeah sure, you go and have a good time!"

Before leaving, Leroy pressed a small collection of roll-up papers and a handsome pinch of herb into the skinhead's palm. "Enjoy!" he told Del simply. It seemed like a good idea to help the young skinhead unwind.

* * *

Ralph and Greta were having dinner together, complete with the formality of candles and a delightful Rhine Valley hock, served chilled in cut glass goblets.

"I think Simon is doing really well for the cause," Ralph said to the young girl.

Greta nodded as she cut a piece of beef from her steak and popped it into her mouth.

135

Ralph looked at her in marvel. She was a girl of many parts - beautiful and vivacious, able to be flippant and fun one minute, formal and mannered the next. There was a lot about her background he didn't know and she wasn't prepared to volunteer the missing information. Rather than heighten his sense of curiosity, he was content with what he understood. He never once questioned what she saw in him, an overweight man approaching his late forties, nor whether she had an eye for other men. That didn't matter to him. They were close on a level that no other could reach, that he was sure of. It was a spiritual feeling of being soul mates, trapped in a time that wasn't of their choosing and certainly not suited to their romantic notions of joy through strength.

"He's ambitious for sure," Greta said after swallowing the mouthful of food.

"Yes, I can see I'll have to watch that tendency, but while it serves our purpose I feel it should be encouraged!" Ralph had it in the back of his mind that he could remove Simon from the picture just like Himmler did to the S.A. when the time was right.

"Where is he tonight?" Greta asked. She had stayed away from the office during the day and wasn't up on the latest developments.

"He's, um, organising some punitive action against the National Front!"

"What?" It came as something of a revelation to Greta. She knew a power struggle would be unavoidable between the two parties, but it seemed too early in the GBP development to fire the first shots in the war. "Is that wise?"

"I thought it necessary. We need to demonstrate total independence from the Front, and as the national press is beginning to show an interest in our party, there is a certain sense of urgency to provide tangible evidence."

Unashamedly, Ralph had just presented Simon's words from earlier that day as if they were his own. At first Ralph hadn't been convinced himself, but it didn't take long for Simon to convince him of the merits of the attacks. In fact, by the end of it, Ralph had even come up with a couple of names from his NF past that he wanted sorted out.

* * *

While Ralph and Greta were enjoying their dinner, Simon, Dave and two other members of the gang were borrowing a Ford Capri from the car park at the back of Hackney Pavilion. Having hot wired it, they drove away and headed west.

"Where we going?" asked Greg, a thug hand-picked for the job by Dave who was sitting in the back of the car.

"We're going to pay a social call on an old friend of Ralph's!" Simon said, looking back over the headrest at Greg with a grin on his face.

"Right!" Greg nodded, before settling back into his seat to light a cigarette.

Forty five minutes later they were cruising around Kennington High Street, searching for the address on the slip of paper that Simon was carrying. Ralph had confused the issue by saying the residential road was on the left of the High Street heading out towards Hammersmith, when in fact it was on the other side of the street.

"Stupid fat cunt!" Dave said, laughing at Ralph's mistake, as they found the road and nosed the car into the bend.

"Bit like Clockwork Orange this!" Greg added, referring to the scene in the film where the droogs drive out into the countryside and invade the home of a novelist.

"Don't look like there's anywhere to park," Simon moaned as he scanned the line of cars on both sides of the well to do road.

He tapped his fingers on the edge of the steering wheel as he peered through the windscreen, wondering what number they were looking for. Still driving along, he pulled the piece of paper from the breast pocket of his jean jacket and passed it to Dave. "Here you are, mate. See what number we're after. We can't be far off now."

"Forty six," Dave said. "That's it, just over there."

"You ready?" Simon asked the pair in the back as he looked for a response in his rear-view mirror.

"Yeah, sure!" Greg said.

The other guy was fairly new to the gang, but Greg knew him from school and was happy to vouch for him when Dave had asked for a suggestion on who else to take along.

Simon halted the car next to an immaculate Sixties Bentley. "Number forty six," he said, looking at the property. It was a three storey affair with large bay windows.

Dave drew out his toy from underneath his seat and tested the weight of the night stick in his palm. He always thought it was a great joke that a police implement could be used on the other side of the fence too.

"Okay, let's go!" Simon said, jerking at the door handle.

137

They stepped out into the street together, each looking furtively around the neighbourhood. Further up the road, a young lady was walking her dog, but she was heading away from them and there were no other potential witnesses to be seen.

The car engine was still running and Simon reminded them that it was to be a lightening raid Pulling a ski mask over his face and making sure the others had covered theirs, he took the lead and went through the garden gate. At the door, Simon rang the bell and helped himself to one of the empty milk bottles down by his left foot.

Inside the house, Desmond Brooks, the owner of a firm of chartered accountants, was sipping at a glass of expensive wine he'd been given that day by a grateful client. Disturbed by the doorbell's chimes, he glanced at the carriage clock on the mantelpiece. Obviously the young lady was impatient for his company as she wasn't due for another half an hour. Not that he was about to complain.

On his way to the front door, he paused momentarily to regard himself in the gilt-edged full length mirror fixed to the hallway wall. With a sense of satisfaction, he lightly adjusted a lock of hair. Desmond was a stickler for perfection and despite his age and the fact that he would be paying the young lady for her company, he still fancied himself as a lady killer.

Slipping the catch, he opened the door with an assumed air that he thought would create the right impression. Then, on seeing four masked faces, he dropped the glass in shock and tried to slam the door. Simon stopped the door's progress before it could close and was soon in the hallway, with Desmond cowering down on one knee, holding a hand up to ward off any attack. It proved an inadequate defence as Simon rushed forward and smashed the bottle across the man's head.

The pain of the blow and the shards of glass in his scalp allowed the ball of fear caught in his throat to find its release in a howling "No!" Dave moved in to cut the cry short with a blow from the police stick which added a further laceration to Desmond's head and knocked him clean to the floor.

Greg, trembling with anticipation, stepped between them as Desmond tried to push himself up on both hands. Like a rugby player going for a winning conversion, the young attacker grinned as his steel toe capped boot smashed into the man's face, flipping him completely over on to his back. Like a pack of wolves, they savaged the lifeless body for over a minute until Simon decided they had done enough.

"That fucked him!" Dave said, kicking him a final time.

138

Greg laughed. "Sure did!"

Simon took one of the GBP flyers and let it flutter down on top of Desmond's bloody body. "Something to read when he wakes up!"

"Yeah, it's only good manners to introduce yourself if you turn up uninvited!" Greg's friend added.

Dave laughed and clapped his hand on the newcomer's shoulder. "You done all right, mate!"

Howard Ritter was just contemplating retiring for the night when the 'phone rang. Picking the receiver from its cradle, he glanced at his watch - eleven-thirty. "Hello!"

"Howard?" The voice on the other end of the line inquired.

The American recognised it as Hubert Crawford's. "Hello Hubert, what can I do for you?" Howard said amiably, moving to take a seat in the armchair next to the telephone table.

"I've just had the Executive Council breathing fire down my neck. They want to know what your plant is playing at?"

"Sorry you've lost me." Howard was a little perplexed, but Hubert's tone of voice told him something wasn't quite right.

"The Front's treasurer was admitted to hospital earlier this evening suffering from fractures to the skull, cheekbone, jaw and ribs."

"And?" Howard had a feeling he knew what it was leading up to, but feigned ignorance all the same.

"The police recovered a GBP handbill from the scene of the attack."

"I thought that was the idea of using fall guys. To demonstrate a split of intent!" Howard wondered what Hubert was getting so upset about.

"The trouble is, Desmond wasn't a sanctioned target!" Hubert replied angrily. "The Council suspects there's a double-cross being performed here. I mean, they were talking contracts at one point . . . "

"Tell them from me, I don't take kindly to threats!" Howard was beginning to get irate, but he was as angry with Simon for dropping this on him as he was with the paranoia of those he was dealing with.

Hubert relinquished his manner slightly. "Well, there's no need to worry about that at the moment. I guess it was something said in the heat of the moment. I've staked my reputation on the fact that your behind us one hundred percent, but they still want to know what is going on."

It was obvious that Hubert was sincere in his support. Howard considered the situation for a moment and realised he would have to talk to Simon to find out exactly what was happening. "Leave it with me, Hubert. I'll get to the bottom of it. If there is a problem, then I'll deal with it!"

"Thanks Howard, I think they'd appreciate that!"

"No problem, Hubert. I'll ring you in the morning, okay?"

"Yeah sure. Goodbye!"

"Later!" Howard said, closing the conversation. He stayed sat in the chair for a couple of minutes, thoughts churning around in his head. Deciding there was only one course of action, he went to the wardrobe in his bedroom. Slipping his jacket off momentarily, he reached into the cupboard and removed a coat hanger that held a shoulder holster containing a Beretta pistol. It was standard embassy issue, even in postings considered safe from terrorist attacks. Putting his sports jacket over the top of it, he fastened the single button and slipped on his shoes.

Arriving at the GBP office, Howard stabbed at the entry phone with his finger. Upstairs, Simon was in the middle of a drinking session with his companions when he heard the buzzer sound. Their drunken talk fizzled instantly as each looked at the other.

Simon was about to answer the call when Dave warned him, "It could be the police!"

Simon stopped short of pressing the answer button and decided to check first. From the window that overlooked the side street, he peered cautiously out and saw Howard standing in the pool of light made by the lamp that hung over the entrance. "No problem, he's one of ours!"

Dave went to the desk and pressed the button that released the electronic lock. "Come on up, the door's open!" he called into the intercom.

Pulling on the handle, Howard entered the hallway and began climbing the stairs.

"Howard!" Simon called with an alcoholic slur to his voice as the American entered the office. Then, noticing that Howard wasn't in the mood for idle exchanges, he lapsed back into a controlled frame of mind.

It was obvious that this wasn't a social visit. "Tell your boys the party's over. We've got some business to discuss!"

"Simon?" Dave wasn't sure if he liked the manner in which the visit was unfolding, but Simon's look told him that it was time to wrap things up.

"Catch you lot tomorrow okay!" Simon said to the others.

"Yeah, see ya later!" Dave said, picking up his flight jacket before heading for the door with the other two.

Simon sat down on the edge of Ralph's desk. Howard stood in the middle of the room, his hands cupped in front of him, head slightly cocked listening for the sounds of the entrance door closing behind them. His face was swathed in shadow by the desktop lamps.

"So, what can I do for you?" Simon asked, looking at the American with mock earnest.

Howard wasn't in the mood for playing games and moved within inches of the skinhead's face. He spoke in soft tones that both hinted at and masked his annoyance. "Cut the crap!"

"Sounds like someone's upset you a bit Howard!" Simon mused before finding a pen within easy reach. He then began doodling nonchalantly on a scrap of paper that was lying beside him.

Howard looked at Simon for a moment. The flippancy being displayed goaded him into reacting and he pulled the pistol out and cocked it.

The skinhead froze in mid-sketch.

"Got your undivided attention now?"

Turning his head towards Howard, Simon's eyes travelled the length of the barrel, over the hand holding the pistol and up the arm to the American's face. "Yeah!"

Though his voice was controlled, Howard could read the suppressed feelings of anger and fear in the skinhead's eyes. He let the pistol sit more loosely in his palm, allowing the situation to lose some of its tension. "Good. Now, the Front is under the impression that you have turned rogue. They're not very pleased with tonight's little episode!"

Simon found enough arrogance to smirk before adopting a defensive tone. "You mean that guy we turned over tonight?"

"Turned over?!" exclaimed Howard in disbelief. "Jesus, he's lying in hospital like a tenderised steak!"

"A casualty of war!" responded Simon, not even attempting to mask his lack of remorse.

"Yes, but he wasn't supposed to have been!" the American pointed out. "That's what has put their noses out of joint!"

141

Standing up and straightening his jacket, Simon didn't waver in his attitude. Looking Howard straight in the eye he said, "Fuck 'em - it was a judgement call!"

"What?"

Simon paused for breath, collected his thoughts, then took a piece of paper containing a list of names and addresses from his pocket. "If you look at that," he said, holding it out to Howard, "It's Ralph's additions to the hit list. There is no way I can carry out the intended declaration of independence without using any of them! Jesus! How do you think I'm gonna keep the guy's trust, if I give him cause to question my motives?"

"Point taken," Howard agreed, lowering the gun. With a certain sense of relief too because it meant the scam was still in order. Glancing at the list prepared by Ralph, he added, "You'll have to leave the rest of these alone though!"

"Hey no problem!" Simon said, indicating that he had already thought about it. "Tell them to increase the security around these guys and I'll tell Ralph I can't get near them. Then if he has any spies in their camp, my story will check out!"

"Smart move. You should have warned me though, about tonight I mean," Howard said, shouldering the pistol.

Simon nodded. "Didn't have any choice though. Ralph decided he wanted it done then. I could only play along with it."

"Jeez, they were pissed off with you!" Howard found he could laugh about it now. "They wanted to put a contract out on you!" he told the skinhead in a friendly manner.

"So give them the same warning I'm giving you!" Simon said coldly. "Point a gun at me again and I'll kill ya!" With the words out, he tensed up in readiness.

Howard looked at him, face set in grim determination, and began to apologise. "Hey, sorry about that Simon. For a moment I thought . . . "

"Yeah, you thought I'd sold out!" Simon raged, wagging an accusing finger. "You're a cunt - I stick to my word, always have, always will!"

"Hey, let's chalk it up to experience?" Howard asked, offering a truce.

"All right," Simon agreed while thinking to himself that if the opportunity presented itself he was going to get even.

"I'll go and square it with that lot, "Howard told him, mopping the sweat from his forehead with the sleeve of his jacket. "You get some sleep and I'll get in touch either tomorrow or the day after."

"Yeah, sure," Simon said, not moving from the desk while Howard collected himself and left with a curt "Ciao!".

"Cunt!" Simon hissed under his breath as the door closed behind the American.

Will I write?
Yeah, once in a while
I'll send my love
And a molotov cocktail!
LOVE AND A MOLOTOV - THE FLYS (1977)

CHAPTER ELEVEN

LEROY had returned from the African arts display in a buoyant mood. As he had gleefully explained to Del, the president of the student's union who had hired them for the Police gig had approached him at the community centre and enlisted his help in planning an open-air music event under the banner of Rock Against Racism.

"Hey, congratulations!" Del said, jumping out of his chair and shaking his hand to show how happy he was for him.

"There's a slot there for you," Leroy said in all seriousness. "In this way you can show them not all skinheads are media stereotypes!"

"Cheers!" said Del, his imagination already working overtime. "What kind of crowd they looking at?" he asked.

Leroy's lips drew back in a big grin exposing his yellowed teeth. "Get this - fifteen thousand!"

"Shit!"

"Say that again! This is big time man!"

Suzi, who had been dozing on the armchair, stirred. "What is it?" she asked in a hazy voice.

"You're still half asleep!" Del told her.

"Oh!" she said, raising her eyebrows without opening her lids, and returned to her slumber.

Del and Leroy chuckled at the response.

"Come into the kitchen and I'll tell you all about it," Leroy said, indicating Del to follow him. The rasta loaded the filter machine with coffee powder, then while sitting at the table making a spliff, he explained about the meeting and the fact that he would be responsible for getting some reggae bands to appear.

"Can you do that?" asked Del, accepting the reefer after Leroy had taken a few puffs.

"Yeah, I've got some solid contacts with Steel Pulse, Matumbi and Black Uhuru. Shouldn't be a problem to get some support!"

"Home and dry then ain't ya!" From where Del was sitting it looked a dead cert and his imagination was trying to picture what it would be like to spin records in front of such a big crowd. Just thinking about it was giving him an incredible buzz. Together they grinned like Cheshire cats over a bowl of cream.

"You staying the night?"

Del looked up at Jenny who had come into the kitchen after making sure Stephen was okay. "Yeah, I guess, if it's all right with you?"

"Hey, no problem," she assured him, responding in kind to his smile.

Leroy and Del discussed possibilities for the forthcoming show well into the early hours until they were disturbed by a groggy Suzi, who stood dreamily wincing against the glare of the kitchen light. "I'm going to bed, see you in the morning!" Her words were lax and slurred.

Glancing at the clock on the wall, Del wondered where the time had gone. "Jesus, I've gotta go to work tomorrow . . . "

"Yeah, I know." The rasta said yawning. "See you in the morning."

Ralph was in his glory. The morning had yielded a trio of reporters interested in the Great Britain Party. He knew fine well that they were going to deride him for his beliefs, but he also understood from previous experience that press, whether good or bad, served a useful device for recruitment. It was the difference between being local and being national. National and becoming international.

In anticipation of a photo call, he told Greta and Simon that they'd be required to wear their uniforms. Wondering whether personal publicity was a good idea at this stage in the game, Simon said, "Ralph, I'm gonna have to drop out of the shoot!"

"Why?" Ralph asked looking at the skinhead. It hadn't occurred to him that there might be a problem somewhere along the line.

"Hey, think about it a minute." Simon gave him the room to form his own conclusions, but from the momentary silence it seemed that the leader of the GBP wasn't going to get the idea. Sighing mentally, Simon filled in the gaps. "Look, when I got back from Angola, the Home Office gave me the full treatment. They made certain threats, gave certain warnings - if you know what I mean? It wouldn't be prudent to draw attention to myself at this stage - especially when we're in the middle of running a campaign of action!"

Ralph, rare to concede a point outright, said, "You won't be able to dodge the public eye for good!"

"I'll cross that bridge when I come to it. For the moment there's no point in going looking for it," Simon said with a conviction that told Ralph he wasn't going to be swayed.

"Okay," Ralph conceded. "Tell you what, organise it for Dave and a couple of the others to take your place."

Simon nodded. "Yeah, no problem!"

* * *

"Twenty five pence," Del said, swapping the bag of tomatoes for the money. "Thanks lady!" he added, checking it was the correct amount before shoving it in the pocket of his apron.

Glancing around, he saw a young girl who looked like she was from the nearby offices. Turning his attention to her, Del said, "Yes, love, what can I get you?"

She gave a small smile that tickled his ego, and pointed to the vegetables. "One pound of celery, one of spring onions and an iceberg lettuce please!"

Del grinned as he remembered the rugby song about a girl and her celery. Methodically and with practised movements, he rounded up the order. "Here you go. Twenty, thirty and fifteen - that's sixty five pence all together!"

"Have you got a carrier bag?" she asked.

Del nodded, went to the back of the stall and removed one of the bags from under it. Holding it open for her, she smiled once again and placed the produce inside.

Del was just about to say something in the flirtation department when Stan and Rob stepped off the pavement behind him, and Stan gripped him in a friendly headlock. "Don't move or I'll snap yer neck!" he said, copying a line he recalled from a kung-fu movie he had seen recently at the cinema.

"Get off!" cried Del, struggling to free himself from the hold.

Stan grinned at Rob as Del's attempts were easily countered.

"Okay, let him go!" Rob decided that the game had gone far enough.

Grateful for the release, Del turned and gave the black skinhead a playful jab. "Good to see you out, mate!"

Stan danced back like a boxer. "Good to be here. Jesus, it was fucking boring in the hospital!"

"How's Alan?" Del said, seeing that the swelling was still pretty livid on Stanley's face.

"Better, I guess. He's having a difficult time talking at the moment, with his face all wired up!" Stan helped himself to an apple from the stall and took a large bite from it.

"Got everything arranged for tonight?" Del asked Rob while jingling the coins in his apron pocket.

Rob stood there with both hands jammed into his jeans' pockets. "Yeah, pretty well. There's still Richie and Frank to sort out. Warren's gonna see if he can drag them out!"

"Looking forward to giving them the pay back?" he asked Stan who gave a curt nod in reply. The black guy's imagination had painted the picture a thousand times while he lay in the hospital bed and he couldn't wait to see it happen for real.

"Okay, I'll catch you guys tonight," Del said, noticing another customer hovering around the other end of the barrow.

"Yeah, tonight!" Rob responded, jerking his head at Stan to indicate it was time to go.

* * *

Dialling the number Hubert had given him during their meeting at the West End wine bar, Howard stood looking out of his window at the street below. Lifting the blind slightly, he watched a couple of kids playing football in the street.

"Hello, Hubert Crawford speaking."

"Hi, Hubert, it's Howard!"

Hubert had been waiting for this call all morning. "Howard - thanks for calling!" He had to be a little guarded as his secretary didn't know about his double life. He didn't like giving out his office number, but it was necessary to be available at all times for the cause. "Have you sorted out our little problem?" Hubert said guardedly.

Howard understood from it that Hubert wasn't in a position to speak freely. "Depends on the Committee. That business last night was necessary to maintain our operative's cover. It was one of a series of targets proposed by McLare."

"I see, so it was just a market quirk!" Hubert trusted Howard to read the hidden meaning.

"Yeah, I guess so. There are some others, but our man suggests that you tighten up security around them to give him an excuse to be unable to meet the obligations placed upon him. That way he can revert back to the original list that you supplied."

"I think that sounds like an amicable solution. Tell you what Howard, give me the list of names and I'll see what I can sort out, okay?"

He sat there mindfully watching the secretary, as he scribbled out the names that Howard recited. Looking at the list, Hubert saw no problem in pacifying the committee members with the explanation. And being able to produce the list would show good faith on the part of Howard's operative. "Okay, let me sort this out Howard, but I don't see a problem at all."

"Okay. Thanks Hubert," Howard said in closing.

"No problem, Howard. Bye!"

Howard felt relieved and more able to receive the deputation from the Young Farmers organisation, as arranged by the embassy in his capacity as trade attache. It also crossed his mind that he would have to have another clandestine meeting with Simon. Still that could wait until later.

Using the directions supplied the night before, Leroy found himself hopelessly lost on arriving at the University. Colin, bought along for moral support, was chuckling to himself as he held out his hand. "Let me see that!"

Leroy looked flustered and readily handed over the slip of paper the organiser had torn from his address book. Colin eyed it then looked at the nearest door. "It's no wonder we can't find it - we're not even in the right place. This says A16, the door says D16. You starting to get the idea, man!"

A passing student stopped and asked if they were lost. Leroy was about to say no, but Colin held the piece of paper up for the girl to see. "Yeah, can you tell me where we find this room?"

Adjusting her glasses, she took a second to digest the scrawl. "D block is on the other wing!"

"There you go, man. I said we was in the wrong place!" Then, to the girl he added, "My friend's a great DJ, but never trust him as a navigator. Can you tell me how we find our way to D Block?"

"Yeah if you take the stairs there." She pointed to the staircase at the other end of the hall. "Turn left at the bottom and follow the corridor to the end. Turn right there and you'll be on D Block. D16 is on the second floor, first on the left!"

Colin got her to repeat the instructions again, just to make sure, and then they both thanked her for her help.

"Nice girl!" Colin said loud enough for her to hear as she went to a room further up the corridor.

"Business before pleasure my man!" Leroy said, gripping Colin's face in the palm of one hand and lightly shaking his head.

Colin brushed the hand off and took a deep bow, his hands and arms tumbling in a flamboyant movement ending in a presentation. "After you, sir!"

"Thank you my good man!" Leroy said, putting on the airs and graces of a titled gent as he took the offered lead towards the staircase.

The meeting was already in progress when Leroy and Colin cautiously opened the door and peered round. All heads turned to the new arrivals and the speaker of the moment cut short what he was saying.

"Sorry we're late!" Leroy said, feeling a touch conspicuous from having so many unknown faces looking at him.

"Yeah, kinda got lost in the corridors!" added Colin.

Martin Langham, the student president, was pleased to see them. For a while he had been wondering if the rasta had taken him seriously the night before or not. Standing up to shake Leroy's hand, he called to the others. "If I can have your attention. This is Leroy of The Ethiopian Express, a reggae sound system, and his companion . . . ?"

Leroy realised it was a question and responded with a little hand wave to the seated members of the meeting, mostly young guys, a couple of girls and three older males. "This here is Colin - he's part of my team!"

Martin pointed to a stack of chairs in the corner of the room by an overhead projector screen. "If you and Colin would like to grab a chair, we'll make some room for you at the table."

While the two black guys helped themselves to a chair a piece, Martin asked Diane Phillips to move round and make room for the new arrivals. With a minimum of fuss, Leroy and Colin were soon seated at the table with the rest of them.

Martin then began to explain the situation. "For the benefit of those who weren't present at the earlier meetings, we have agreed that

149

something needs to be done to curb the rising tide of fascism!" Pausing to take a sip from the glass of water that sat on the desk in front of him, he continued, "The public has become apathetic to the threat that these extremists pose. Therefore we feel there is a need to educate them and rally mass support like this country hasn't seen since Grosvenor Square!"

Leroy knew he was referring to the Student Power movement of the Sixties. It occurred to him that perhaps Martin was trying to instigate his own mark upon the history of political sociology, though for what reason he was unsure. It could have been a rebel stance, a power play or even sincerity of heart. Either way, self-gratifying political masturbation was of no interest to him. "This is where the idea for the festival comes in?" he asked.

"Yes, it was the brainchild of Meena Patel . . . " Martin pointed to the Asian girl sitting between Peter Sergeant of the SWP and Martin Polaski of the borough council. Meena let a light smile of embarrassment play over her lips. "Perhaps she would like the honour of explaining it to you?"

Meena gave a curt nod and stood up with several pages of her summary in hand. She was currently doing a business course, studying public relations and advertising, something she had readily equated with the needs of this sibling movement. "Since the early Seventies, there has been a rise in the membership and diversity of nationalist movements, from the National Front and its 160,000 members, to obscure concerns like The League Of Saint George, the November 9th Movement and the Great Britain Party. Each represents an uneducated and intolerant perception that must not be permitted to find root in today's society. In spite of the obvious lessons that history teaches us about the nature of these parties, they still remain a prime attraction for the mid-teen to early twenties white males. The question we must ask ourselves is why?"

Meena paused momentarily to regard the meeting. Leroy watched her quietly. She was a natural at public speaking - precise, but warm. Since no answer was offered up to her somewhat rhetorical question, she ploughed on regardless. "The reasons are many fold. Social and environmental issues are obvious factors. Yet the attraction lies more in the nature of adolescents than in their background. The restless romanticism of the struggle is something that mirrors their arrival into adulthood. It also offers an alternate identity from the majority of the older generation as it is viewed as forbidden fruit by all in living memory of the Third Reich."

"So, what you are saying is it's human nature."

Meena looked at the pocked-marked face of Kevin Bates, the first year sociology student. Seventeen years old and with scraggly mouse coloured hair, he looked more like a guttersnipe than the son of a merchant banker. "Yes, although I prefer the term 'teen nature', as they are the ones who form the fighting force of these movements. They are the ones by nature who test their physical prowess and readily embrace combat!"

"What is this leading to?" asked Donald Princeton who sat at the opposite head of the table. It was easy to see he was an experienced radical suffering from the after effects of a hyperactive childhood. He was a direct action man and this pussy-footing sociology was a waste of time in his book. His solution to this and every problem was to identify and eliminate the opposition.

"Simply this," Meena continued. "In order to make a lasting effort against such a long-term problem we have to form an effective plan. We have to counteract the outlaw attraction of these groups. It's obvious that the current campaign of fly-postering the message that fascism is an evil, is ineffective at rallying widespread support. What we need is a bit of panache. With apologies to our friends from the SWP, what we need is a commercial hard sell."

Peter Sergeant laughed at the remark, but the audience was still attentive enough to encourage her to continue.

"What are the prime motivations for a teenager?" It was a question levelled at the meeting. Her gaze swept around the faces, awaiting a response.

"To explore life?" volunteered Zeb Hibberts, a refugee from the Congo.

"Yes, in a broad sense you are right, but the prime motivation for a teenager is enjoyment. Enjoyment that is identified as being found in the old adage of sex and drugs and rock 'n' roll. Obviously there's no way we can use sex to achieve our aims, although one or two here might like to try . . . " Her eyes fell on Diane Phillips momentarily. The blonde girl just smiled, leaving Leroy and Colin to wonder what the hidden meaning behind the gentle snipe was.

"Drugs . . . Unless we produce our own beer with a purposeful label, or press tabs with a message on them, there's little we can do in that field either!" Shuffling her papers, Meena went on. "Which leaves us

151

rock 'n' roll as the means to reach the apathetic. Reaching this point I suddenly realised there was a wealth of possibilities.

"For instance, we can easily counteract the forbidden fruit syndrome of the fascist's appeal by offering an alternative, namely the bands that make up this punk rock phenomenon. They're topical and anarchical by nature, which not only carries the right sort of appeal for your average teenager, but also means that the bands are ripe for conversion to our cause!"

"Why punk? It's white music," called Zeb from his seat.

"It's not only going to be punk. We intend to have a reggae sound system too which is why Leroy and Colin are present, as well as several bands of a Caribbean nature. By mixing the line-up in this way we subtly promote a cross-cultural introduction. There's no point or sense in preaching to the converted. Growth will only occur by reaching out and gaining the attention and support of the uninformed."

"What do you think we have been trying to do all these years?" cried David Collins, Steve Sergeant's companion from the Marxist organisation. He sensed that Meena's words were a belittlement of his efforts.

"Settle down please, Dave!" pleaded Martin Langham, feeling that perhaps he was letting his temper get the better of him. "Give her a chance to speak freely. You are on the same side!"

Dave glared across at him, but Steve intervened with a restraining hand and the anger died down as quickly as it had flared.

"What I am trying to say," began Meena, looking coldly at Dave, "Is that the method and style of campaigning hasn't really changed since the Nineteen Twenties. The artwork for instance on both nationalist and Marxist flyers and stickers is archaic to say the least. I have prepared a photocopy collection to demonstrate what I mean."

Giving the wad of sheets to Leslie Woods, she asked her to hand them out to all present. DEFEND YOUR NATION! proclaimed one, depicting an incredibly muscle-bound individual with a protective arm around a lithe woman and child. Another showed a swastika being broken by the blow of a red hammer, with the slogan SMASH FASCISM.

"Society has moved on since these images held any real P.R. value. Today they only really appeal to the hardened supporter, or the romantic who wishes to recreate the past. Quite simply, most people have outgrown this approach and are far more sophisticated than the radicals recognise. To be successful we must use modern commercial practices to promote our campaign."

Meena took another look around at those seated at the table and was pleased to see several approving nods. The two SWP representatives were hurriedly exchanging words, as even David could see the attractions of what she was proposing. Through the use of music they could boost their claimed attendance and use the figures as a political lever, and it would provide a captive audience for SWP recruiting. "Yes, we can go along with that!" said Steve.

"Thank you, Meena!" Martin said, taking over the proceedings. "In case you haven't already guessed, Meena is to be our press liaison officer, along with Donald Princeton seated opposite me. A respected music journalist, he has agreed to write some of the literature that will be handed out at the event!

"The movement is to go under the banner of Rock Against Racism which we feel is punchy enough to become a catchphrase on everybody's lips. Our two artists, Leslie Woods and Diane Phillips have designed several logos and would welcome your comments as to the appropriate one. To save time, this will be performed at the close of the meeting."

"Martin Polaski on my right represents the local council who we are informed will provide us with the facilities of Finsbury Park free of charge, as well as making a substantial donation to our launch fund. I trust that the SWP can pledge some money to the cause as well?" He eyed the pair present. "It will be necessary. So as to get the maximum effect from our efforts, any events will need to be free until we gather enough momentum to support a subsidised entry charge. Now, to the next matter . . . "

"So you believe repatriation is the key to making Britain great again?"

Ralph smiled at the journalist, one of a group of three sitting around his desk. "Yes, that's about the size of it!"

He leant back in his chair. Dave stood stock still behind him to the left in the military at ease pose, while the GBP flag provided the pair with a backdrop. Something Ralph had formulated to have a good psychological effect on the press perception so they would view his party as paramilitary in nature.

"Don't you think that is somewhat condescending to the immigrants who have given their working lives to this country?" chipped in one of the three hacks.

"I didn't asked them to, did you?" Ralph loved playing with words and meanings. It was a trait he had enjoyed from his first days in political life. "As far as I can recall there was never a referendum to find out if the people wanted this influx of cheap labour. It seems to me that it was a decision taken to profit a few at the expense of the many!"

"When you were in the National Front, you once stated that Hitler was right. Would you care to explain that?" another asked, taking over from his rival.

Ralph understood full well that another hook had been baited for him. With relish he accepted the morsel. "What I meant was Hitler was right to take the radical steps he did in Germany in 1933. Understand his country was broken and bankrupt, floundering upon the rocks to which it had been consigned by the Versailles treaty. I was merely saying that desperate times require desperate measures, and was not endorsing the indiscretions of the Third Reich!"

"I'd hardly call six million gassed an indiscretion!" retorted the inquisitor, finding Ralph's amiable manner offensive when applied to the subject in hand.

"An indiscretion is no less an indiscretion because of the scale of its affects. What about the carpet bombing of Dresden? Or the troop ship of Italian POWs sent back from the UK to Italy without an escort, through U-boat infested waters? Were not the Americans indiscreet when they flattened Hiroshima? Or the Japanese in the way that they handled British POWs? Everybody is indiscreet in war - because war is the ultimate indiscretion of them all!" Ralph declared, triumphantly wagging his finger as if at the gods.

Dave mentally chalked up another point to his leader. He admired the way Ralph had turned some of their own principles against them. Ridiculing the belief that the victor was a good guy merely because he had won was a master stroke in Dave's eyes.

At least one of the hacks was sharp enough not to be thrown, however. Latching on to the closing point, he countered with, "Yes, but if the Second World War was the ultimate indiscretion, who was it who committed this heinous act?" His eyes fell upon Ralph and his features settled into a self-satisfied goading expression.

Ralph banged his hand on the table hard enough to make the journalists jump at the noise it made. "It was the Jews in the world banks. They feared the economic strength of the united Germany since they realised it would move the centre of world finance from America to Europe, and put them in the shadows!"

"Jews?" The hack looked pleased with himself, as he scribbled something on his note pad. His companions sensed a breach had appeared in the subject's verbal armour and together they sought to exploit it.

"Yes, Jews - those manipulators of the masses!" Ralph declared, flushed with the passion of his beliefs.

"Can you explain how you feel the Jews were to blame for the war?" One of the hacks was doing a good impression of being earnest. They each sensed that self-condemnation was lurking below the surface.

"World leaders change every few years. Leaders of the financial institutes don't! Therefore it should be easy for even you to understand that bankers own the countries, and elected politicians are merely the puppets they play with!"

"Yes, but how does this apply to the Jews?" The hack was getting impatient for a more committed statement from the party boss.

"They are the ones who control the world banks. They stripped Germany of its natural assets following World War One and wrecked the German economy. They are the ones who laid the path to Hitler's rise - they created their own nemesis, if that is what the Third Reich was for them!"

"So you think it was their own fault if they were gassed?" asked one of the hacks, wondering how the man could be so strictly cold-blooded in his beliefs.

"God is with us!" answered Ralph cryptically.

Divine retribution? thought the first hack, jotting it down on his pad. *It might be an idea to ring the London School Of Psychology and see if it is synonymous with any known disorder!*

The rest of the interview was taking up with the purposes of the GBP and a further parrying session when they tried to attribute the recent spate of attacks on opponents on the GBP. Ralph countered by pointing out that they distribute the leaflets freely at street markets, football grounds and youth clubs so anyone could be dropping them at scenes of crime.

"Why would someone else drop them?"

Ralph looked at the man as if he was a simple child. "Why, to implicate and discredit the good name of the GBP of course!"

The journalist smiled with suppressed humour as he considered what possible good name the GBP could have.

Ralph threw a spanner into the hack's train of thought though, by adding, "The police have admitted it is a possibility!"

It was a veiled warning that the line between cold fact and libellous opinion was very thin. To exploit it as anything more than circumstantial and not conclusive evidence would invite retaliation.

Don't wanna be a martyr
To anybody's cause,
Just wanna break free
From this cell of yours.
Don't wanna change the world
Just my own - sometimes I feel so alone!
ENEMIES.- RADIATORS FROM SPACE (1977)

CHAPTER TWELVE

DEREK had returned home to an argument with his mother. She hadn't seen him for a few days and here he was, getting changed into clean clothes, with the intention of going straight out again.

"Quit moaning will ya!" he called down the stairs as he struggled to force a boot on to his foot. The clock that stood on his window sill told him that he had ten minutes to get round to the pub.

"This ain't a hotel, young man!" she retorted. If Del had the time to stop and consider, he would have realised his Mum was feeling lonely and ignored, but the fire of youth obscured any sensitivity.

Thinking to himself that she's always going on, Del hurriedly pulled on his jean jacket and stormed down the stairs. Unlatching the front door, he called out, "Bye Mum!", and was off down the street. Whatever she thought about his abrupt departure was behind him now. Ahead lay the adventure of teenage kicks.

On reaching the appointed venue, he was happy to see that all the stops had been pulled out and the majority of the gang were there. A quick scan of the faces at the bar and around nearby tables, told him the only obvious absentees were Bob, Neil and Warren.

"Hello, matey!" cried Joey from behind, clamping his arms around Del's waist and lifting him off the ground.

"Put me down you idiot!" snapped Del, fighting to loosen the other's grip.

"Is it my imagination, or are you getting taller?" quipped Rebel.

"Very funny!" said Del, looking down on her before finally getting Joey to concede that his feet were supposed to be touching the floor.

At the bar, there was a lot of talking and a lot of catching up to be done. As the beer flowed, the talk became more aggressive and the mood shifted on to a warlike footing. Everyone wanted to know from Del what they were going to do about getting revenge.

Del leaned against the bar and surveyed the gang. "Give it till nine o'clock and we'll go and pay off the debt. Frankie, you still driving that mini-bus for the elderly?"

"Yeah!" Frankie answered from his table to the right of the bar. Knowing he was going to be collared into driving, he had wisely limited his drinking to a single pint.

"Okay, you can take a dozen in that. Adam, Jerry and Alex can take the rest in their cars!"

"Okay," Frankie said, "but I'll need a lift back to my place to pick up the old bus."

Del looked to Adam, but didn't have to say anything. His mate drained his glass and got out his car keys. "Lets go, Frankie!"

When they returned half an hour later, Adam was proudly flashing about a home made cosh he had picked up while at home. The air was full of chat about who to look out for, who wasn't worth worrying about and similar banter.

Dead on nine o'clock, the gang finished up their drinks and Alex called out to the landlord that they'd be back later.

"Don't do anything I wouldn't do!" he cheekily called back. He knew exactly what the full turnout meant with its air of confrontation. Still, it had been the same in his day. He chortled at the memory of standing in the middle of a dancehall in his best drapes, flashing a cut-throat razor and daring the Simmons mob to "Come and get it!"

On the pavement in front of the pub, the mini-bus and cars formed a rank of their own. Del jumped into the front seat of the mini-bus, next to Rebel who had voted herself as the other front seat passenger. Leaning out of the window, he called to Adam to follow them in his sorry state of a Zephyr. Adam held up an acknowledging hand, and jumped in his motor.

"Where to?" Frankie asked as he started to lead the convoy on its mission.

"Hackney - I'll sort the details out when we get there," Del told him.

As they drove along, Del ferreted about in the glove compartment and withdrew a set of brass knuckles with the tut-tut of mock disapproval.

Frankie grinned. "Put 'em away . . . They're for a rainy day."

"It's pissing down now, can't you see it!" Del said, pointing to the clear night sky.

* * *

At the same time as the Trojan convoy was on its way to Hackney, Simon, Dave and Greg were on another one of their little errands for the party. This time to the back streets of Deptford and a print workshop that was being used by the SWP. All the way there, Greg had eyed the plastic jerry can that Simon had placed at his feet. He didn't need to hear it from his mouth to work out that the merc intended torching the place.

The address they had been given turned out to be a row of lock-ups on an access road for the High Street shops. The single lane road itself was in terrible condition. Hardly any tarmac survived from its proud conception, and tuffs of grass sprang up where they could find a purchase. Adding to the sense of abandonment were the overhanging branches from the few trees that stood to the rear of the shops, ensuring that the lock-ups stood in eternal shadow.

"Bloody dismal looking area!" commented Dave, as he surveyed the scene ahead.

Simon held up the jerry can and joked, "There goes the neighbourhood!"

An infectious laugh rippled through the trio. Dave edged the car forward until the small thoroughfare opened up into a larger courtyard that had lock-ups on all sides. It didn't take long to find the one they were looking for. Rotten timbers formed the padlocked front doors and a tatty peeling sign proclaimed it to be the home of PRIME PRINT.

"Turn the car around," Simon ordered, stepping from the car with the can. "We need to make a quick exit."

"Anything I can do?" Greg asked from the rear passenger window.

"Yeah, scout around for a piece of rag will you!"

Greg jumped out, banging the door behind him, and began looking around for a suitable piece of rubbish. Dave then climbed over into the driver's seat and drew the car slowly to the top end of the forecourt.

Simon stepped up to the workshop and peered through the letter box. To the left and right he could see stacks of printed material going back a fair way. Below the slit, he could just see the edge of a pile of mail.

How thoughtful, he told himself, uncapping the can and extending the spout so he could pour the contents through the letterbox.

Greg returned with what looked like a fragment of an old boilersuit. "This do?" he asked, holding it out to Simon.

159

Simon looked up from his act and grabbed the cloth. "Yeah, that's fine!"

Greg watched him as he stopped pouring the petrol through the letterbox and doused the rag. The remainder he poured through the small window to the right, after knocking out one of the panes, and slopped over the doors.

Dave was back level with them by the time Simon was recapping the container. Handing it to Greg, he motioned for him to get into the car. While that was being done, he placed the rag into the letterbox and quickly scanned the floor for something to poke it through with. Fragments of a shattered palette held the answer.

"You ready for this?" he asked the two skinheads watching from the car.

With his zippo in his hand, Simon lit the rag. The flames leapt and rolled across the surface of the doors as the fire devoured the fumes from the dousing. Using the stick to push the blazing rag through, Simon was delighted to see what was left of the side window light up with an orange glow. If getting caught wasn't a possibility he would have loved to stay around and watch the fire develop.

With bravado, he walked casually to the car and got in. "Time to go home, James!"

"Yes, sir!" Dave said, playing along and taking the chance to watch the smoke begin to emerge from rotten breaches in the door via the rear view mirror.

With the passenger door shut, Dave nosed the car out of the access road and back into the traffic.

* * *

"That's the place!" Del said, pointing as they passed The Lord Nelson. "Take the first right and look for somewhere to park."

Frankie indicated to turn and paused on the bend for a few seconds to make sure the cars following got the idea. There weren't many vacant slots available, but luckily a recent demolition job had created an unofficial car park a hundred yards further down.

"This will have to do!" Frankie said, guiding the mini-bus slowly against the curb and bouncing it up on to the builder's wasteland.

160

By the time the last car had pulled over, the passengers from the mini-bus were out and standing around waiting for the order to move out.

"Get everyone together first," Del told Frankie. "I'm gonna take a quick look down there. Check it ain't a wasted effort!"

"Okay Del, be careful mate!" Frankie answered back.

Del strolled casually down to the corner, his heartbeat rising as tension entered his being. It was a strange mixture of exhilaration tempered by intrepidity. As the pub loomed closer, he slowed down and edged his way to the nearest window. Peering in, he saw that the bar was lightly populated. A few ardent regulars and about nine skinheads. Ferret was there, in the middle laughing and joking, but there was no sign of Dave or Simon. Probably for the best, Del mused as he carefully backed away from the window and returned to the car park.

"Okay, quit messing around!" Frankie said to those who were indulging in horseplay.

The gang formed a semi-circle around Del as he stood before them. "Okay, we're on. I've counted nine of them in there. Stan, you'll be happy to know Ferret is one of them!"

The black skinhead smiled with a malicious glint. "Let's go and say hello then!" Without waiting for a cue, he began marching in the direction of the pub.

"You heard the man, let's do it!" Frankie called to the mob.

Del turned on his heels and gently trotted after Stan, falling in with his footsteps. The crunch of so many Dr. Martens on the loose gravel sounded off loudly, and created a sense of power and determination among the gang members. Their descent on the pub was watched by passing motorists in sheer amazement.

Ferret, having turned round from the bar, saw Stan pass by the window. His grin quickly faded and a sense of entrapment filled him, as the others sauntered past.

"They've seen us!" yelled Joey as he made eye contact with Ferret.

"Let's go!" shouted Frankie as he pushed through the door behind Stan.

The skinheads at the bar weren't too sure what was taking place. A couple sought to move behind their companions, as first Stan and Frankie faced them from the other end of the bar, and then Del and the rest of them rushed in to take up position. The regulars decided that perhaps it was a good idea to take their drinks into the street.

161

Del watched them go, then turned back to the mob. Stan was silently mouthing to Ferret that he was going to die. "No one fucks with us!" Del stated flatly.

"Hey, we don't want trouble with you!" Ferret said, hoping to salvage something from the situation.

"Should have thought about that before you turned over two of our boys the other night!" snarled Frankie, wagging his finger.

"What are they talking about?" asked one of Ferret's companions. Whether he was truly unaware or just feigning ignorance didn't matter, as it was a comment falling on deaf ears.

"Hey, that was a mistake!" Ferret said with fading hope.

"You know what they say about learning from your mistakes!" Stan said, quick with the snappy comeback.

"Oh, fuck this!" cried one of the East End skinheads, losing his patience with the dead-end diplomacy. Stepping to the left of the huddle, he raised his fists. "Come on then, if you want it!"

Del and Frankie looked at each other and silent agreement passed between them. Together they led the assault, crossing the gap and tearing into the mob.

Within milliseconds, Stan had Ferret by the collar and had him across a table, pinning him down with a flurry of blows. Frankie, making his play for the guy at the ready, was surprised by the other's fast reactions. Before Frankie knew it, a fist had crashed against his jaw, splitting his lip. Lowering his chin and ignoring the pain, he moved in and retaliated with a few sharp jabs of his own.

Del had punched out at three different targets, fists swinging like a whirlwind, before landing a headbut on a face that suddenly loomed up in front of him. Before he could follow up, Joey was pushing past him to bring his boots into play on the fallen victim. Backing away and letting Joey finish him off, Del realised there was little he could turn his attention to. Most of the opposing gang were finished, felled by the sheer weight of numbers. Looking up, he saw the landlord talking down the phone behind the bar. A conversation that could only mean one thing - pigs!

Grabbing hold of Joey, he pulled him off and propelled him towards the door. "Get going mate, the guvnor's called the filth!"

For a second Joey stood there, chest heaving, as if he couldn't comprehend what was going on. Wild-eyed, he looked first at Del and then to the landlord who was a mere shadow in the doorway that led

162

from the bar to the private living accommodation behind the pub. The meaning slowly sank in and Joey took off towards the door.,

"EVERYBODY OUT!" Del yelled to the others, watching as the gang broke away from the fight.

Frankie backed off from his opponent and said to him, "Another time!"

"I'll be waiting!" promised the other, still at the ready in case it was some kind of trick.

A wry smile crossed Frankie's face. The guy had bottle, something he could respect, even if they weren't on the same side.

Out on the street, a mad dash for the vehicles began as distant sirens wailed into action. "Fuck, this is too close for comfort!" laughed Frankie as he ran.

Fucking mad sod! Del thought to himself. He could feel the same buzz, but he didn't relish it as much Frankie seemed to. The idiot seemed to thrive on it!

Arriving at the van, Del was about to wait for him, but pulled the rear door open and jumped in when Frankie waved his arm and yelled, "It's not locked!"

With a certain amount of pushing, shoving and panicked laughter, the mini-bus filled up and Frankie fired up the engine. He pulled out with wheels squealing in a cloud of gravel and dust. Joey nearly fell out as he fought to close the rear doors. And if it hadn't been for Terry grabbing him, he probably would have.

Jerry and Adam's motors were hot on Frankie's heels, but Alex's car had picked that moment to suffer a transmission problem. The starter motor laboured to no avail as he tried to start it.

"What the fuck are you doing?" screamed Neil from the rear seat, panicking at the sight of the other vehicles disappearing down the road while they were stuck there, not moving.

"It ain't me you cunt, it's this fucking motor!" Alex growled back as he turned the ignition key and pumped the accelerator pedal.

"That's clever ain't it!" moaned Sean. "You've fucking flooded it now!" Opening the door, he got out.

"Where you fucking going?" called Alex, ducking his head to see Sean through the opened passenger door.

"Legging it! I'd suggest you do the same!" he replied. Not bothering to hang around to argue the toss, he broke into a run, only halting momentarily at the mouth of the car park to decide which way to go.

163

Neil and Pete looked at each other. From the back seat they could sense a horrible sensation of impending doom that hampered the need for a quick decision. Only the maniacal anger of Alex swearing at his every failed attempt to kick the engine into life tipped the scales of indecision. It was obvious that to stay there would guarantee being arrested.

"Leave it!" called Neil, getting out at the same time as Pete. They both hesitated momentarily as Alex ignored them and continued to try and will the car to work.

"Leave it for fuck's sakes!" pleaded Neil.

"Forget him!" called Pete, giving up on the driver.

Not wanting to be left alone there, Neil gave up and followed Pete in pursuit of Sean.

"What the fuck?" Dave exclaimed, surprised to find the pub where they had left the rest of the gang crawling with police.

"Don't stop!" Simon warned as the car slowed.

Glancing sideways, Dave realised that it wasn't a good idea to get mixed up with the police. Curiosity could wait till later! Checking that the way was clear first, he turned the car to the right and let the scene drift from sight.

"Must have been some heavy shit!" Simon said, noting that the three cars and a transit van meant around fourteen uniforms were on the scene.

I don't need anyone,
Don't need no Mum and Dad
Don't need no good advice
Don't need no human rights.
I've got some news for you,
Don't even need you too!
SONIC REDUCER - THE DEADBOYS (1977)

CHAPTER THIRTEEN

SIMON woke with a fuzzy head, wondering what time it was and who the hell could be buzzing up to be let in. He guessed from the quality of light coming through the small window over the sink that it wasn't much more than seven-thirty.

A yawned "Shit!" hissed between his teeth, as he swung his feet to the floor and walked through into the office area, scratching his arse through his boxer shorts as he went. Leaning across the desk, he stabbed at the intercom switch. "Yeah?"

"Simon, it's me . . . Dave!" rasped back the speaker.

"Come on up, I was just making coffee!" Flicking the intercom off, he pressed the electronic release for the door down stairs. Leaving Dave to see himself in, he returned to the back room and filled the kettle, plugged it in and then turned his attention to slipping on a pair of jeans. Which reminded him to talk nicely to Greta today. His spare clothes were in desperate need of a trip down the launderette.

"Simon?" Dave's voice drifted in from the office area.

"Yeah, out back mate!" Simon called out, holding a milk carton to his nose and sniffing suspiciously. There was a slight odour of ageing, but nothing that he couldn't live with. Dave came through. "Alright, mate - you want a coffee?"

"Nah, can't really stop. I was on my way to work."

"You working now?" Simon asked, looking at his friend as if it was a major revelation.

"I told you two days ago, I've got a bit of work on with me brother!" Dave reminded him.

Simon nodded. Now that he mentioned it, he did recall something being said. "So what brings you here now?" enquired Simon, switching off the boiling kettle and preparing himself a drink.

165

Dave took a deep breath, held it for a second, then said, "I found out what last night's police raid was all about!"

"Oh yeah?" Simon looked up from what he was doing. When Dave didn't speak he felt obliged to prompt him. "Well?"

"Remember those two skinheads that got turned over by our mob?"

"The nigger and his side kick!" Simon confirmed.

"Yeah, well their mates didn't take too kindly to it!"

"Oh, I see!" The picture became clearer. "So what was the final score?" he demanded. The tone in his voice tightened slightly, yet apart from that there was very little indication that the revelation had provoked a reaction.

"The boys got kicked about a bit, but no one copped it too seriously!"

"Who won?" Simon asked flatly.

"Put it this way, it was twenty of them and nine of ours - who do you think won?" Irritation had crept into Dave's voice.

Simon was about to bark back, but caught himself in time. There was nothing to be gained from working their frustrations out on each other. "Give me time to think it over and we'll organise something later, all right!"

Dave nodded and looked at Simon one more time. "I better be going mate, it ain't getting any earlier!"

"Where's the job?" Simon felt obliged to help Dave put the matter out of his mind.

"Aldgate."

"Plenty of office tarts then?"

"For sure, mate!" Dave answered with a grin.

* * *

Leroy had to go around to Colin's house because he didn't have a telephone himself. He had had his own 'phone cut off by the G.P.O. and was on their bad debt list, owing some seventy pounds in unpaid charges. He would have cleared it, but for the attitude of the woman he had spoken to. She was a firebrand in the mould of DHSS officers. Apparently they would accept his money to pay the debt, but even then wouldn't permit him to be reconnected. "What's the point in paying then?" Leroy had asked.

Arriving, he found Colin in charge of his nephew Martin. His sister had asked him to baby-sit as she needed time to sort out a claim for

166

furniture from the Social Security. Spending hours down at Gestapo Central was enough to drive anyone mad and a kid in tow only made it worse.

"Use the phone, man?" Leroy asked.

Martin smiled a broad grin, making Leroy feel kind of special.

"Yeah sure, you know where it is!" Colin said, stepping back from the door with Martin in his arms.

Leroy entered and went to the stool that stood next to the telephone table. Sitting down, he took his address book from his breast pocket and began thumbing through the pages.

"You calling someone about that little bit of business?" asked Colin who from the other side of the kitchen doorway where he was holding Martin above his head and gently shaking him. The baby giggled with enjoyment.

"Yeah, I tink I give dem Brummies, Steel Pulse, a ring - a maybe dem wanna join our little soiree!"

"Tis a wicked idea, man!" Colin agreed, as Leroy began dialling the number in his book.

After several rings it was answered by a guy claiming to be the band's manager. It wasn't something that Leroy had expected as when he had met the band at a gig and had been asked to play, there hadn't been the slightest sniff of a manager. He naturally thought the number he had been given belonged to one of the band's members.

In spite of the surprise, Leroy felt there was nothing to lose in outlining the proposal to him. The fee was basically expenses only, but the manager seemed quite amicably disposed to the idea. Smiling with delight, Leroy realised the guy was counting the publicity side of the deal as being more valuable. With the expertise of an angler, Leroy laid the groundbait of anticipated media exposure. Playing the hook in the manager's direction was a guaranteed catch.

"I like dis business!" declared Leroy as he put the phone down.

"Dem interested then?" Colin asked.

"Sure dem interested, dem hooked!"

"That's good for me!" said Colin returning to the game, much to the squealing delight of his nephew.

Derek was happy too see Suzi when she appeared from behind his stall. "Hello girl!" he responded, giving her a peck before handing

167

back the change to the old dear who stood waiting. "Sorry, love!" he told her.

"Oh, don't worry about me. I'm just an old lady, but I was young once too you know! No, it's nice to see young people in love!"

Derek grinned and shook his head. Her words had struck his humour as well as his sensitivity.

Suzi smiled and said, "What a sweet old lady!" as she watched the old girl move away.

"Takes all sorts!" murmured Del.

Suzi wasn't too sure if that was a positive answer or a cryptically negative one. Not bothering to question it, she asked instead about how it had gone the night before. Derek grinned and told her the account was closed, meaning it had gone well. She nodded and agreed that it was good. Then changing subjects, Suzi told Del that she had just been passing through on her way to see Gillian and wanted to know if he was interested in going down the Roxy tonight. Chelsea and Bloody Sunday were playing.

Del paused to consider. "Yeah, why not?"

Suzi smiled and said she'd be back when he finished up for the day.

Del felt a warm glow inside as he watched her walk away and melt into the crowd. He congratulated himself on getting off with her in the first place since she made him feel good about life.

Ralph, Simon and Howard were in a huddled meeting at the GBP office. A copy of a music paper lay on the desk between them, open at an article introducing Rock Against Racism and giving a build up to a festival going to be held in Finsbury Park.

"It's obviously a commie front, but the question is what do we do about it?" Ralph commented from behind his hands which were clasped together in front of his face.

Howard paused for thought, while Simon didn't really feel it was his place to comment. Back in the army such decisions had been the officers' prerogative. It was a situation he had come to accept and a hard habit to break. Howard was inclined to agree with Ralph. It occurred to him that R.A.R. could soon become a major force on the scene.

"There's going to have to be some kind of response - what about a protest march?" suggested Ralph, imagining the opportunity to boost his media profile.

Howard looked at the party leader. He knew the idea had potential, but he couldn't see the authorities granting approval, especially given the size of crowd the proposed festival expected to draw. "No, I think this is more a job for Simon's talents!" Howard concluded. "The media would make mincemeat of a few hundred nuts protesting against a festival attended by thousands!"

Simon grinned at the cruel edge to Howard's words, but he was only pointing out the obvious. "We can't do much against a crowd that size," the skinhead said, "but perhaps we can get people's attention if we attack the stage during the festival?"

Howard and Ralph smiled together. It wouldn't take much of a confrontation to guarantee them front page news.

"Yes I like it!" declared Ralph gleefully.

Dave was surprised to see The Squire, a skinhead from Fulham in the pub his brother had selected as suitable for a lunchtime drink.

"Alright mate?" Dave said.

The Squire was named after the handmade shoes he chose to wear. Squire nodded and joined them at the table they occupied. "Not too bad, mate!" he replied, nodding to Dave's brother, although he didn't know him personally.

"What brings you over this side of the water?" asked Dave out of mild curiosity.

"Checking out the street markets, rents, type of trade, you know."

"Thinking of going into business then?"

"Yeah, something like that."

They talked about the kind of stall Squire had in mind, the merits of Fulham and West Ham and the appearance of a new band called Sham 69 whose lead singer had an affinity with the skinhead cult.

"Do you know where I can find the Trojan crew?" Dave asked a little later, fishing for information.

"What Del, Frankie, Alan and that?" asked Squire unsure.

"Got a couple of black skinheads in their number," Dave said when the names meant nothing to him.

"Yeah, that's them!" Squire confirmed. "Try the Seven Seals in Brixton High Street."

"Cheers, I will!" Dave said with a grin, raising his glass and draining the contents.

"You fit?" his brother asked, wanting to return to the job.

"Yeah sure! Catch ya later mate!"

"Later!" Squire replied.

Dave was chuffed with his little bit of undercover work and knew Simon was going to be pleased with the information.

Del was in the process of dragging the stall away to the lock-up when Suzi arrived. It was obvious from the pinpricks that represent her pupils that she had been dipping into her merchandise for the night. She giggled as Del fought first to get the wheels of the barrow moving, then fought to slow it up as it threatened to overshoot the entrance to the courtyard where they were stored.

"Where's your boss?" Suzi asked, leaning against the wall as Del snapped the padlock into place and checked that the doors of the lock-up were secure.

"He went about lunchtime, had something to sort out."

"Should ask him for more money if he expects you to run the stall single-handed!" said Suzi.

"I do it as a favour, not because I get something from it."

"You'll never make a businessman!" she pointed out.

"Can't say it bothers me!" Del answered as he pocketed the padlock key.

"You ready now?"

"Yeah, sure girl, let's go!" Del answered, slipping his arm around her waist. Together they headed for the traders' pub as Del was feeling in dire need of a drink.

By the time they decided to go to Covent Garden, Del was buzzing nicely from a cocktail of lager tempered with amphetamine. Approaching the club, Del was first surprised to see there was no queue outside, then realised they had spent longer in the pub then intended. *That bloody speed don't half make time fly!* Del told himself as he examined his watch.

"What's up?" Suzi asked.

"Hey, nothing!" Del replied and gave her an affectionate kiss.

Paying the guy on the door his £1.50, they descended the staircase into the basement club. The interior was dimly lit, but the stage was picked out by an ill-conceived lighting rig that barely did the job. The place was more packed than their last visit and Del looked around the crowd with a sense of pleasure. Pleasure that was short lived because a jarring blow crashed up against the side of his head. He didn't even

170

have the chance to know his attacker before he was brought down by the weight of numbers as more joined in.

Suzi screamed out, "Leave 'im alone you bastards!", grabbing one of the guys and scratching for his eyes.

Suzi was violently thrown aside as the group sought to savage Del. From his point of view he was dead in the water, on the floor, and unable to get up without exposing himself to another telling blow. Suzi scrambled to her feet and went to have another go, as the security and several members of the audience moved in to break it up.

Del was helped to his feet by a security member, his nose streaming with blood and the wild expression of cornered animal on his face.

"What you doing helping this Nazi bastard?" snarled one of the attacking punks with his arms pinned behind his back, as he struggled and kicked.

Now Del recognised them. *The fuckers from the squat!*

"He ain't no Nazi!" said Suzi, upset at the implication.

"He fucking is!" declared the punk. "Him and his mates beat us up cos we were Irish!"

"You're gonna fucking die!" Del said, fighting to shake off the bouncers. Freeing up one hand, he took a wild shot at the punk guy, but missed. He didn't get a second chance as the bouncer twisted his trapped arm and used his weight to force Del to the floor.

"Bullshit!" snarled Suzi. "You fucking robbed me, that's why you were turned over!"

"Yeah?" the Irish punk said, trying to pretend that Suzi was making it up.

Their attempt at turning the crowd against Del might have succeeded if it wasn't for Snake-Eyes who had been lurking among the surrounding by-standers. "Yeah!" he said, striking the guy with an unopened can of bitter across the bridge of the nose.

A bouncer punched out at Snake-Eyes and sent him staggering back. It goaded his mates to attack the bouncer and within seconds, everything was out of control and the scene had degenerated into a free for all. Del didn't get to see much of ti though. He was hauled to his feet and forced back up the stairs, thrown out into the street and told not to come back.

"I'll get me mates down here next time - see if you're so fucking hard then!" Del promised.

"Suck my dick, you wanker!" called back the bouncer.

Del reacted angrily. Forcing the sleeves of his Harrington up his forearms, he held his hands up as fists. "Come on then!"

Whether the bouncer was going to accept the offer or not was lost to the intervention of Suzi and Snake-Eyes emerging from the club. They dragged Del back, ignoring his wish to stay and fight it out.

"Take the cunt home and make sure he don't come back!" the bouncer advised the two punks.

* * *

When Dave presented Simon with the name and location of where the mob from the previous night's raid could be found, Simon was hellbent on taking instant revenge. In a short space of time, three carload of his cronies were heading over to South London.

They found the Seven Seals just down from the tube, pulled over and parked outside without any regard for the double yellow lines.

"You lot ready?" Simon asked as his mob assembled on the pavement.

Murmured agreement and nodding heads assured him they were. Simon took the lead as they entered the premises and felt a sudden overwhelming sense of shock when he realised there wasn't a white face in the place. It was packed to the hilt with dreads and other fashionists, and a stunned silence defined the vortex that stood between the two cultures. Unsure, the skinheads looked around. Everywhere, intense stares were fixed on them.

The table near the door held three dreads in a huddle who, despite the unexpected turn up, were still looking very relaxed. One of them pulled a machete from a secret pocket in his jacket, then held it up and ran an illustrating thumb along its edge. "So what do you want white boy?" he asked in a loud voice.

Shit, this is heavy! thought Dave. In the back of his mind, he was vowing all kinds of hell on The Squire if he got out of this in one piece. Looking around, he imagined that the entire pub's clientele was packing weapons of one description or another.

Simon knew they were caught in a delicate situation. "Guess we're in the wrong place!"

"I tink so!" said the other black guy to the left of the machete holder.

A nervous shuffle began in the ranks behind Simon when the speaker produced a handgun that Simon recognised as an American service piece.

"Hey, there's no need for this man!" Simon said, holding up his hands calling for all to be calm. "We're leaving!"

"Ummm - me tink that's a good idea!" replied the gunman, smiling.

Looking at his gang, Simon jerked his thumb to leave. They turned around and filed out through the door to the pearls of laughter from the blacks still inside. Subdued and with damp spirits, they got into the cars.

Simon didn't want to lose total face and called to Dave to start up the engine. Kicking her over, Dave watched as Simon wrenched a nearby rubbish bin from its perch and threw it through the nearest pub window.

All hell broke loose. Simon dashed for the open passenger door as the first of the angry customers burst out into the street, with the other cars pulling away. Ferret nearly had a heart attack as Dave started accelerating up the road. He was sitting in the back of his car when he looked back and saw himself on the wrong end of the pistol barrel. Whether he had been close to death or not was thankfully lost by the action of the gunman's friend, who wrestled it away and prevented him from firing.

* * *

Del had been fuming all the way back to Brixton, pushing off Suzi's attempts to clean up the blood spilt from his damaged nose. Snake-Eyes had opted to accompany them after seeing the way Derek was reacting. Not that he was sure he could do anything to lift his spirits, but not to try would have seemed a little inconsiderate.

All three of them headed for Jennifer's place. Suzi silently wished that Del would snap out of his melancholy. She was still buzzing and didn't want to feel the touch of paranoia that his mood was promoting.

Speeding from the clutches of the dreads, Simon was surprised to see Del, Suzi and an unknown punk walking along the pavement about a hundred yards beyond the overhead rail bridge. "Mother fucker - that's one of 'em!" he cried.

Dave looked over, snapping out of his own depressed state. "Let's get him!"

173

Squealing to a halt, they drew the attention of all three pedestrians. Del saw the faces through the windscreen and realised in shock who it was who was in such a hurry to stop. "Run!" he yelled, cutting through his companions' bewilderment.

The car was emptying as two other motors screeched to a halt next to it. Breaking for an alleyway, Del, Suzi and Snake-Eyes ran helter skelter down its length. Barely halfway in, the sound of running feet registered behind them. Not stopping to look, the three friends reached the junction where the alleyway emerged out on to the street at the rear. Snake-Eyes and Suzi froze momentarily, but Del had no hesitation. These streets were his and he knew exactly which way to go to escape. "This way!" he called, turning to the left and putting even more effort into his flight.

Suzi was struggling to keep up and Del felt obliged to slow down. Chancing a look back, he saw Simon emerge from the alleyway with a baseball bat tucked under his arm. "Come on girl, this ain't the time or place to take it easy!"

A nervous grin, meant as encouragement, flitted across his face. Suzi also saw the bloodthirsty mob clamouring for them and felt a sudden burst of energy. The weariness fell away like it had only been a passing mist.

Cutting across the road, Del dodged around the back of a passing motor and ran across a green into a commercial yard used by several businesses. Once inside and out of sight of the pursuers, Del ran to a fire escape, leading up on to one of the roofs. Snake-Eyes thought he was mad. The last thing they needed was to get cornered up high. He would have preferred to go on to the High Street where there was plenty of people. Suzi was following Del without question, running up the iron steps that spiralled the three floors. Feeling he was in a minority of one, Snake-Eyes felt obliged to do likewise.

They made the roof at the same time as Simon and friends entered the courtyard. Halting at the gates, eyes scanned the seemingly empty open expanse.

Gotta be hiding somewhere, Simon thought.

Meanwhile, Del, not pausing for one moment, ran across the flat roof, crunching the gravel spread across the asphalt under foot. Suzi and Snake-Eyes stayed with him as he went to the opposite end of the roof. The punk soon realised that the roof hadn't been the dead-end he had thought it was. Del's target was a steel hoop and Snake-Eyes deduced that it was the top of a fixed wall ladder.

"It's a bloody assault course!" cried Suzi, as Del swung himself on to the parapet and began climbing down the rungs of the ladder towards the ground floor roof of the garages.

"Go on!" urged Snake-Eyes, his ears picking up the sounds of the others in the courtyard behind them. "Quickly!" he hissed as one of the voices called out, "Try the rooftop!"

As soon as she was climbing down, Snake-Eyes joined her on the ladder. Hurriedly they descended its length and made it safely to the bottom.

"What now?" Suzi asked Del.

He turned with a smile. "Now we jump!" he said, pointing to the edge of the roof that overlooked someone's garden.

"Oh you gotta be kidding!" cried Suzi.

"Come on, the ground's soft on the other side!" Del said, pulling her to the edge. Suzi looked down at the ten foot drop into the moist, well kept flowerbeds, but the warning voice of inbuilt vertigo made her hesitate at the edge.

"Get going!" Del said loudly, giving her a push. With a cry, she fell into the flowerbed, landing on her feet before toppling forward and rolling over the top of a miniature conifer.

Del and Snake-Eyes jumped simultaneously, landing to the left and right of her. Hauling her up between them, they ran for the gate that led down the side of the house to the road beyond.

Simon and Dave reached the edge of the roof in time to see the three of them disappear from sight. "Fuck, fuck, fuck!" screamed Dave as he banged his fist on the parapet.

"Forget it man, get 'em another time!" Simon said laying a hand on his shoulder.

Punk rockers, dem a next to reggae rockers!
PUNK ROCKERS - THE BLACKSTONES (1977)

CHAPTER FOURTEEN

IN the two weeks that followed the double incident, Suzi found it was her turn-to worry over Del. When questioned he always claimed to be all right, but she knew that there were things on his mind. A heavy depression had gripped him in the two days immediately after the aggro and it seemed to have lingered like an emotional fog. On one of the rare occasions he had opened up to expose his feelings, it had been in the shape of a short cryptic statement, "Skinheads should be above this shit!". Attempts at gaining clarification of what he meant were met by a stonewall reply of "It doesn't matter!".

Even Leroy was unable to reach into his soul. None of his philosophical prompting could induce more than a curt response. So having to second guess the reasons, Leroy told Suzi that it was most likely a response to the conflict of ideals tempered by grief for his brother's death.

"See, he worshipped his brother tremendously. I guess his murder was something he never fully got over. You know he became a skinhead out of respect for his brother?"

Suzi could tell Del wasn't the only one feeling at odds over the past. Leroy's heart was heavy with guilt too. "Is that why you became a rastafarian?" she asked.

"I don't know," Leroy said honestly. It hadn't occurred to him that there might be a connection. After all, he hadn't changed over night, but then again it might have had a possible bearing.

"What was his brother like?" Suzi asked. It was something she had wanted to know, but hadn't felt comfortable asking Derek.

"A great guy. Cocky, very quick with a quip. There was one time I remember some hippy chick asked him if he was a racist. That was the time the newspapers were making a big thing out of the paki bashing you know? He just looked her in the eye and said, 'Yeah - Grand Prix, horses - I like all sorts of racing!'"

Suzi smiled as Leroy chuckled at the memory. So long ago yet still only yesterday in the vivid recollection.

"I thought the skinheads and hippies didn't get on?" Suzi murmured, unsure of her facts.

"In general we didn't. I mean it depended on where you was. Like take Southend on a bank holiday - then, yeah, there was no love lost between the two. Yet like in this case, it was at the local youth club and you kind of tolerated each other's presence. By and large we kept ourselves to ourselves. I mean, you knew it at discos. The hippy chicks used to be in the corner by the stage, greasers by the pinball and us skinheads down the other side. Yet many of these people were the ones you'd been to school with. So in spite of the way things were, there was a basis for getting along."

"Was that the case with this girl?" Suzi asked.

"Nah, she was one of dem rich bitches from Hampstead. Come to see some friends you know. First off she was trying to wind him up, then later she went over the field with him. I guess she fancied a bit of rough for the night!"

"Didn't see her again then?" Suzi wanted confirmation of what she sensed.

Leroy shook his head and sighed, "Nah!"

Looking to Jenny who was resting against the kitchen sink, he asked her to rustle up some coffee. He was feeling thirsty and was sure Suzi could do with one. Dutifully, she set about fulfilling the request. As she held the kettle up to the gushing tap, Jenny spoke to Suzi. "Don't worry too much about Del. He's still keen for that show this weekend. I guess that's when he'll find himself again!"

"Yeah, I guess so," Suzi agreed, with a smile that said she wasn't really convinced by the words of encouragement.

"Hey, don't let it get you down girl," said Jenny. "Dis is relationships for you. You have to be their lover, their friend and sometimes you gotta be their mother too! Dem never grow up, dem always like kids!"

"Hey, I didn't hear you complaining last night when we . . . "

"Hush your mouth Leroy. Respect our guest!"

Suzi found them amusing. This attitude of scathing sarcasm towards each other masked the real affection they held for each other.

Leroy grinned sheepishly at Suzi and held a finger to his pursed lips as if calling for hush. He peered tentatively at Jenny from the corner of his eyes and earned himself a light cuff on the back of the head.

"Damn dem. See what I mean?" Jenny asked Suzi. "Like Peter Pan dem never grow up!"

"Come on, we're going to be late for the meeting!" Lesley called to Diane as she popped her head around the artroom door.

Diane was in the process of printing the R.A.R. logo on to another yellow t-shirt. Their tutor had approved the use of college facilities to produce the shirts needed to identify those working for the festival from those attending. "Hold on a second!" she answered.

Scraping the tar-like printing ink into the safe corner of the screen with the squeegee, Diane then wiped her hands on the apron she was wearing. Still feeling sticky, she opened the bottle of metholated spirit and soaked a nearby cloth in the liquid. Lesley watched impatiently as she used that to clean her hands more effectively. Then all she needed to do was wash away the smell of the meths. "Don't want them to think I'm a wino!" chirped Diane.

All right for them to think you're a slag though, Lesley thought to herself. That was the only side of her friend she had trouble dealing with, although sometimes she wondered whether she was just a little bit jealous. After all, some of the guys that Diane had been with had been more than a little bit appealing to her.

Before leaving the room, Diane removed the t-shirt from the template and placed it on a hanger above the industrial heater they were using to proof the ink. Then the two girls hurried along to the meeting.

"What kept you?" asked Martin Langham, looking up from the papers he held in front of him.

Lesley looked sheepishly around the gathered faces and pointed to Diane. "She did!"

Martin smiled. "So how's the t-shirts going?"

Diane sat down before looking up and answering. "I guess there's about another ten to do."

"Make that another fifteen. Steve Sergeant has added more names to the security contingent," he informed her.

Diane sighed. That guy was becoming a bloody nuisance. They needed his members' ability in crowd control that was for sure, but it felt like he was using the security provision as his own private army. This was the second time he had insisted on an increase in personnel.

"Okay," Martin said, starting the meeting proper. "Everything is set for this weekend. *Melody Maker* and the *NME* have donated free advertising space for the event. Confirmed acts include The Clash, Chelsea, The Police, Dead Wretched, Teenage Vampires, Steel Pulse and The Regulars. Johnny Kidd And The Pirates might put an appearance in, as might Wreckless Eric. We'll know about them later this week."

"The t-shirts for sale to the general public will be with us tomorrow. This is item three-one on the agenda. A vote on whether to sell them at commercial prices or to keep them to a small mark-up of say twenty pence on the shirt. This will realise a return of about two hundred pounds per thousand. All those in favour of the small mark up, please raise your hands."

All around the table, hands went up. Martin smiled with satisfaction. He loved it when things came together with a minimum of fuss. "Item four-two . . . "

* * *

"Right, so that's sixty bodies confirmed for Saturday!" Simon declared as he faced Ralph across the desk. "What I propose doing is organising them to slip into the concert in twos and threes. Then we can reassemble in these areas."

Unfolding a sheet of paper, he pointing to a drawing of a stage with six circles surrounding the oblong. "By standing back about four or five ranks from the front, we can use the crowd as cover. Timing is important so I've allowed an hour and fifteen minutes for everyone to be inside the park before we attack the stage. By using a countdown, we can ensure that everyone makes their play at the same time rather than risk a disjointed attack if people fail to see a given signal!"

"You're going to have to ensure each group has a synchronised watch," Greta pointed out.

"Yeah, I've called a meeting here tonight to explain the situation and to tell them whose in which group," Simon told Greta. "And if we have to act sooner, I'll give a signal by blasting an airhorn."

"What about arousing suspicion from the police?" asked Ralph. "If you're going in in dribs and drabs, where are we going to hide those waiting their turn?"

"There's a pub on a side street near the Seven Sisters tube that's a right dive. The Woodman or something. I found it last week when I was going over the area. Doesn't pull many punters, so I guess the landlord will be grateful for the unexpected boost to business. From our point of view, it's far enough off the main drag to avoid being noticed, and the tube trains run every fifteen minutes to Finsbury Park. So it's a simple matter of letting a group of fifteen go every quarter of an hour from the pub. Then they can use the crowds to stagger themselves into groups of twos and threes outside the park - simple but effective!"

"What happens if it takes longer to get into the event than the time you've allowed?" Greta asked, knowing a delay or slow moving queue could wreck the carefully formulated plan.

"Yeah, I wasn't too sure about that myself. Give me time though and I'll come up with something else before tonight. Trust me!"

Del was surprised to see Frankie arrive at the fruit stall just as he was breaking down for the night.

"Wotcha!"

"Alright mate?" Del said, looking up from his work.

"Not too bad!" For a minute or two Frankie watched in silence as Del repacked the produce.

"Ain't crossed your mind to lend me a hand has it?" Del asked, stacking one box of Golden Delicious on another.

"Oh, sorry mate. Wasn't thinking!" Stepping down from the pavement, Frankie joined Del in placing some bananas back into the box they had come out of that morning.

"So what brings you down here then?" Del asked.

"You ain't been about for a while. Thought I'd check things were all right with ya!"

"You're getting worse than me mother!" chided Del with humour.

"Don't take the piss mate. I saw Snake-Eyes down the Kings Road Saturday. He told me you had been on the receiving end of a kicking the week before."

"Hey, that weren't all. We got chased by that Nazi mob half way round Brixton!"

"Yeah he told me!" Frankie said.   "That was down to The Squire. He phoned Alan last week to say he'd been asked for our hang out!"

"What? He set us up?" asked Del, pausing from his labours to look at Frankie.

The other's eyes shone with amusement. "No man, he sent them to the Seven Seals. You know, the yardies' place on the High Street!"

Del grinned at the thought of the shock they must have got when they wandered into the joint."

"So, we gonna grab a beer or what?" Frankie asked.

"Yeah - why not?" Del responded. He was feeling better for seeing a friendly face.

With the barrow away, they went to the trader's pub and were pleasantly surprised by having their drinks bought by Del's neighbouring stall holder. He knew that his daughter had the hots for Del and appreciated his discretion in handling her advances.

Sitting at one of the window tables, the two skinheads supped their pints. Frankie strained his eyes to try and make out a blonde form that floated past the frosted window, causing Del to laugh at his efforts.

"You doing that festival this weekend?" Frankie asked when the vision had passed.

"How do you know?" Del asked. It was something he hadn't had the chance to tell anyone about.

"I saw Leroy's sound system mentioned in one of the adverts for it."

"Yeah, Leroy has included me in the team."

"Great. That's what we thought!"

"We?" asked Del looking from Frankie to the drink sitting in front of him.

Frankie lit a cigarette and dropped the still burning match into the ashtray. "Yeah, me and the rest of the mob. You remember them don't ya? You know, your mates!"

"All right, don't take the piss!"

"Who's taking the piss. I ain't the one who's been missing these last two weeks!" His words were soft, but the meaning was intended to sting Del's conscience a little.

"I'm here now ain't I?" Del responded.

"Okay, so let's get pissed eh? You've got a few days to catch up on!"

Del laughed and nodded.

Suzi was beginning to worry about Del's non-appearance when there was a knock at the door. Being the only one in, she felt a bit cautious about answering it, but at the same time couldn't really ignore it. Slipping the catch, she drew back the door to find Frankie standing there with Del leaning on him for support.

"Thought I'd better help him get back. He's had a skinful!" Frankie's voice told her that Del wasn't the only one.

"Hello baby!" Del chirped as he looked at Suzi with a ridiculous grin on his face.

"I'll fucking hello baby you!" Suzi replied. Stepping away from the door, she said to Frankie, "Bring him into the front room!"

Frankie wasn't too sure if coming around had been a good idea, and the expression on his face said as much.

"Hey, don't worry Frank," Suzi said. "I was only joking you know. Seriously I think he needed to get out. Only wished he'd let me know first!"

"How could I?" slurred Del. "Frankie turned up unexpected like, and Jennifer ain't got a phone!"

Suzi felt there was no point in arguing with him in that condition. As soon as Frankie dumped him on the sofa, he promptly fell asleep anyway.

"Cheers Frankie!"

He looked at Suzi, not too sure if she was genuinely grateful or being sarcastic. "Hey, no problem!" he responded.

"You want a coffee or something?" she asked.

"God, no!" Frankie responded. The idea of ruining a good buzz was against his religion. "Anyway, I'd better be going!" he added.

Suzi followed him out into the hall.

"You going to this gig at the weekend?" he asked as he opened the front door.

"Yeah I'll be there!" Suzi replied.

"Okay, see yah then!" Frankie said as he took his leave.

"Yeah, see ya!" Suzi said before closing the door.

On the morning of the festival, Del woke up around ten-thirty. As he got dressed, he felt the need to go back home and get a change of clothes. He wished he didn't have to after the way his Mum had reacted the last time he was home, but he was feeling grubby from wearing the same shirt for three days. The dirt on the collar was thick enough to grow potatoes.

Suzi was still in bed, enjoying the luxury of just lying there. Her breasts were exposed uncaringly, and Del leaned over and kissed one of them on the nipple, causing her eyelids to flutter.

"Morning, sweetheart!" he said as her eyes opened.

"Morning," she responded, her hand groping for his. Locking the fingers, she gave his hand a squeeze and he responded in kind.

"I've gotta go and get some fresh clothes for today. What do you wanna do? Meet me back here or at the festival?"

182

Suzi shrugged, trying to clear her mind so she could think straight. "No, tell you what. I'll meet you there. I wanna see if Gillian can sort me out with a larger stock."

Del nodded. "Okay, give me a kiss then!"

Leaning up, she kissed him, while his hand gliding softly across her body, exploring her shape and intimate features.

"Later!" Suzi said as she felt the tip of his finger circle her womanhood.

"That's a promise!" Del said, withdrawing his hand and turning his attention to putting on his boots.

"The last of the dirty stop outs!" declared Derek's mother, as she heard the front door being opened.

Del shut the door behind him and followed her voice into the kitchen. From the hall she had sounded somewhat conciliatory.

"Hi, Mum!" Del said.

His mother looked up from the washing up she was doing. "I take it there's a young lady involved in you not coming home these days?"

Del grinned nervously. He hated going under the microscope like this. "Yeah, her name's Suzi."

"Has she got her own place?"

"No. Remember Leroy?"

"The coloured kid, your brother was always with?" his Mum asked.

"Yeah, she's staying with his girlfriend," Del told her as he eyed the lemon pie that stood steaming on the table.

His mother followed his gaze and smiled. "Take a piece if you want!"

Gratefully he cut a slice and after fishing a plate out of the cupboard, sat down to eat it.

"Bring her round tomorrow!" his Mum said, causing Del to freeze in mid-mouthful.

"Why?"

"I've got to meet her before I decide if she can move in with us or not!" she answered.

It was a shock to Del. He hadn't even thought of asking his Mum when Suzi had been kicked out the squat. "You mean that?"

She laughed at his doubt. "Of course I do. It's the only way to ensure you come home of a night. Besides it'll be fun to have another female about the house. Give me someone to talk to!"

Del understood what she meant. Before she had married his Dad, she had been living at home with her four sisters. Since then home life had been predominantly male-orientated and it had never occurred to Del that she might have been lonely for some company of her own gender.

"Don't let the way she looks put you off," Del muttered. "She's really a great person!"

The rushed statement caused his Mum to raise an enquiring eyebrow. "Pardon?"

"She's one of those punk rockers and you know they dress weird!" Too embarrassed to look her in the eye, Del concentrated on the dish in front of him.

"It's not what's on the outside that matters, it's what's on the in!" she pointed out. "Besides, how much weirder can she be than that Karen your brother came back with that time?"

Del grinned. He remembered Karen all right. She was a devout David Bowie fan, to the point of imitating the face make-up of Ziggy Stardust and having thunder streaks dyed into her hair. "Okay, I'll bring her round tomorrow!"

"Okay, that's settled. After you've finished that, I'd suggest you get out of those things and get a bath. They look almost alive from where I'm standing!"

Leroy and Colin were setting up the sound system on the right of the stage, next to the steps that led up from the ground. The lighting rig was high overhead in the canopy that was intended to protect the equipment from any rain. Not that the day looked like offering a drop of the stuff. The sun was reaching its mid-morning position and sparkled like a jewel when seen through the tree tops that lined the boundaries of the park.

Leroy had decided to put his speakers on stage even though the decks would run through the main PA. He said he felt naked without them, and needed them to be on display even if they weren't being used. Colin walked another bass bin into position as Leroy checked the decks via the monitor channel on his console. Satisfied that each worked perfectly, he looked over to Colin. "Don't forget to pick Del up at twelve o'clock."

"What's the time now?" Colin asked.

"Eleven!" Leroy responded.

Both their heads turned to the sound engineer up behind them, as his voice rumbled through the speaker banks. "Can we have The Clash on stage for their sound check please?"

Leroy watched as the band members came slowly together. Out in the arena, several catering trucks were moving into their assigned position. A troop of St John's Ambulance people were settling into a small marquee and the police were talking with the organisers just below the stage.

Spotting the uniforms below them, Joe Strummer exchanged a few words with Mick Jones and then cheekily called out, "Okay, *Police And Thieves*, 1-2-3-4!"

Leroy and Colin nodded approvingly as the disgorged chords of Junior Marvin's hit burst from the stacks. The sound engineer took each input in turn, peaking its sound above the rest before dropping back into a considered volume level. Satisfied with the balance, he began tweaking the sound, adding a little more treble on the vocals, turning backing ones down a touch, a bit of echo on the drums, and a little less bass to hold clarity.

* * *

Simon had decided that to avoid arousing the suspicion in The Woodman, they would go there early and spend a few hours as customers. The cover story was that they were a stag party, making out that Simon was marrying Greta that afternoon in the local register office. Before heading for the pub though, Simon had gone to a bicycle shop to buy an airhorn. The signal to attack early would be three blasts on that.

Arriving at the pub, Simon found 20 or so GBP members already there. "He's the one!" cried Ferret from the bar, pointing at Simon as he came in.

Simon gave him a quizzical look as he stepped up to the bar. The barman set him mind at rest though by saying, "Congratulations on tying the knot, son - first one's on the house!"

Simon smiled. A freebie was an unexpected bonus from the ruse. "Cheers! Light and bitter please!"

With the drink and a curt thanks to the barman, Simon moved away to the corner table. Out of earshot of the bar staff, he took a sup from his drink and then asked the others if they were packing anything. It was too public an act to be using weapons.

185

As time wore on, the pub gradually filled up with the rest of the GBP active members, and the festival was guaranteed a surprise it would never forget . . .

* * *

Del was ready with his vinyl selection in boxes when Colin called. Both of them were feeling a sense of excitement about the show. "Yeah man, sweet little set," Colin said. "Good sound, know what I mean? Radical bro!"

"Yeah right!" Del responded as he shut the van's back door on his boxes and stepped round to the passenger door. Both he and Colin climbed in at the same time, and as Colin turned the engine on, Del slammed his door shut.

"Jez man, you trying to break it?" complained Colin, wincing at the force Del had put into the act.

"If you had a proper van instead of this heap, you wouldn't have to worry!"

"Hey man, I don't see you walking!" Colin answered back.

"One-each!" exclaimed Del as the van moved off in the direction of Finsbury Park.

By the time they arrived, Frankie and Rebel were already there and were talking to Leroy. Frankie spotted Del as he approached and called out, "How was your hangover the other day?"

Del grinned as he sauntered up to them. "Didn't have one!"

Frankie looked at him in disbelief. "Bollocks! After what you drunk?"

"Straight up!" Del insisted, before turning his attention to Rebel. "How's my favourite bootgirl then?"

Rebel looked at him in a funny way. "Since when?"

"Hey Rebel, you were always my favourite!" Del said, placing his arm around her waist and giving her a hug. "Just waiting for the day when you want to envelope with me!"

"That's elope, dummy!" she said, correcting his grammar.

"Nah, envelope - I wanna lick you all over!" he said, sticking his tongue in her ear by way of a demonstration.

Rebel cried out and shied away. When she had regained her composure, she slapped Del on the shoulder. "You dirty sod!" she complained, trying to remove the moisture from her ear with a tissue.

186

"Hey man, I got something for you!" Leroy said to Del, holding out what looked like business cards. "If you wanna hotdog or something, you use these instead of paying for it - part of the expenses. Also we have a case of light ale as hospitality extras."

"Yeah, but you and Colin don't drink!" Del said before thinking about it. Then he sussed what Leroy meant. "Hey all right, where is it?"

Leroy smiled at Del. "Little bit slow there bro!" he said, jerking a thumb at the decks up on the stage.

"I'll put these up there and grab a couple of tins!" Del said, lifting his records.

Frankie decided to give him a hand, and picked up a record box before following him up the stairs to the disco set-up. Leroy had had the foresight to bring the pair of steel framed paste tables he occasionally used to arrange records on at gigs, and Del placed his two boxes down on one of them, close to the turntables. Frankie did the same with the box he was carrying.

"Brought some good sounds?" Frankie asked, eyeing the boxes that at a rough guess held a hundred singles each.

Del looked at him with a sarcastic stare, as if to say, "What do you think?"

Knowing it was a silly question, Frankie changed the subject. "Dig the beers out then," he said, reminding Del of the other reason for going there.

It took a little looking around before they discovered the case of tins under the decks. Taking a four pack from it, Del peeled off two tins for Frankie and kept two for himself. Then, tearing off the ring pull and discarding it carelessly, he supped at the tepid liquid, letting out a sigh of satisfaction as he did so.

Together, the two skins looked out over the park. Soon it would be throbbing with people. Looking down below, they could see a guy talking to Leroy while Rebel looked on. The rasta nodded and turned to face the stage.

"Stick some music on," he shouted to Del. "They're opening the gates!"

Del gave him the thumbs up and, dancing around Frankie, he took hold of the first box and began flicking through the records. He had it in his mind that something a bit laid back was right to start with since the party wouldn't really start till the first band. Pausing momentarily on *Tons Of Gold*, a Val Bennet horns cut of *Liquidator*, he decided against it and plumped for *Cassius Clay* by toaster Dennis Alcapone. Practised hands centred the disc, dropped the needle on the leader and stabbed the start button in a smooth flow of action. Allowing a few seconds for the blank segment to burn off, he dragged the slider on the mixer to deck one.

"Coming from the top of the mountain, the man called Cassius Clay is back . . . !"

"Fucking hell!" Frankie laughed as the man's voice came booming out of the speaker banks like the voice of God.

Del grinned and looked down at Leroy who was giving him three shakes of the hand in a flicking motion, meaning the tune was hot, a killer! Del knew his music and guessed the early roots sound was a safe bet until he had a chance to work out the tastes of the crowd. Leroy and Colin had it worked out that their contribution to the set should centre around the two reggae bands, while the prime slot before The Clash would be Leroy's prerogative.

Del set up the other deck to play an Upsetters / Versatiles cut of the classic *Stepping Razor*, while Frankie leaned against one of the canopy supports and looked out on the arena that was defined by the wall of tents and marquees. Several were being used as information points by the likes of CND, the SWP, local councils and the Race Relations Board, but the largest one was reserved as a refreshments tent.

In the middle area people were beginning to congregate and fill the empty ground with bodies. Frankie waved to Rebel to come and join them, but she was halted at the foot of the stairs by a steward who demanded a stage pass.

"Oi! She's with us!" Del called down to the guy, but it was lost in the noise from the PA output.

Sliding out from between the decks, Del was about to descend the steps and have a word, when Leroy got there first. The steward nodded and stepped aside, and as Rebel began to climb the stairs, Leroy gave her stage passes for the three of them.

"Here!" she said handing Del and Frankie a pass each. "Nice view!"

"Sure is from where I'm standing - on cloud nine!" Del declared, obviously pleased with life as he watched the area in front of the stage begin to fill.

After an hour, Del had settled into the routine enough to feel confident at delivering some of the toasts Colin had patiently taught him. "Heavy like lead, so knock 'em dead, like a bullet to the head -

that's what I said. For this is your boss record jock speaking from the very top, going out on high with sounds that'll groove you - no word of a lie . . . !"

Out beyond the stage, the park was throbbing with a life of its own. The attendance had swollen to cover the available space within the confines of the tents and catering pitches, and a queue could already be seen leading to the mobile toilet vans. The fact that some people were moving to the feel of the music gave Del an even bigger sense of satisfaction at how the event was shaping up.

Alan and Stan appeared at the bottom of the stage steps and tried to attract Del's attention. He didn't notice them, but Rebel did. Nudging him, Del looked to her first then to where she was pointing. He held up his hand in acknowledgement and Alan called him over with a beckoning wave.

Indicating that his mate should hold on a minute, Del checked the disc that was playing - *DJ's Choice* by Winston Wright. It was about half way through, so taking hold of Rebel's shoulder, he leaned over so his mouth was close to her ear. "When that one finishes, press this button," he said, pointing to the start button on the right-hand deck. "Then move this across to the other side!" he added, showing her the slider.

"Sure, but if I fuck it up don't blame me!" she replied.

"I got faith in you girl - besides it's too simple to fuck up!"

Leaving her to it, Del descended the stairs to where Alan and Stan were waiting. Before he reached them, a coloured guy took the time to compliment Del on the music which gave his ego a real boost.

"Alright chaps!"

"Yeah, how's things with you?"

"Never better mate, never better!" Del answered. "The others here?"

"Over there somewhere, getting something to eat!" Stan said, jerking his thumb in the general direction of the perimeter.

"Lot of people here!" Alan noted as he looked at a girl in a day-glo green bikini top and jeans that were shortened to the shins and shredded at the bottom of the legs in a Robinson Crusoe castaway style. Her ample breasts gave a good enough display of cleavage for him to add, "Jesus!"

"You'll go blind if you keep looking at those!" joked Del.

The girl noticed them looking and smiled while moving to the music.

"Excuse me a minute!" Alan said, deciding to chance his luck with her.

Stan slapped Del on the shoulder. "Catch ya later, bro!"

"Yeah, sure man!"

Leaving them to work their charms on the young lady, he turned to go back up the stairs and was met by Leroy. "Del, them gonna put the M.C. on for the show in about ten minutes. Some guy called Clark, okay?"

"Yeah, sure!"

"Oh, by the way, I hear from them at the gate we got an audience of nine and a half thousand just now!"

Del was impressed. In the one-upmanship world of disc jockeys that was going to take some beating.

* * *

Things weren't running so smoothly for Suzi.

"Clive's had a bit of trouble getting the pills," explained Gillian. "Something to do with a customs bust at Dover!"

"Shit!"

"Hey, don't worry. He's out trying to sort it now if you wanna hang on till he gets back. I'm sure he can do something. How many were you thinking of?"

"Say two hundred this time?" Suzi said, hoping it wasn't too much to ask for.

"You got something big on?" Gillian asked, knowing it was over three times her normal quota.

"Yeah, there's a big show on at the park in Finsbury. Should be a cinch to off-load a couple of hundred."

"I don't know if he can lay on that many. He's got other commitments to meet as well you know."

"Well, whatever will be fine!" Suzi said from her seat at the kitchen table.

"How's the boyfriend?" Gillian felt like indulging in a little women's talk to pass the time until her husband returned.

* * *

For an hour, Simon waited as the numbers in the Woodman dwindled and eventually it came to his group's turn to move. Dave

190

looked at his watch and spoke across the table crowded with empty glasses. "The next tube is due in about five minutes."

Simon nodded and looked around the faces sitting at the table. He thought about leaving Ferret behind. It was obvious he had drunk too much and he was a potential liability, but in the end Simon decided to let him come. "Okay let's go!" he said, draining his glass and standing up.

The others had been feeling the build up of anticipation and were grateful for the chance to be on the move. The last ten minutes of waiting had been almost unbearable.

"Have a good day lads!" the landlord called as they headed for the door.

"Yeah, cheers!" Dave responded, holding in a desire to laugh until he was outside.

The walk to the tube took about three minutes. Inside the foot tunnels leading to the platform, they heard the train rumbling distantly.

"Leg it!" called out Andy from the back, prompting a mad dash for the platform.

All eyes were on them as they burst out on to the platform. Simon grinned, knowing full well that the sound of running feet was threatening to those who felt intimidated by such things.

Ferret managed to cause a ruction during the one stop to Finsbury Park. A teenage girl was blowing bubbles with a lump of Bazooka Joe gum. Grinning sickly with glazed eyes, and holding on to one of the handrails, he leant over and undid his zip. "If you wanna blow on something, blow on this darling!"

He was too drunk to realise the woman sitting next to the girl was her aunt and not one to take kindly to his antics. She was a big woman with a lot of power in her arms, as Ferret found out when the corner of her handbag found the tender part of his groin. He fell heavily to the floor, like a puppet with the strings cut, gasping for air.

His companions fell about laughing with the exception of Simon who had had enough of the little runt. If Ferret had expected sympathy or back-up he was about to be disappointed. Stepping across, Simon kicked him viciously in the stomach. Then to the lady and the girl he said, "Sorry about that. He's an ignorant sod at the best of times!"

The laughter died down, cooled by the aggressive behaviour dished out by Simon. He looked around at their faces and thought he could detect an air of disapproval, but it was lost as the train braked for the required stop.

Simon was out and walking as soon as the doors slid open.

"What about Ferret?" called Andy, standing in the doorway, looking down on his friend who was struggling to find his feet.

"Leave him. He can find us later!" shouted back Dave on Simon's behalf.

Simon was grateful that he understood even if no one else did. Leaving the tube station behind, the atmosphere between the members of the group remained subdued, but Simon guessed that once they went into action, the doubts would melt away.   At least, that's what he was banking on . . .

* * *

Del watched the thin wirey guy with a wild mop of hair going through his Master of Ceremonies routine.   Snippets of poetry and postulating gave way to the kerrang of a lead guitar's strings being struck. "So, without further ado, please welcome - Dead Wretched!"

The drummer began a roll as the lead vocalist and bassist bounded out on to the stage. "It's really great to be here, m-a-n!" the frontman cried into the mike with an almost sarcastic drawl.

Whether or not the crowd understood he was taking the piss out of the rock and roll circus didn't matter to the young punk. His t-shirt was tastefully torn and bore the legend, I'M A MESS. Five minutes of glory and total oblivion was preferable to a lifetime of arse-licking excellence as far as he was concerned. "*Dole Limbo* - 1, 2, 3, 4!"

They were a new name to him, but Del was impressed. Despite the heavy massacre that was being carried out, the tune still held the elementary sound of The Booker T & The MG's instrumental it had been derived from. The lyric, if it could be called that, was a running dialogue of questions and answers that could have come from any DHSS office.   "Have you done any work since you last signed on?" seemed to serve as a chorus.

As they played, Del thought it was an ideal time to take it easy. Grabbing a four pack from the case, he wondered for a moment if he was drinking too much, but he could always put some back later if need be. Standing on the steps, Del surveyed the crowd and saw his gang towards the middle, just behind the punks who had commandeered an area immediately in front of the stage to pogo and do their own thing in. The energy being released by this activity rippled through the crowd like waves.

At the bottom of the steps, he had to tap one of the security guys on the shoulder to make way so he could step down on to the grass. Pushing his way through the crowd, he found himself feeling embarrassed when a large chested girl chose to press forward, just as he ducked low to squeeze past two blokes. His nose touched and buried itself momentarily in her cleavage. Eyes wide, he pulled back in shock. The girl just laughed at his wild-eyed look of surprise.

"Sorry!" he murmured, and pressed on till he reached the area occupied by his friends.

"What was you saying to her?" Alan asked, having noticed him coming part of the way.

"I was saying sorry. I got a faceful of her tits by accident!"

"Fuck!" exclaimed Alan looking over at her. "I'd been more like Oliver Twist!" he said, thinking she was a good looking girl.

"What?" Del wasn't with him.

"Oliver Twist - you know, can I have some more please?"

"Oh, very droll, pal!" Del responded with a grin.

For a while he stayed to talk with his friends, mainly passing comment on two girls who had latched on to Joey and Adam. Then deciding the grumbling of his stomach couldn't be ignored any longer, he decided to go and get something to eat. "Catch you later, Alan!" Del said.

"Where you going?"

"Get something to eat, then back up there!" Del replied, using a thumb to indicate the stage.

Alan nodded. "Okay, later!"

At the nearest hotdog van there was a healthy queue, causing Del to mentally curse. He was going to give up when he noticed the rear door of the van was open to let in some air. Going there, he stood poised in the doorway, watching the two girls rapidly filling orders.

When he caught the brunette girl's eye he didn't waste the opportunity. "Can you swap these for a couple of burgers? I would queue, but I gotta be back on stage in about ten minutes!" he said quickly, holding out a couple of the vouchers Leroy had given him.

Without any fuss, the girl got two burgers ready. "Sauce?"

"Yeah, tomato please!" Del said politely, knowing that good manners didn't cost anything, but often worked wonders.

Armed with the burgers, he made his way back to the steps munching on the food. He was slightly annoyed when he got to the stage and the security guy didn't recognise him as a DJ, forcing him to juggle the food and beer tins so he could free up a hand and pull the stage pass from his pocket.

With a nod the large-built guy stepped aside just long enough to let him pass, before once again blocking the access route. As he stood by the decks finishing his grub, the band bowed out and Martin Langham stepped out to the microphone. The student leader had about five minutes to explain to the audience the facts and feelings that were behind the formation of the Rock Against Racism movement.

From what Del could tell, his speech was getting a mixed reaction. Some were avidly hanging on his every word, while others like the punks and party-goers were getting impatient for some more music. Taking a chance that it would be welcomed, Del searched his selection and pulled out the Heptones' Studio 1 cut, *Be A Man*. Taking the dub side, he dropped the volume down low so it would act as an underlying theme for Martin's speech.

The addition of music earned Del a sideways look from the speaker and a momentary transfer of understanding. Satisfied, Del looked out to the audience as he popped the last bit of food into his mouth.

Yeah, that was more like it!

As he opened a can of light ale, something in the audience caught his eye. Nah can't be, he said to himself, straining for another look. There were too many people in the way for him to be sure, but when a girl moved to one side he knew that he wasn't mistaken. "Shit!"

* * *

Simon had seen Del up on the stage a minute before he had called Dave's attention to the fact. "Look, it's that slag Peterson!"

Dave peered between the heads just as Del was looking directly at him. "He's sussed us!" he hissed.

Simon knew there was no more time left and was immediately reaching for his airhorn. Del was calling to the security guards at the base of the stairs when he heard three long blasts from the claxon.

All hell broke loose as the six bands of GBP members began to punch and kick their way towards the stage. In some areas it was easy to make headway across the thirty or forty yards to the stage, with the panicking crowd parting like the Red Sea did for Moses, but elsewhere things didn't run so smoothly.

Frankie and Alan had turned to see the disturbance erupting behind them, and had seen some familiar faces emerge from the pack. Thinking they were the intended target, they didn't wait to see if the rest were ready to back them up. Frankie scythed his way towards them, hell bent on getting at the guy who he had promised a rematch to. Alan was blazing with rage, having missed out on the previous pay-back. They were quickly joined by Joey and Adam who burst through from another direction and cut into the group.

For a moment it was four against ten, as the rest of the crowd stood around bewildered as fists and boots went into action. It might have remained like that if one of the GBP members hadn't headbutted a black bloke who was standing close to the edge of the fight. Friends of the guy grabbed at the Nazi and threw him to the ground where they started kicking him, prompting other GBP boys to attempt a rescue.

Rebel, having gone to tell the rest of the gang, returned with a force whose added weight scattered the remaining members of the right-wing group. Simon's intended plan that they should all reach the stage at the same time was falling apart at the seems elsewhere in the crowd too. Half of his strike force had got bogged down in isolated scraps.

Dave had to duck as a baseball bat swished through the air right where his head had been. Coming back up from the low crouch, he punched the bat wielder in the face, then grabbed at the security man's shirt and hauled him off the steps into the main body of the group. Boots eagerly sort to damage the fallen victim, but his companions had other ideas and jumped to his defence.

Looking around, Simon realised that the game was up. There were security shirts coming from everywhere, and the GBP members who arrived at the staging area further over to the right were quickly confronted by half a dozen bodybuilder types armed with an assortment of weapons. One charge and the fascists were sent scattering.

"Shit!" cursed Simon, as he gave the single blast retreat signal on the airhorn. He then looked up at Del who stood watching from the stage. Pointing an accusing finger, he screamed, "You're fucking dead Peterson!"

Del responded with a raised middle finger and a silently mouthed, "Fuck off!"

Dave was grateful, as were the others, that Simon had called off the attack. It was fast turning into a nightmare. Even with the mission aborted, they still had to fight their way back to the park gates, and how they managed to dodge the police was one of the great unanswered mysteries of the year.

"This was not a good idea!" Dave said, breathing heavily, as they emerged on to the street and dashed across the road.

"Shut up and follow me!" Simon yelled, putting a fresh spurt into his dash. He had made provision for the attack ending in disaster. Two streets away was a derelict house he had spotted when he was scouting around the area. It had occurred to him that it would make a good hiding place if it became necessary, and now was as good a time as any to head for it.

* * *

Del had watched the chaos unfold below him with a dispassionate feel. It was almost abstract, kind of unreal. The crowd had backed away and let those who were wanting a fight get on with it. Within a minute of the first flare-up, uniformed bobbies were everywhere.

By the time the trouble had ended, the police had managed to make thirty arrests inside the arena. Much to the dismay of the rest of the gang, Alan and Adam had been lifted too, but at least they were better off than some of the Nazis who had to be ferried to hospital.

Leroy stood beside Del. "What happened?" he asked, his glazed expression giving away the fact that he had been in the camper van used by one of the reggae bands, sharing some weed.

"The GBP happened, that's what!" Del replied.

"Say what? What dem come here for?"

"Well it wasn't to lend their support was it?"

"Don't get upset with me man. Stick a disc on. Let's pull the show back together!"

Del looked at him and then out at the crowd. Stupid as it seemed, it was also the only thing to do. The fighting had died down and those going home were in a minority. In some ways, Simon had done the Rock Against Racism a favour, by vividly demonstrating what they were up against far better than any amount of speaking was going to do.

What the hell! Del thought. Removing a single haphazardly from his collection he set it running.

"Tune!" declared Leroy as Jimmy Cliff's voice flowed sweetly from the speakers.

196

"Well they tell me of the pie up in the sky, waiting for me when I die, but between the day your born and when you die . . . "

The Harder They Come, The Harder They Fall seemed the perfect song for what had just happened.

* * *

Inside the house, Simon waited about ten minutes after the last siren had died down. He was getting angry at the barracking he was getting from the remaining members of the group. Out of sixty, he could only be sure the six with him had got out in one piece.

"You fucked up, fucked up real good!" Terry accused, looking out at the overgrown garden from the shattered window with its filth encrusted shards of glass.

Dave was squatting with his back against the wall. He was as pissed off as the rest of them, but he wasn't directing it at Simon. In his mind the failure had been down to that fucking skinhead from Brixton.

Simon turned on Terry, his eyes blazing. He wanted to tear the guy apart, but a voice in the back of his head held him back. "Fuck you!"

"Terry, Bob, the rest of you shut the fuck up!" declared Dave. Standing up, he pointed across at them. "You knew this wasn't gonna be a picnic, so stop moaning, okay?"

"Yeah, but . . . " started Bob.

"Yeah but nothing!" Dave declared adamantly. He knew that they had had him as a leader too long to oppose his decision. By propping up Simon's shaky hold on the group, he could see them through the feeling of discontent. His and Simon's eyes met and an understanding formed, while the rest of the gang lapsed into silence.

"Look, I'm gonna check if the coast is clear," Dave said. "Then we can get back on our home turf!"

Slipping out from the back door, Dave edged his way cautiously to the front garden. Ignoring the gate, he crossed to where the bushes met the jungle that had once been a well kept lawn. Finding a gap, he then squeezed forward until he got a reasonable view of the road beyond. Looking first to the left he saw it was clear, but to the right there was someone heading this way and he quickly ducked back.

Catching his breath, he edged his face forward again. It was just a girl - and she hadn't seen him. At first he had thought it was a copper or a militant. *Thank fuck for that*, he said to himself.

197

He was about to slip back to the house and tell his companions that the coast was clear, when he suddenly realised who the girl was. He backed off and edged towards the gate.

What a result!

* * *

Suzi's mind was a bit fudged by frustration. She mentally berated herself for spending so much time at Gillian's only to come away empty handed. Clive had given her a lift to a dealer he knew in the Finsbury Park area, but it was the same story all over. Things were dry, try again in two weeks.

She was so wrapped up in her own problems that she hadn't even noticed the house, let alone Dave hiding down behind the end bush. Dave held his breath as she levelled with the gate then jumped from his hiding place. Suzi barely had time to realise someone was there when a hand clamped hard across her mouth, and an arm around her waist lifted her toes off the ground.

Fear gripped like a tight knot threatening to choke her, as she saw the street disappear and become replaced by first a hedge and then a mass of undergrowth, as Dave dragged her backwards. Struggling like mad, she tried to dig her heels into the attacker's shins, catching them once as the wall of a house came into view.

The hand on her mouth wrenched her head back and a harsh voice hissed into her ear. "Do that again and I'll break your neck!"

She was so scared that her bladder felt like it was bursting for relief. The strain placed on her neck made her fear for her life, while her racing mind had difficulty accepting what was happening. Over and over, the voice in her head was saying, "Oh, God, no, no!"

"What the fuck you doing?" cried Terry as Dave entered the front room and threw the punk girl on the floor.

Winded by the fall and petrified with fear, she lay sobbing, surrounded by the surprised group.

"What's this?" asked Simon.

Dave grabbed at Suzi's hair and hauled her face up so they could see it. "Recognise this slut? When we chased Peterson the other night this is the girl who was with him!"

"Alright!" Simon said gleefully, moving nearer to take a closer look.

"Del?" said Suzi blankly, her chin trembling as she looked up at Simon with tear blotched eyes.

"Yeah, Del!" smiled Simon, gripping her face in the fingers of one hand and shaking it. "He caused us a lot of aggravation, girl. He owes us - you owe us!"

"No!" Suzi cried weakly.

"Oh yes!" Simon said coldly, releasing his hold.

Terry knew what was intended. "No fucking way!" he said, setting his jaw line hard with determination.

Simon grabbed at him, snapping, "You'll do what I say!"

Terry shook the hand off and stepped back. "Fuck you!" he said. Then pointing at Suzi he added, "This ain't me pal! I'm going!"

"Yeah, well fuck off then, I don't need you!" Simon declared.

Terry looked at the others. He could see that only Dave and Simon were comfortable with the idea. "Bob, Greg, you gonna get involved?" he asked.

Bob shook his head, while Greg just looked wildly at everyone.

"Come on, lets go!"

Bob and Terry moved for the back door and let a flood of sunlight in as they opened it. To Suzi, it promised freedom and she suddenly jumped up and broke into a run.

Dave caught her after a few steps and slapped her viciously around the face, sending her spinning with a bloody nose on to a dilapidated armchair. Quickly he pinned her into a crouch position, struggling to stifle her shrieks in the chair by pushing her face into it.

Greg was unnerved by the animalistic noises that were escaping muffled from her throat. The grunts of exertion from Dave, and his shout of "Pin her fucking hands down!" as she tried desperately to release her head, left Greg shaking his head.

Simon knelt behind her and reached around her hips to undo her jeans. A louder moan escaped her throat as they suddenly loosened. Victoriously, Simon pulled them halfway down her thighs and wrenched at the delicate underwear, ripping them completely off.

Feeling the touch of cool air on her naked behind goaded Suzi into trying to get free again. Pushing up, she found that Dave was able to cope easily with her efforts, and pushing back to try and slide under his grip caused an electrical jolt of shock, as she realised she had unwittingly aided Simon in his penetration.

Greg found it all too much. Dumbly he walked for the door. He wanted nothing to do with it and after pausing momentarily to regard the struggling trio, he left.

Suzi gave up the fight after the realisation that there was nothing she could do to prevent it caused a numbing blanket to descend over her mind. It blotted out all but the rocking motion of Simon's thrusting, and the pain that came from her unyielding vagina.

"No pain, no gain!" declared Simon as she winced from his attempts to push further into her dry cavity.

After Simon had finished, Dave tried to force her to have oral sex with him, but her teeth remained clamped hard together and no amount of force or threats was going to make her submit to him. Frustrated, he let her slide to the floor, zipped himself up and kicked her in the teeth. "Suck on that!"

Simon laughed, spitting at her trembling form as she buried her face in her hands, trying to hide and stem the pain in her mouth.

"Let's go, eh?"

"Yeah!"

The two occupants of the patrolling police car were stunned to see a girl staggering blindly along the curb, her shirt in tatters with one breast exposed and jeans burst open, showing her pubic hair off to all and sundry. Pulling up behind her, the girl didn't even seem to notice them.

Paul Morgan, the passenger, jumped out. "Hey, love, what's happened?"

Suzi turned around like an unseeing automotive, letting them see her damaged face clearly for the first time.

"Jesus!" the young cop breathed in shock, dashing forward as the girl collapsed in a heap.

Del was becoming worried about Suzi. She should have turned up hours ago. He feared that perhaps with all the trouble there had been, she might have been searched and busted for possessing drugs. Sitting on the steps watching The Regulars perform, he noticed that Jenny was with Leroy and they were both heading his way. He looked to see if Suzi was with them too, but couldn't see her.

"Hello Jenny, didn't think you was coming girl. Should have been here earlier. Well then again, maybe not. There was a bit of trouble you know!"

He froze when he realised Jenny's stony look wasn't going to soften. "Something the matter?"

"It's Suzi, she's in hospital!" Jenny's tones were sober and deadly serious.

Del was shocked. "Hospital? Why, what's up? What hospital?"

"She's been raped," Jenny said flatly, spelling it out. "The cops came round and told me - she gave them my address!"

Not that Del heard her explanation. He was feeling strange, kind of sick and disorientated. Jenny took hold of his arm. "Del?"

Taking his face in her hand, she guided it so she could see into his eyes. "I've got a taxi outside the gate, let's go and see her!"

Gently she pulled him up and took his hand to guide him through the crowd.

"Leroy . . . " Derek said numbly.

"Don't worry man, I'll look after your records!"

"What's up?" Rebel asked, as Del and Jenny came past her. She felt worried when Del acted as if she wasn't even there.

Frankie came over to her. "Where's he going?"

"I don't know, I think something's wrong."

"Like what?"

"Oh shit! Suzi!" Rebel said, looking into his eyes. "I think it's Suzi!"

Frankie didn't want to let Del go on his own, and together with Rebel, he headed after his mate. By the time they got to the gate though, they could only watch as the taxi pulled away with Del and Jenny in it.

I live off you and you live off me,
And the whole world lives off of everybody
See we've gotta be exploited
See we've gotta be exploited
By somebody!
I LIVE OFF YOU - X-RAY SPEX (1978)

CHAPTER FIFTEEN

DEL sat silently in the corridor outside the single room that held Suzi. They had to wait while a C.I.D. officer attempted to find out what had happened. A little way down the corridor was a grieving family who had lost their young son in a road accident. Their crying and wailing made Del shiver. He felt so lost, and despite Jenny's company, so alone.

The corridor was darkened by the shadows of an evening sun through its few windows. Nervously Del bit at his fingernails, then when he ran out of nails he chewed at the skin surrounding them. He was only dimly aware of Jenny hugging him and rubbing her hand on his back. "Don't worry Del, I'm sure Suzi's gonna be fine!"

"Listen, there's a canteen up by casualty. You wanna get a cup of tea?" said the duty nurse from her desk situated in an alcove with the ward pharmacy behind her.

"Fancy it, Del?" asked Jenny.

Del shook his head and murmured. "No, I'll stay here."

"They do takeaway," the nurse added helpfully.

Jenny was grateful for her concern. "If I get us one, you promise me you'll drink it?"

"Yeah, okay," Del said.

"Where is it?" Jenny asked, getting up with her handbag in her hand.

"First right, second left!" the nurse said, pointing back the way they had come in forty-five minutes earlier.

Del sat huddled with his head down, until Jenny returned with two polystyrene cups and a plastic spoon. "I've put sugar in it already. It might need stirring though."

Del gratefully accepted the cup then felt a pang of collapsing emotions as his hand trembled violently.

"Hey, hey, hey," Jenny said softly, taking the cup from his grip.

Del just kept on staring blankly at his shaking hand. To break the spell, Jenny pushed her hand into his and squeezed it hard. "Listen up Del, don't go losing yourself, man - that girl in there needs you. You gotta be strong!"

His chest heaved heavily as he loosened his grip on the tension he felt. "Yeah, guess so!"

Lighting a cigarette, Jenny passed it to Del. He had actually given up six months ago, but he felt like one now. Accepting it, he puffed on it, alternating sips of tea with clouds of smoke. The nurse looked on, knowing that there was a no smoking regulation in the hospital away from casualty and the canteen, but deciding to turn a blind eye.

The cop came out just as Del finished the cigarette. "How is she?" he asked, getting to his feet.

"In shock I guess. The doctor's in there with her at the moment."

"So who are you?" Del's voice was harsher than he had wanted it to sound.

"Detective Sergeant Roist - Islington C.I.D."

"What did she say then?"

"Not a lot really. She was grabbed off the street and dragged into a house where she was raped. We're having difficulty finding out which street or the description of the attacker or attackers. We'll try again tomorrow." Taking out his notepad and pencil, the policeman wrote down the number of his station and his extension. "If you find out more from her, please give me a call!"

Del accepted it from him, then was overcome by an aggrieved sense of foul play. "How come you get to see her, the doctor gets to see her, everyone gets to fucking see her, and I've gotta sit here like a fucking lemon for an hour not knowing what's going on!"

His voice rose steadily with each word until he was shouting the last sentence. An irate man in a white coat emerged from the room. "What's going on here, who's making all that noise?"

"I am!" Del admitted. "I've been sitting here the last hour waiting to see my girlfriend and no one will tell me how she is or what's happening with her!"

Pointing to Suzi's room, the doctor asked, "This your girlfriend?"

"Yeah!"

"And you are?"

"Derek Peterson!"

"Hold on there and I'll see if she wants to see you!"

203

With that he disappeared back into the room, while the cop patted Del on the shoulder and told him to take it easy. Halfway down the corridor, D.S. Roist turned and called out to remind them to give him a call if they learned anything new.

The doctor returned after two minutes. "Okay, you can see her."

As Del went to go through the door, the doctor stopped him. "She looks worse than she is. There's some facial bruising and there's a couple of broken teeth we've had to seal with dental cement. It looks messy because frankly I'm not a dentist. He'll be by tomorrow morning to see what can be done about that. Also treat her gently, she is suffering from a mixture of shock and hysteria. I'll be back in five minutes to administer some sedatives. Then you'll have to go. Okay?"

"Yeah, thanks doc," Del responded

The room was sterile and empty except for the bed and cabinet. Suzi was lying there in a white gown, staring at the flowers a nurse had taken from one of the wards to brighten up the room and make it feel less impersonal.

Del felt a surge of sympathy for her. There was bruising on the throat that the doctor hadn't mentioned, her lips were puffy, and her cheek was an angry purple colour, but if anything it was less intense than that received at the hands of the squatters. The real damage had been done to her mind.

"Hello babe!" he said, walking around the bed to her side.

Her eyes wandered slowly from the flowers and looked at him, almost through him. Like a little child, she murmured almost silently, "They hurt me!"

"I know . . . I've been told." He thought he'd spare her the need for an admission. He just wanted to hold her, to tell her it was all right, but she shrank from his hand he had intended to stroke her forehead with.

Bitter words escaped her lips. "Don't touch me!"

Del was shocked. "Hey, it's me!"

"Please don't touch me!" she pleaded hysterically

"All right, I ain't gonna touch ya. See . . . " he said, holding his hands up in the air.

She looked and the wild expression softened. "I don't wanna be touched," she said in a deadpan tone.

Jenny could see there was a tear in Del's eye as he took the chair from the other side of the cabinet and sat next to the bed. Each move he made was drawn out, slow and deliberate, so as not to startle Suzi.

204

"Jenny's here!" Del said pointing to her, mainly because he didn't know what else to say.

"Jenny?" said Suzi with a stir of interest.

"Yes, I'm here honey!" Jenny said, coming over to the bed and sitting where she could look into Suzi's eyes.

Suzi's lip moved as if struggling to form a word, then began trembling as tears welled in her eyes. Jenny's hand slowly reached out for the girl's cheek with a gentle caress. The touch caused Suzi to end the struggle to keep her emotions down. Racked with sobbing, she grabbed at Jenny and buried her face into the black girl's shoulder, her hands clawing in anguish at Jenny's arms.

Del looked on helplessly as Jenny cradled Suzi in her arms.

"I couldn't stop them . . . He said I wanted him, but I didn't. I didn't and he didn't care. He just laughed and forced me!"

"Who did?" Del demanded angrily.

Suzi lifted her head to look him in the face. Her eyes were bloodshot and wet with tears, and mascara streaked her cheeks, marking the path they had used in running down her face.

"That skinhead you've been having all the aggro with. He said you had caused him trouble today and he was going to make you pay. You?! He fucking raped me - ME!"

Jenny pulled her head back into her shoulder.

"Simon!" Del snapped. He got up and walked straight out of the room with Jenny's voice ringing in his ears, asking where he was going.

Only one thing was on his mind. Quickening his pace, he threaded through the hospital corridors, went out of the main doors and started running. He ran and ran. It didn't matter where, he just kept running until his lungs were burning with the exertion.

Eventually he stopped next to a modern sculpture commissioned by the nearby insurance company headquarters. Panting and fighting to control his breath, Del felt alone enough to shed some tears. It was all his fault. He should have kept her out of it. There was no way Simon should have put it on her.

Bastard!

Del lifted his head and shouted to the stars. "Fucking bastard!" And with those words he lashed out with his boot at the blob that amazingly passed as top of the range art.

Emotionally drained, he wandered around aimlessly until he came upon a tube station. He went down to the platform serving the District and Circle line and waiting for a train, staring right through the people who looked at his raw eyes.

Simon was feeling okay with things. He had been told by the Desk Sergeant at Islington nick that only three of his boys faced serious charges of affray. The rest had been booked under breach of the peace and everyone knew that it was just a Mickey Mouse charge, requiring a minimum of supporting evidence. Two officers backing each other's story or a single public witness was enough.

Dave was still solidly behind him, and the half dozen hangers-on quite liked the fact that they had become the gang's hardcore, albeit temporarily. Those he had fallen out with, like Ferret, Bob and Greg, would be back with their tails between their legs - that he was sure of. Even if they didn't, he couldn't care less. He didn't need them. Once the story had hit the newspapers he would have an army of volunteers to pick from.

Propping himself on the bar with his back to the door, he waved his glass to attract the barman's attention.

"Be with you in a minute!" the barman said as he set up a Guinness for the old boy in the corner.

Dave was telling the others his version of what had happened at the festival and failed to notice Del enter the pub through the door which had been locked open to let the humidity find an escape. The barman saw him march over to Simon and thought nothing of it. Just another skinhead. That was until Del swept up the empty glass sitting in front of Simon and smashed it into his face.

"Fuck!" cried Simon, knocking over a stool as he tried to back away from the pain. There was no escape though as Del thrust the glass into his neck and Simon felt the jagged edge of the glass bite again.

Dave and the other gang members quickly came to Simon's defence as soon as they heard his first cry of pain. Del tried to turn the weapon on them too, but he was badly outnumbered, and they had little trouble disarming him.

Now they could tear him apart at their leisure, but even as he was being kicked unconscious, Del was grimly satisfied with what he had achieved with the glass. The last thing he saw through the sea of legs laying into him, was the barman holding a bloodied beer towel over Simon's face, trying to stem the flow.

Got you, you fucking bastard!

It was a strange netherworld into which Del slipped. Silent and pitch black. Solid, yet flowing like the undercurrent of a river and occasionally punctured by a beacon-like flash. Then there were the disembodied sensations, not unlike pins and needles and motion sickness, that flowed around in the darkness, ebbing against him like rippling waves. They caressed his being, teasing him, before fading again into the unseen distance.

How long he was suspended in this world seemed irrelevant. It didn't matter at all. In fact nothing really mattered because nothing existed. He didn't have the will to escape and he didn't feel trapped. It was just him and this nothingness.

Del may have forsaken time, but it had not forsaken him. At first the ending of this suspended state was suspected rather than fully perceived. The blackness was gradually replaced by a turmoil of sensations boiling around him, and then he was overcome by a feeling of being driven by an upward velocity that was unmistakably nauseating.

Then came the sensation of having broken the surface of some oceanic depth, coupled with a burst of intense light. Red at first, then brilliant white. It intensified further before settling down into blurred outlines that announced his arrival back in the real world.

The nurse saw Derek's eyelids open and shut several times, blinking at the lamp beaming at him from above his head. In an effort to make it easier on him, she twisted the lamp's hood away from his face.

"Hello . . . How are you?" she asked. After feeling his forehead, she took her thermometer from her breast pocket, shook it, and placed it under his tongue. While she waited for it to do its job, she found the pulse in his left wrist and began to count his heart rate.

Del surrendered like a weakened lamb. He had no choice given his present condition and was still not sure that the sensation of drifting had finished with him yet. The only real awareness he had was of dull pain all over his body, both inside and out.

"Where am I?" had been the intended words, but they were blurred by a hoarse gurgle.

"Stay still while I take a reading!" ordered the nurse, scooping the thermometer up from his chest and placing it back in his mouth. She noted that the pulse was slowing a little, but that was to be expected with the mixture being fed into him by the saline drip.

"You're lucky to be alive," she said quite matter of fact, as if she was imparting a piece of trivial gossip. "We had to use twelve pints of blood and two of plasma before we could stabilise your condition!"

Del did not really grasp the significance of what the nurse said until he tried to move. Muscles refused to co-operate, but the trying caused a wave of pain to wash throughout his body, and his midriff section in particular.

"Ah, fuck!"

The words broke from his lips clearly and concisely, prompting the nurse to berate him like a school teacher. "Lay still you silly boy. Your kidneys will need time to heal before they are fully functional again!"

"Kidneys?" queried Del, giving up the fight and letting himself go floppy.

"Don't you remember anything?" she asked, removing the thermometer from his mouth and reading the temperature - ninety-nine point four. Replacing it in the pocket, she took the clipboard from the end of his bed and noted the time, the pulse reading and his temperature.

"There was a fight . . . that's all!" responded Del.

"Ah well. You were admitted four days ago with multiple stab wounds, one of which had punctured your kidneys and gave us quite a time. Minor fractures of the cheekbone, left wrist and index finger plus numerous contusions."

"Sounds like a failed M.O.T. report!" Del said, trying not to laugh because it only added to his pain. Then he realised she had said four days ago. "Jesus, why do I still feel tired?"

"Well at least you're not a write-off!" she retorted in kind to his car theme.

Ralph had treated Simon with kid gloves for the past two days. Like a bear with a sore head, there was an element of danger in the way the skinhead brooded. What didn't help a squeamish Ralph was having to look at the bloody stitches that lined Simon's face. Starting with a uneven star shape just above the forehead, they ran down, missing the left eye, before starting again at the cheek right down to the jaw-line. An extra two stitches had been inserted into a smaller wound in his neck.

Despite being wounded so severely, Simon had retained the foresight not to go to a hospital local to the incident, but insisted that

Dave drove him to Saint Thomas' in Central London. There he had explained it away as a motiveless attack in the street by persons unknown. A couple of phoney descriptions kept the records straight and the cops off his back. They couldn't prove he was involved in the Finsbury Park fiasco anyway.

Dave was morose, racked with guilt for not seeing Del enter the pub. Simon knew it wasn't his fault, but didn't say as much. He was suffering so why shouldn't Dave and the others? It was only Greta who he'd permit to be close to him. She fussed over him like his Mum used to when he was a kid, and he enjoyed the attention.

The attack on the Rock Against Racism gathering might have failed, but the publicity generated by sensationalism in the press was already paying dividends. When the morning post arrived, Ralph gleefully eyed the heap of letters asking for membership details, offering support and words of encouragement.

His joy wasn't shared by Dave and Simon, who both felt let down by the way the gang had fallen apart. Instead of everyone returning to the fold, some faces had not been seen for days and others had called to say they were dropping out of sight for a while because of the press coverage. Only Roy could be convinced that the photos in the 'papers were too blurred to be used to round them up.

The following day, Del had to endure a parade of visitors. The police were the first in, wanting to know who had attacked him, but he just said he didn't know and pointed them back in the direction of the pub landlord. Then his mother had spent an hour at his bedside offering little sympathy and much anger that he had adopted his brother's lifestyle and nearly ended up dead and buried like him too.

It was just after an unappealing lunch that Leroy arrived with two other blokes. One Del recognised as Martin Langham from the college and festival gigs and the other introduced himself as Steve Sergeant. "I believe we have a mutual problem in the shape of the GBP? And it occurred to me we could be of assistance to each other!"

"We? Who's we?" Del demanded, wondering why the hell Leroy had brought two virtual strangers with him.

"We're an organisation who can help you get revenge for what you and your girlfriend have been through . . . "

"Hold up!" Del indicated he wanted to think by using his hands to call for silence. "By organisation, I take it you're some kind of left-wing group, yeah?"

"That's about the size of it," admitted Steve.

"Forget it!" Del declared.

"Why, what's wrong?" Martin asked, sensing the mood had turned sour in the twinkling of a eyelid.

"When I was in Leroy's place, I read a newspaper story about skinheads and it was one of your lot who wrote it. If you think the GBP are the only fuckers you should try looking closer to home!"

"He was talking about racists!" responded Martin, guessing it was the feature following the attack on his student union meeting.

"Well he didn't fucking say that did he? As far as he was concerned, we're all scum!" Del was feeling slightly aggrieved as he recalled the context of the article.

"Well, the only thing I can suggest is . . . "

"Don't suggest anything, pal. You're already out of order!"

Martin took umbrage at Derek's remark and responded with a scathing, "How can we be out of order, eh? We're fighting the intolerance and racism that this scum perpetrate!"

"Yeah, well I was beaten up down the Roxy because of that fucking article. I ain't a racist, but who's gonna believe me after reading that shit? You just use what I am as the bogeyman to justify your own actions, like some kind of promotional device. I'm the one whose gotta live with the consequences, not you!"

Fuming, Del used the cuff of the night-gown to wipe away a fleck of spittle he could feel on his lower lip.

"What was said isn't untrue. The GBP are skinheads!" pointed out Steve.

"Yeah, but without comparisons it ain't strictly true either!" Del argued back. "Nobody bothered to point out there was another side to the story. Not all skinheads support the GBP and not all racists are skinheads either. You bastards are fucking using us as much as the GBP are. You're fighting for liberty? What about my liberties? You say your fighting oppression and ignorance? From where I'm standing you're all the fucking same!"

"What?" cried Martin in outrage. "We're pole opposites!"

"Yeah, only if you think in terms of a straight line, but on a circle you're bang next door to each other. You're just too blind to see it!"

"Forget it," Steve said. "Let's go!"

"Might as well he's so wrapped up in himself, he can't see he's helping the fascists!" retorted Martin in spite.

"Yeah, fuck you too!" snapped back Del.

As they left, Del turned to Leroy. "What did you bring those arseholes here for? I've had enough of nutters to last me a lifetime!"

"Hey man, I didn't know they were gonna be like that!" Leroy offered as an apology.

"It ain't your fault mate. You did what you thought was right. I'm just wondering if I done what was right by you?"

Leroy walked to the window, then looked at Del lying in the bed. The rasta shrugged his shoulders and spoke softly. "Hey man, everybody got the right to live the way they wanna live. Jah tell you that! You've done nothing wrong to me. It's dem coloured glasses again man. There's a lot of people wearing dem these days!"

"Heard anything of Suzi? I asked the nurse, but she couldn't get through to the hospital she's at."

Leroy took on a grave expression. "I was gonna tell you later man."

"Tell me what?" A knot of dread gripped Del.

"Jenny went to visit yesterday and find that Suzi's parents had come and taken her back home with them. She ask the hospital where it was, but dem say they were asked not to tell anyone."

Del was stunned. It felt like a part of him had died. Worse because he didn't know if it was what Suzi wanted because he hadn't had the chance to say goodbye or hear it from her own mouth.

Fuck! Fuck! FUCK!

Ralph McLare was preparing himself for probably the most important GBP meeting to date when the television's evening news caught his attention. There had been a riot involving members of the National Front and various anti-fascist groups in the streets of Lewisham.

Eagerly, Ralph absorbed all he could from the facts and footage, certain that he could turn it to his advantage when addressing the gathering later on. By all accounts it would be the largest attendance to date at a GBP meeting if the pledges and promises were anything to go by.

After grabbing something to eat, Ralph drove by the office and picked up Simon and Greta. As they headed for the library where the hall had been booked, it seemed that Simon was finally back to his old self. He was cracking jokes as they arrived at the library, but their humour was cut dead by what they found.

Ralph halted the car against the curb some way down from the meeting place. He could see a handful of uniformed police standing outside, turning away people who were hoping to attend the meeting, after taking what could only be their names and addresses.

"What the . . . ?" Simon peered hard through the windscreen. He didn't like the feel of it at all. He watched a small group of party members walking away from the library towards their car and waited until they were level with the passenger door before winding the window down. "Richard!" he hissed across to the forty year old milkman who had just been appointed to the GBP's Executive Council.

Richard bent down to look into the window and saw Simon and his leader. "Ralph, don't go there my friend!"

"Why, what's happening?" asked Ralph.

"I'm not too sure. They're refusing to let the meeting go ahead and they want to talk with you. They're putting heavy emphasis on their meaning of talk too!"

"Did they have a court order to postpone the meeting?" Ralph didn't pay much attention to the personal threat, confident that he could talk his way out of any situation they cared to concoct.

Richard shook his head. "Can't be certain, but they didn't show me one."

"Well then, they've got no right to do this!" exclaimed Ralph, as if it was going to make a difference.

"Right or not, they're doing it!" Simon pointed out to him.

"But they shouldn't!" Ralph was irate. Knowing that the blockade was illegal didn't help because, dressed as he was in the full GBP regalia, he couldn't approach the police to argue his case without risking arrest under the 1930s law banning political uniforms in public places. "Damn!" he swore, and banged his hands on the steering wheel.

"Well, that's the end of that!" declared Simon.

"Not necessarily!" smiled Ralph as a thought occurred to him. Leaning over towards Simon, he whispered in his ear, "I think it would be a good idea to see if our American friend knows anyone in a position to stir things up. If they haven't got a court order . . . "

"Then they've got to pack up and go!" Simon said, filling in the gap. "Yeah, could be worth a try."

212

Ralph prepared to drive off. "Stay by your phone Richard. We might yet have our way!" And with that he turned the car around and headed off in search of Howard.

As their car passed by the library, a dark blue Rover fired up its engine. The passenger lowered his camera with its zoom lens, gently into his lap. "Stay with them!" he ordered as the driver pulled out behind Ralph's car and went in lazy pursuit of it.

Howard was surprised to see the deputation on his doorstep. At first he was bewildered while Ralph excitedly explained the situation, and then he became angry when he found out that the costumed clown expected him to actively get involved.

"Come into the kitchen!" he said, making it clear he wanted to have it out with Ralph alone.

Greta and Simon just accepted it and settled themselves into the armchairs that adorned the living-room. Simon waited for them to leave and then helped himself to a drink from the executive bar Howard had in his apartment. He had just recapped the Southern Comfort bottle when the sound of ranting began in the kitchen. Looking to Greta, Simon grinned. "The course of true love never runs smoothly!"

Greta smiled back. She wasn't too sure she understood what he meant, but his expression told her it was English humour.

Steve Sergeant was sitting in the backroom of the bookshop that fronted his operations centre. On a notice board above his head was a series of photographs. Several had been taken at the Finsbury Park debacle, while others were cropped enlargements containing the head and shoulders of various subjects.

Ralph McLare was first, with a basic biographical description below it. Next was Greta or Eva Stein as the caption stated. Her biographical details were limited to country of origin. After that was Simon's picture with the details of his mercenary career and jailing in Angola. Then there was the photograph of the mysterious Howard. They had only been able to ascertain his first name from the unsuspecting neighbour who thought she was talking to the television licence people. Other shots included the GBP office, Ralph and Howard's homes and various cars used by and places frequented by the subjects.

213

Thomas Gearheart, a black American, entered from the bookshop beyond. "Yo, Stevie. The team you put on that guy have just called in. Apparently our Howard X is a countryman of mine!"

"How did they find that out?" Steve asked.

"They tailed him to the U.S. Embassy!"

"Visa application?"

"Nope. Staff entrance!"

"Oh really?" mused Steve with genuine surprise. He knew some people who would be very interested in identifying the subject for him, providing of course he shared his intelligence with them. If his suspicions were confirmed it would be a real feather in his cap.

It was four-thirty in the morning when Simon was rudely awakened by the sounds of someone trying to break the door in at the foot of the building. At first he didn't comprehend what was going on, then he realised it was an attack of some sort.

Rushing out into the office, he picked up the baseball bat and went out to the landing beyond, just as the door gave way. "Come on you fuckers!" he roared, lifting the bat ready to strike the first person who tried to reach him.

A shadowy figure came in from the cold. "Drop it - armed police!"

"Prove it!" shouted back the skinhead.

Suddenly everything went dark, then Simon was blinded by a sudden flood of brilliant light. Adjusting his vision he could just about make out a flak jacket and arms raised pointing a pistol at him. Letting the bat fall and clatter down the stairs, he raised his hands.

With the area secured, other officers rushed up the stairs and spun Simon around. Pushing him hard against the wall, they cuffed him, read him his rights and led him downstairs to an awaiting patrol car.

On the way to the station, Simon refused to answer any questions or be goaded by their childish references designed to provoke the egotistically macho. He knew the situation was lost - the presence of armed officers said as much. The only thing he could wonder now was what did they have on him.

Back at the station, he was led past a series of interview rooms, each with a window. Through each he saw in turn, Ralph, Greta and Howard. Now he was certain the game was up and he felt his confidence disappearing. Meekly he allowed himself to be stripped of his possessions and ended up in a solitary cell awaiting the police's next move.

Breakfast had been served over three hours ago and Simon was beginning to wonder what sort of psychological games the law was playing. He was approaching his fifth hour of being held without charge when the door unlocked to reveal two uniformed police officers. "Come on, son," one of them said, grabbing at his arm. "Time to sing for your supper!"

"Get off will you?" Simon said with bored detachment.

"Like this or in cuffs, it's up to you," the copper answered.

Shrugging, Simon accepted the restraining hand and allowed them to lead him to one of the interview rooms he had passed earlier. Inside were two guys in civilian suits, surrounded by a minimum of furniture. A table, three chairs and a bench on the opposite wall. The expected bright light was suspended above the suspect's side of the table.

The cops released Simon when the more portly member of the duo told them they could leave. "If you need anything, Sir, we'll be down the hall, one of the uniforms said.

"Maybe later, Constable," answered back the second member of the team. Then as the two officers left them alone, he turned to Simon. "Sit down please."

It was both firm and polite, making Simon wonder who he was dealing with. "Who are you then? C.I.D. never say please!"

"There you go, Tom. Our young friend isn't the moron you thought he was!"

"If that's supposed to wind me up, forget it all right. It got boring enough when Laurel and Hardy out there were doing it!" Simon informed them.

"No, seriously. My friend thought you were just a two-bit punk. I wagered you were more than that. Looks like I won doesn't it?" said the portly guy with a beaming, almost charming smile.

"Everybody's entitled to their own opinion," Simon replied flatly. If this was going to be the sweet and sour session, he wasn't going to be any more responsive to the nice guy as he was the nasty one.

"No, you're right about us. We're a different kind of cop. "They look after a single borough," he said, indicating the building and its people beyond the closed door. "We look after the entire nation. You could say I'm Number Five and he is Number Six."

215

The cryptic message wasn't wasted on Simon. He knew instantly that they were Military Intelligence.

"I thought that would make an impression!" declared Five, still smiling sweetly in spite of the stunned expression on Simon's face. Continuing, the government agent spelled it out for Simon. "You've put us in an awkward situation with that Noddy outfit of yours. Why didn't you relax and return to normal life after that episode in the bush?"

"A change is as good as a rest," Simon offered sarcastically.

"Don't get flippant boy. You're not talking to PC Plod now!"

"Always the same story," mused Six. "They think they're the big fish in the pond until they meet us and realise all too late that they were only minnows!"

Simon knew the situation was heavy. He didn't need them to point it out. The fact that the cops were reduced to mere errand boys indicated how serious things had become.

"You know this man?" asked Five, pulling a photo from a dossier file and dropping it in front of Simon.

Simon looked down at it. "Yeah, that's Howard. You know that already. You had him in here last night!"

"Correct. Ten out of ten. Go to the top of the class. Now, what do you suppose our friend Howard does for a living?"

Deciding that they already knew, Simon felt it would be more beneficial to play ball and see where it led. "I don't know exactly, but he's some kind of trade official at the U.S. Embassy!"

"He does work for the American government, but not as a trade rep. Your friend and mine is an operative for the C.I.A.!"

"Do what?" declared Simon, surprised.

"Yes, afraid so! Now normally, we accept the presence of allied agents on British soil because we have the same reciprocal arrangement in the States. But here we have an allied agent dabbling in a situation that is detrimental and threatening to the security of the realm. Why do you think he was doing that?"

"Search me," Simon responded, still trying to digest the revelation about Howard and wondering what new light it placed on their association.

"What's it feel like to be suckered?" asked Six.

"Yeah, but how? Why?" voiced Simon.

216

"The Americans say he's a maverick. Turned rogue for some reason. They insisted on taking him back to the States to interrogate him. See if he's been got at."

"That makes even less sense," declared Simon. "What can the Russians gain from sponsoring a right-wing party?"

"Our thoughts exactly, but his transfer was approved by those on high. So it's an explanation we have to live with."

"So where's the problem in all this?" asked Simon, knowing the story didn't end there.

"The intelligence that exposed Howard was supplied to us by a British left-wing organisation. Its disclosure could have led to a major diplomatic incident, wrecking the close ties we have with our American allies. To prevent that, we had to pay a price. A heavy price. Within the next three months, a motion will go through Parliament, curtailing the freedom of right-wing groups, while not affecting their opposite number. Then the GBP will be formally disbanded after an inquiry has discredited them. We also had to provide a bit of tit for tat intelligence concerning the sexual practises of one West Country branch of the Front, which will itself prove good ammunition for the press."

Then, Five took over. "The other problem is you and keeping you silent. If you had been working for the Russians that would have been dandy. Up before the judge in the morning and twenty-five years in Dartmoor. But you were effectively working for the Americans and the trial would only lead to the publicity we are trying to avoid. We don't even think you could live up to the Official Secrets pledge you took on entering the army. Problems, problems . . . "

For a moment, Simon was sure he would face a summary execution, but Five was about to put his mind at rest.

"We have found a solution however, or rather the Yanks did. As you can imagine, they are more than a little embarrassed about the whole affair and have offered to take full responsibility for you."

"What are you saying?"

"We want you to go into voluntary exile. Basically leave and never come back. There is a sweetener to this bitter pill though. Our American friends have agreed to employ your talents in Columbia and Paraguay - after suitable training, of course. In return you'll be given several operational and residential addresses as well as a healthy bank account. Well, what do you say young man?"

"Do I have a choice?"

"Do you need me to spell the alternative out to you?" warned Five.

217

"Sunnier climes it is then," declared Simon. In fact the more he thought about it, the more he realised it might be the best move he ever made.

"Oh by the way, recognise this?" asked the agent, showing Simon two sealed plastic bags containing items of crockery and cutlery.

"Someone's washing up," responded Simon, seeing the marks of a past meal still on them.

"Correct, but more importantly they are yours from breakfast!" declared the guy, obviously enjoying the sense of theatre.

Simon looked at him in a puzzled way.

"Insurance dear boy. Right now there is a forensics expert going over your cell, collecting all the hair and clothing traces he can find. If for any reason you return to the U.K., this collection will be added to the next suitable unsolved murder and you will be tried and convicted for it. During the trial, a renowned psychiatrist will provide the evidence to have you ruled criminally insane with megalomaniac tendencies. Basically, you will be detained at Her Majesty's pleasure and nobody will believe another word you say! So if you breath a word about this little fiasco, it will be dismissed as the rantings of a mad man!"

"Cute!" Simon said.

"Yes, I thought so!"

"Okay, what happens to Greta?" Simon asked. She had been the one person who had made his time back home enjoyable, and he regretted not having taken advantage of her interest in him.

"Eva Stein actually. She's on Interpol's wanted list for a bank raid in Zürich which left one guard and an innocent bystander dead. The Italians have also expressed a desire to talk about her involvement in the Bologna station bombing!"

Simon whistled. There was always something about her that was different. At least that explained why she was with that fat slug, Ralph. Any port in a storm.

"I take it Ralph is a goner too?"

"Yes and more over he's the main player. Through the tie-in with Eva, we have a story of collusion with foreign terrorists. A desperate man suffering from the delusion that he can overthrow the government. By the time we've finished, he will be looking at seven years minimum and we will have the scapegoat we need to explain away any minor indication of what really went on. Can't be too careful you understand. There's a lot of curious people about and we can't watch all of them."

* * *

Ralph sat in his cell contemplating the future. He wasn't Simon's keeper and he could hardly be held responsible for all of his actions. At worst, he was looking at three to six months and he knew Greta would be waiting for him! All his followers would be waiting!

Oh my God, he thought. *It's like Hitler. I'll be a martyr to the cause! Just like him!*

In a strange way, Ralph felt it was his destiny to go to prison. Just long enough to follow Adolf's lead and write a *Mein Kampf* of sorts before returning to his adoring supporters!

Yes, yes, yes! That's it!

* * *

As the jet's engines roared and the 747 hurtled down the runway, Howard looked out of the airplane's small square window pane. As his mind drifted back to the debriefing, he wondered what would become of him.

Jackson, the head of Embassy security had waltzed into the room fuming, almost unbalanced by rage. "Howard, what the hell did you think you were doing getting caught working against the government of a friendly power?"

"I wasn't working against the government, Sir. I was working against those who wished to bring down the government - the Marxists!"

"In case it had escaped your attention, the right-wing also wants to overthrow the government!"

"Firstly, I would never have let it get that far, and secondly, they're not capable of such a strategy anyway," argued Howard in his defence.

Jackson banged his hand hard on the surface of the mahogany desk and looked desperately at the star spangled banner for inspiration. "You stupid, jerk! If we hadn't been able to cover this up, do you think the British press would have thought that you were promoting a right-wing party for the fun of it? And like some pansified gardener, gonna pull 'em out by the roots when they were good and ready? Get real, mister!"

Jackson looked at the aide who stood by the door and yelled at him to get out. Then he turned his attention back to Howard. "Your job was to be Washington's eyes and ears. To report back what you saw and heard. Not to go blundering about like a poor man's James Bond. The reds were restless because of our instigation! All we required was some independent observation."

"Our instigation, sir ?"

"Yes, us you cretin!" shouted Jackson.

"But why would we support our enemies?" It was all getting a bit beyond Howard now.

"Simply because for generations we have enjoyed a central political and economic role in the western world. This is currently under threat by the discovery of oil in the North Sea."

"I didn't think it was such a significant find," Howard responded. All the information points to a short-life operation!"

"Thats the information they released to the public. However, our survey ships show it to be infinitely larger than the fifty year lifespan they are talking about! If the North Sea went into full production, the balance of power would swing from our continent to Europe. We would be overshadowed by the new wealth it would generate and be left in the wings by the geographical divide."

"What's this got to do with the revolutionary groups?" wondered Howard aloud.

Deciding he owed Howard the full story, Jackson patiently explained. "There have already been several attempts to buy into the operation by some of our high financiers. They were turned down despite our attempts at subtle diplomatic pressure. This Premier Wilson is proving a tough cookie to crack. Obviously, we need someone more amicable to our needs in the top job to ensure that the oil field is milked slowly enough to maintain the status quo as it currently stands.

"Since Wilson refuses to play ball, we have two options. Assassination or undermining confidence in his Government."

"Execute our allies?" The idea stunned Howard.

"Believe me the Premier is no friend of America, and should it become necessary we can always make it appear to be the work of the IRA. You nearly upset our mission with your tinpot dictator and his friends. We were slowly, but surely pushing Wilson out of office by increasing people's fear of the far left."

"Oh God!" Howard now realised he had made a terrible mistake. "What's going to happen to me ?"

220

"The agency can still use you, but your career as a field operative is over before it even started. I guess you'll end up in some administration post - once they've put you through retraining that is!"

Howard's stomach lurched as the aircraft took off. Though depressed, he was doing his best to convince himself that his career as an administrator was going to be a good move. To convince himself it had been his choice was the best way he knew of dealing with it.

Del was sitting up in his hospital bed. Rebel had telephoned earlier to say she would be coming to see him at two o'clock. He looked forward to seeing her. Much as he liked the rest of his mates, he needed someone he could to talk to who would understand him and overlook his confusion and weaknesses. Someone like Alan or Frankie would take the piss, but Rebel was always prepared to hear his joys and woes with the discreet confidence of a priest at a confessional.

When Rebel arrived, she was beaming with delight. "Read that!" she said, tossing today's 'paper over to Del.

On the front page was a picture of a fat guy and below it was the caption, GBP BROKEN AS LEADER IS ARRESTED! Del studied the story closely, absorbing it word for word.

Twenty members of the GBP, an ultra right-wing group, were arrested in a series of dawn raids. A police spokesman said that the GBP had been targeted because information received showed that their overtly violent approach was being orchestrated by Eva Stein, an international terrorist wanted by Interpol in connection with bombings and shootings.

It is expected that the defendants, mainly skinheads, will be remanded in custody this morning when they appear before Magistrates at Peckham's Queens Road courthouse to answer charges arising from their involvement.

"Good, ain't it?" Rebel said.

Del looked over at her. He felt happy that it was all over, but it felt like a hollow victory. For him, the skinhead cult had been sold down the river. They should never have become pawns in the games of others.

221

Everybody's talking about revolution,
Everybody's saying "Smash the state",
Sounds to me like the final solution
Left-wing, right-wing - full of hate!
WATCH YOUR BACK - COCK SPARRER

PROLOGUE

Del and Alan were already legless as they led the mob towards the bar in the Kensington Rooms. There was a real air of anticipation about the place, something that had been missing since punk had become a sterile wave of alternative pop.

Trying to find some room between the other drinkers, Del became quickly frustrated at the lack of attention his waved tenner was getting.

"Push forward!" urged Alan from behind him.

Accepting it was the only thing to do, he spoke into the ear of the rude girl in front of him. "Excuse me, love, can I get through?"

The girl turned around and Del's expression fell into a stunned blank. "Suzi?"

There was no mistaking that smile.

"Suzi!" he cried out in delight, giving her a hug.

She was as happy to see him as he was to see her.

"Let me look at you!" he said, holding her hands and stepping back as far as he could. "This is a big change!" he said, looking over the fashion she had adopted. Black and white panelled skirt, Harrington, button-down shirt and trilby. Not that he was complaining. She looked great.   "So you back in London?" Del asked, thinking of the possibilities.

"No, still in Coventry. I just came down with the band."

"What this other group - The Specials?" he asked.

Alan butted in when he realised who Del was talking to. "Suzi! How are you, girl?"

"Never better!"

"That's great!" beamed Alan, feeling compelled to give her a hug. "Rebel's about somewhere. I think she'd like to see you!" he told her, taking the tenner from Del's hand. "I'll sort the drinks out. I guess you two got a lot of catching up to do!"

"Thanks mate!" Del responded, looking at Suzi's eyes for a moment He felt the sense of attraction rekindle itself. "I've missed you," he told her.

"Yeah, I'm sorry about that. It was my parents not taking no for an answer and me being too fucked up to stay."

"Could have said goodbye!" Derek pointed out.

"Yeah, well, what's done is done."

"I take it there's no chance us getting back together then?" Del had sensed an underlying mood in her words. He had thought about her a lot over the past two years, and the hurt had eventually faded and been replaced by memories of their happier moments together. He would have liked to give it another go on the strength of that.

"Hey Del, you're special to me. You always were and you always will be, but I'd rather we were just friends. It took me a long time to get over what happened and I don't wanna risk any reminders . . . "

Seeing that he was looking a bit despondent, she added, "Maybe in the future we can be something more!"

"Yeah sure!"

"Let's watch the show together!" Suzi said, putting her arm around his waist.

They skirted the crowd just as the piped music stopped abruptly in mid-chorus and a familiar voice called out to the faithful.

"Hey you! Don't watch that! Watch this! This is the heavy, heavy monster sound. The nuttiest sound around. So if you're coming off of the street, and you're beginning to feel the heat. Well listen buster, you better start to move your feet. To the rockiest rocksteady beat of Madness . . . ONE STEP BEYOND!"

THE END

ALSO AVAILABLE FROM S.T. PUBLISHING

FICTION

The Complete Richard Allen Volume One
Now back in print, the Richard Allen novels that charted youth cults throughout the 1970s. **Volume One** contains three great novels, **Skinhead**, **Suedehead** and **Skinhead Escapes**.

The Complete Richard Allen Volume Two
Three more classics from the king of youth cult fiction. **Volume Two** contains **Skinhead Girls**, **Sorts** and **Knuckle Girls**.

The Complete Richard Allen Volume Three
Another three great novels from Richard Allen. **Volume Three** contains **Skinhead Escapes**, **Skinhead Farewell** and **Top-Gear Skin**, plus an interview and tribute to the author.

Saturday's Heroes by Joe Mitchell
A brutal and horrifying novel that takes you into the violent world of Paul West and his skinhead crew. They do battle with casual gangs, other skinheads and rival supporters as they live up to the graffiti sprayed on the outside of their ground - DEFEND YOUR MANOR - JOIN THE MSS.

NON-FICTION

Total Madness by George Marshall
The rise and fall of Camden Town's favourite sons, Madness.

The Two Tone Story by George Marshall
The history of the 2 Tone record label.

Bad Manners by George Marshall
Limited edition book telling the story of Bad Manners.

Watching The Rich Kids by Arthur Kay
Autobiography that takes you on a tour of the back streets of rock n' roll. A true street classic.

Spirit Of '69 - A Skinhead Bible by George Marshall
The history of the skinhead cult from the late Sixties to today.

All of the above books are available through selected outlets or direct from the publisher. For a full catalogue please write to S.T. Publishing, P.O. Box 12, Dunoon, Argyll. PA23 7BQ. Scotland.